Anthony Gilbert and The Murder Room

》》》 This title is part of The Murder Room, our series dedicated to making available out-of-print or hard-to-find titles by classic crime writers.

Crime fiction has always held up a mirror to society. The Victorians were fascinated by sensational murder and the emerging science of detection; now we are obsessed with the forensic detail of violent death. And no other genre has so captivated and enthralled readers.

Vast troves of classic crime writing have for a long time been unavailable to all but the most dedicated frequenters of second-hand bookshops. The advent of digital publishing means that we are now able to bring you the backlists of a huge range of titles by classic and contemporary crime writers, some of which have been out of print for decades.

From the genteel amateur private eyes of the Golden Age and the femmes fatales of pulp fiction, to the morally ambiguous hard-boiled detectives of mid twentieth-century America and their descendants who walk our twenty-first century streets, The Murder Room has it all. **》》》**

The Murder Room
Where Criminal Minds Meet

themurderroom.

Anthony Gilbert (1899–1973)

Anthony Gilbert was the pen name of Lucy Beatrice Malleson. Born in London, she spent all her life there, and her affection for the city is clear from the strong sense of character and place in evidence in her work. She published 69 crime novels, 51 of which featured her best known character, Arthur Crook, a vulgar London lawyer totally (and deliberately) unlike the aristocratic detectives, such as Lord Peter Wimsey, who dominated the mystery field at the time. She also wrote more than 25 radio plays, which were broadcast in Great Britain and overseas. Her thriller *The Woman in Red* (1941) was broadcast in the United States by CBS and made into a film in 1945 under the title *My Name is Julia Ross*. She was an early member of the British Detection Club, which, along with Dorothy L. Sayers, she prevented from disintegrating during World War II. Malleson published her autobiography, *Three-a-Penny*, in 1940, and wrote numerous short stories, which were published in several anthologies and in such periodicals as *Ellery Queen's Mystery Magazine* and *The Saint*. The short story 'You Can't Hang Twice' received a Queens award in 1946. She never married, and evidence of her feminism is elegantly expressed in much of her work.

By Anthony Gilbert

Scott Egerton series
Tragedy at Freyne (1927)
The Murder of Mrs
  Davenport (1928)
Death at Four Corners (1929)
The Mystery of the Open
  Window (1929)
The Night of the Fog (1930)
The Body on the Beam (1932)
The Long Shadow (1932)
The Musical Comedy
  Crime (1933)
An Old Lady Dies (1934)
The Man Who Was Too
  Clever (1935)

Mr Crook Murder
 Mystery series
Murder by Experts (1936)
The Man Who Wasn't
  There (1937)
Murder Has No Tongue (1937)
Treason in My Breast (1938)
The Bell of Death (1939)
Dear Dead Woman (1940)
 aka *Death Takes a Redhead*
The Vanishing Corpse (1941)
 aka *She Vanished in the Dawn*
The Woman in Red (1941)
 aka *The Mystery of the
 Woman in Red*

Death in the Blackout (1942)
 aka *The Case of the Tea-
 Cosy's Aunt*
Something Nasty in the
  Woodshed (1942)
 aka *Mystery in the Woodshed*
The Mouse Who Wouldn't
  Play Ball (1943)
 aka *30 Days to Live*
He Came by Night (1944)
 aka *Death at the Door*
The Scarlet Button (1944)
 aka *Murder Is Cheap*
A Spy for Mr Crook (1944)
The Black Stage (1945)
 aka *Murder Cheats the Bride*
Don't Open the Door (1945)
 aka *Death Lifts the Latch*
Lift Up the Lid (1945)
 aka *The Innocent Bottle*
The Spinster's Secret (1946)
 aka *By Hook or by Crook*
Death in the Wrong Room
  (1947)
Die in the Dark (1947)
 aka *The Missing Widow*
Death Knocks Three Times
  (1949)
Murder Comes Home (1950)
A Nice Cup of Tea (1950)
 aka *The Wrong Body*

Lady-Killer (1951)
Miss Pinnegar Disappears (1952)
aka *A Case for Mr Crook*
Footsteps Behind Me (1953)
aka *Black Death*
Snake in the Grass (1954)
aka *Death Won't Wait*
Is She Dead Too? (1955)
aka *A Question of Murder*
And Death Came Too (1956)
Riddle of a Lady (1956)
Give Death a Name (1957)
Death Against the Clock (1958)
Death Takes a Wife (1959)
aka *Death Casts a Long Shadow*
Third Crime Lucky (1959)
aka *Prelude to Murder*
Out for the Kill (1960)
She Shall Die (1961)
aka *After the Verdict*
Uncertain Death (1961)
No Dust in the Attic (1962)
Ring for a Noose (1963)
The Fingerprint (1964)

The Voice (1964)
aka *Knock, Knock! Who's There?*
Passenger to Nowhere (1965)
The Looking Glass Murder (1966)
The Visitor (1967)
Night Encounter (1968)
aka *Murder Anonymous*
Missing from Her Home (1969)
Death Wears a Mask (1970)
aka *Mr Crook Lifts the Mask*
Murder is a Waiting Game (1972)
Tenant for the Tomb (1971)
A Nice Little Killing (1974)

Standalone Novels
The Case Against Andrew Fane (1931)
Death in Fancy Dress (1933)
The Man in Button Boots (1934)
Courtier to Death (1936)
aka *The Dover Train Mystery*
The Clock in the Hatbox (1939)

The Fingerprint

Anthony Gilbert

An Orion book

Copyright © Lucy Beatrice Malleson 1964

The right of Lucy Beatrice Malleson to be identified as the author of this work has been asserted in accordance with the Copyright, Designs and Patents Act 1988.

This edition published by
The Orion Publishing Group Ltd
Orion House
5 Upper St Martin's Lane
London WC2H 9EA

An Hachette UK company
A CIP catalogue record for this book is available from the British Library

ISBN 978 1 4719 1024 1

www.orionbooks.co.uk

I

On that first Sunday after the big snow, Sara Drew was walking with her son, Mike, in the woods behind Fell Cottage when she heard the sound of approaching engines, and a few seconds later the two cars shot into view. Although the road was slippery with ice they were traveling at a tremendous, maniacal speed, and her first impulse was to snatch her four-year-old son's hand and vanish among the trees. Ever since that unforgettable day two years ago when she had opened her door to find a policeman on the step, requesting her to accompany him to the station—euphemism for the mortuary—to identify the victim of a road accident, she had felt herself begin to tremble with apprehension whenever she saw a fast-moving car.

But Mike was earnestly making a snowman so he waited and the cars flashed past. She saw they were both Albions, the new pocket model racing car put out by one of the more enterprising motor companies. They were advertised as achieving the maximum speed with the minimum expenditure of fuel; less, she recalled, was said about their safety. The farther of the two cars was a bright red, the other a pale blue picked out with Oxford; they seemed to pass her with the speed of light, yet not so fast that she couldn't realize each contained a single occupant. The road was wide enough for two cars to travel abreast, but the conditions underfoot and the tall banks flanking it made such speeds nothing short of criminal madness. It didn't seem to occur to either driver that anyone might want to travel in the opposite direction. As the cars went by she saw that the nearer driver was wearing a coat of what was called rainbow tweed, very colorful and distinctive, and she found herself thinking, He should wear something quieter in these conditions, something that won't attract another driver's eye.

She saw them flash down the hill, then Mike called proudly, "Man," and she turned to praise his handiwork. In his dark blue snowsuit and his ridiculous little fur hat, sent from America by his paternal grandmother, he was singing cheerfully:

> You be my honey-honeysuckle
> I'll be the bee.

Only he said bunny-suckle.

Where on earth did he pick that up? she wondered, and then remembered mad old Mrs. Cameron, who came in one day a week to iron and do any odd jobs that appealed to her, but nothing heavy. She was always warbling something or other—a metrical psalm one day and the latest from the hit parade the next. "I'm broad-minded," she claimed. And Mike, who was the world's copycat, picked them all up in turn. Michael would have loved her, thought Michael's widow. Oh, how *could* you? she breathed. Even two years later she couldn't accept her grief, such a senseless finish to so much happiness.

She turned to admire Mike's snowman, then her gaze went back to the road. Some distance away, though still within her range, it dipped sharply to the left. The cars still appeared to

2

be racing each other, what could be called a photo finish; she held her breath. One ill-judged movement on the part of either driver and there would be disaster. As they neared the curve she thought one of them would have to drop back, then realized with a shock of sick horror that neither intended to give way.

"You fools, you fools!" she shouted. "Don't you know it's blind?"

The red car drew a yard ahead of its companion; it seemed to be spinning dizzily on the perilous surface of the road as its driver gave a triumphant toot on the horn. A second later tragedy came. Around the curve marched the grenadier figure of an elderly woman, wearing a brown tweed coat and a cap *en suite*, like a female Cossack, thought Sara, dazedly. Attached to this apparition's gloved hand was a leather leash and at the end of the leash was a large elderly clean-shaven dog. In any ordinary landscape it would have appeared white, but snow makes even freshly washed dogs appear dingy. This specimen was either very old or very lame, because it waddled at a slow trot at the full extent of its lead. The grenadier must have heard the cars before she saw them, because already she was tugging at the strap and pulling against the snow-piled bank. She tugged frantically, but without avail.

The dog was stubborn, possibly deaf—white dogs, Sara had heard, were often deaf; it moved perhaps six inches nearer its owner, but it still occupied a position almost in the middle of the road. It was impossible, even if she could have pulled the dog across, for the pedestrian to climb the bank. It was much too high, as well as impeded by snow, and there wasn't even a ditch into which she could sink. Presumably both drivers realized the impossibility at this stage of braking in time to avoid a collision, so the driver of the red car did something that brought Sara's heart into her throat so that her involuntary cry was choked and smothered. But it was too late. It was too far away for Sara to be able to see whether the driver in the rainbow-colored coat had attempted to brake. As she was to say later, everything happened so fast. At one instant there were two gaily colored cars vivid against the snow, and an old woman and her dog moving inexorably to meet them. Then there came a rending crash and the old woman disappeared. The red Albion was almost jolted topsy-turvy—even at that distance she could see the wheels spinning as it reared into the air. Then, by some miracle, it regained its balance and went shooting around the bend and out of sight. The driver of the blue car had already vanished.

After the tremendous thud there was no sound at all, no howl from the dog—but even a dog that weight couldn't hope to survive such an impact—not a sound from the old woman. She found herself thinking instinctively, there's something to be said for these Albions; my little Waterbury would have turned topsy-turvy. Even Michael's Wyburd would have done the same. She put her hand over her mouth. Am I never to be free? she thought. Arthur Crook, whom she was to meet later, could have told her there's only one place where you can look to be free from memory, and that's the grave, and there are mixed opinions even about that.

Her little boy caught her hand and tugged impatiently.

"Mummy, why are you looking down the road?"

"Oh," she said, with a lightness that did her credit, "I thought I saw a big white dog."

He laughed indulgently, then promised, "I'll make you a dog" and, dropping down into the snow, began heaping it together with small fat hands, coaxing and shaping. . . . Sara looked up the hill whence the cars had come, but no other driver seemed crazy enough to choose this way in such weather. No one came up the hill either; the wind whistled, the snow began to fall again in flakes as fine as feathers. Mike took off his fur hat and tried to catch them.

They're not coming back, Sara realized, incredulously. They must know they hit her, *and they're not coming back*. They didn't know, presumably, there had been a witness; they'd establish some sort of alibi in case awkward questions were asked, by which time their cars would be polished and safely garaged. All the same, it didn't make sense. However mad and bad you are, you don't leave an old woman you've just injured, terribly and possibly fatally, to die alone in the snow. Then she

4

thought, Or perhaps they've crashed too far away for me to hear; perhaps one driver is looking after the other. It was even possible they were both dead. Yet, on this afternoon, with the light just beginning to fade and the clear frosty wind blowing, you could have heard a bird call, a dog bark. There had been no crash; there was no cry, no sound from those two bodies on the hill. It was as quiet as if the world had only just been born.

"I ought to go down," she whispered. "If I don't, I'm as bad as they are." Because the old thing might still be conscious, though this seemed improbable, and though there was nothing much she could do—at least I could hold her hand, she thought, take a last message. Only she didn't want to go. Hated the thought of going. That was another legacy from the shocking suddenness of Michael's death.

Mike distracted her again. "Mummy, look. A dog."

She came to, abruptly. "A dog? Where?"

Then she saw the jumble of snow and saw it was intended to represent a dog begging; Mike had crowned his masterpiece with his own fur hat. She snatched it up and crammed it back on his head.

"Do you want to catch your death of cold?"

"Pooh, people don't die of cold."

That might have been Michael speaking; she knew that since she became a widow she had become ultrafussy about the little boy. Michael wouldn't have approved. "I don't want a milksop for a son," he'd have said. But how could she conceivably drag a four-year-old to that scene? To say nothing of the physical difficulty of hauling him down the hill in the teeth of the snow that had suddenly begun to fall with immense speed, there was the mental effect. True, his chief concern would be for the dog, but, remembering what she had been asked to identify as her husband, Sara shrank from subjecting her son to the ordeal. The poor brute was probably cut to ribbons. No, she determined, catching at Mike's reluctant hand, the sensible thing would be to go home as fast as possible and ring up the police. They could send an ambulance and instruct their men to look out for the two Albions. Whereas to go down now and probably find there was nothing to be done would involve the slow exhausting climb back up the hill, dragging a weary child, and all that time lost. Still she hesitated, inwardly referring all problems as she still did to her dead husband.

"Come on," she said to Mike, "it's time for tea. We've got to go home."

She stopped uncertainly, once more looking over her shoulder. Then it happened. Around the corner a car came creeping. It was too far away in all this flurry of snow for her to see very clearly, but at least it absolved her from the necessity of taking any action. The driver must see the bodies, get out, appreciate what had happened, and it would be his responsibility.

"Come, Mike," she repeated sharply. "It's past teatime already."

She hadn't been living in the cottage more than a few months. After Michael died, she had thought at first she would look for the type of accommodation she could now afford, in familiar surroundings, but she soon understood that she would be perpetually rubbing up against neighbors and acquaintances who were too careful, too discreet; it seemed that salt was forever being rubbed into the wound.

The cottage she had taken was remote and devoid of practically all modern amenities, which made it cheap; her neighbors were scattered and took only a mild interest in her. She didn't even know if they believed her story of being a widow. Probably some of them thought she was a divorcee; others might even disbelieve in the validity of her wedding ring, but here it didn't matter. During these months she had begun to fashion a new life; she had a small car and in this she careered around the countryside, attending occasional local events, taking Mike for picnics and the few parties to which he had invitations. Solitude was all right for her, she thought, but a child mustn't be separated from his contemporaries, and in this place a strange youngster was quickly absorbed into the community.

Next year he would go to school; by then she might have healed the wound and be prepared to look for some sort of social life for herself. In any case she had the place on a short lease. It belonged to a man serving in the Middle East, whose date of retirement had been postponed for twelve months, and he had been glad to pick up a reliable tenant at short notice. She kept on with a bit of her free-lance journalism, she had a small pension from Michael's insurance and the state allowance. Mike could go to the village school, nothing to pay there, and he was a friendly creature, everyone liked him. . . .

They had been walking for a little while when Mike at her side demanded fretfully, "Mummy, why don't we go back?"

"We are going back," she assured him. "Come on."

Relief at what she thought was a reprieve made her voice sing.

"But where is home?" demanded the fretful little voice. He stopped, like a stubborn little engine that has suddenly run out of fuel.

"Oh, don't be silly," she told him. "Home is the cottage."

"It's gone," declared Mike, blankly.

Sara looked around. He was right. These woods were extensive and wild; usually there were individual landmarks, a particular-shaped tree, a clearing, a familiar stump where they sat and ate their tea in fine weather; but the snow turned the place into no man's land. They'd strayed a considerable distance from the familiar path, and now she had no notion where they were. Could you get lost in the woods? Mike had once asked, and she'd said, if you wanted to, yes. Well, now they were lost, without wanting to be. The snow lay like an eiderdown over the world as far as they could see it. Soon, she thought, the old woman and her dog will be covered. A shroud of snow.

She laughed down into Mike's disconsolate face. "We walked farther than usual, and so of course it'll take longer to get home," she assured him. But he didn't smile. The snow didn't help either of them. It blew in their faces, and flakes slipped down between her coat collar and her skin.

"The snow's got into my hat," Mike complained.

"I told you not to take it off. Now, Mike, put your mind to it. Imagine we're explorers. Did you bring your compass, pardner? We can't afford to get lost in the wilds of the Arctic."

"But we are lost," cried Mike sullenly. In another minute,

she thought, he'll start whining. She repressed a desire to shake him. Poor little boy, it wasn't his fault. He was cold and wet and he wanted his tea. Like a fool she hadn't left a lamp burning in the cottage, and there was no other dwelling quite near. If the snow went on at this rate they could walk around in circles and never get back.

"I want my tea," declared Mike.

"Well, you can't get it in the middle of a wood, can you? If you were an Indian, Mike, and wanted to get back, which direction would you take?"

"We're not Indians," Mike pointed out. "And it's the Indians who are after us."

She repressed a sigh. "All the more reason to hurry." She caught his hand again and dragged him resolutely along. But the snow was thick and the ground uneven, and his little fat legs were clotted by it; he tripped on a stump and said loudly, "You hurt me."

"Oh nonsense," she cried, with the impatience of a growing fear. "Don't be such a baby. You know you can go faster than that."

She yanked at his arm.

"You're hurting me," he repeated furiously.

"All right." She let go, and down he plumped in the snow and began to bawl. But she didn't pay any attention, because, quite suddenly, she knew where they were; she recognized, with a relief as sparkling as champagne, a peculiar formation of trees—the magic circle, Mike called it. And just beyond this landmark was the cottage. She ran forward, heedless of her enraged child. She had just fitted the key into the lock of the back door, to see the red glow of the kitchen fire penetrating into the passage, when there were hearty sounds behind her, and a voice cried, "Hi, feller, what gives?"

She was so much surprised she let the key fall. A tall young man, wearing a rainbow tweed coat, had got Mike by the arm and was bending to look into his flushed, offended face.

"I told you the Indians were after us," Mike reproached her.

"You've got very sharp hearing," she told him, and it was like listening to a machine begin to talk; the words seemed to have no connection with herself, and it was an uncomfortable thought that they had been neatly stalked through the snowy woods.

The stranger still had Mike's hand, and was smiling down at him.

"Indians, eh? Too bad I left my scalping knife at home."

Mike chuckled. Impulsively Sara came forward. Drop his hand, she was commanding the stranger silently, and aloud she exclaimed, "Mike, come in out of the snow. You'll be soaked and I don't want you down with pneumonia." The clever little boy, she thought. And out of the mouths of babes and sucklings . . .

"Hear what your mum says?" suggested the young man, dusting snow off the little chap's breeches.

"She pushed me," said Mike accusingly, pointing at his mother.

"May as well get used to that first as last, chum," said the newcomer. "They do it all their lives—push us around—women, I mean."

"You know perfectly well you fell over," said Sara, coming forward and snatching at his other hand. "Thank you," she added, rather ungraciously. "We missed the path, he got tired."

She had picked up the key, and the back door of the cottage was open.

"Home, sweet home," suggested the young man, shoving past her. Through the half-open kitchen door the stove glowed redly; warm air floated out to counteract the icy wind outside. Sara wondered if the stranger expected to be asked in and offered tea, but she wasn't going to have him polluting the air Mike had to breathe. She realized now that his must have been the car that had come creeping back around the curve of the hill. He must know that between them he and his friend had done the old woman an appalling injury, but he hadn't even suggested using the telephone, sending for a doctor. He looked as gay and debonair as a fancy-dress Prince Charlie. She stood squarely in the doorway.

"Wasn't it you on the Ridge?" her unwelcome visitor inquired.

"The Ridge?"

"Come on, lower the drawbridge. You be my bunny-bunny-suckle," he sang suddenly. "I'll be the bee," chimed in Mike appearing in the doorway.

"I never met a bee I took to more at first sight," the young man assured him. "Let's hope the bunny-suckle knows its luck. Now, mate, I just want a word with your mum—funny how damp snow is, isn't it?" he added confidentially to Sara.

She drew back reluctantly, allowing him to stand in the narrow passage. "What was it you wanted to say to me? I have to attend to my son."

"Well—it's about that accident."

"Accident?"

"Didn't you notice? Oh, I thought, seeing you were on the Ridge . . ."

"I saw all right," Sara reassured him grimly, "only I wouldn't have called it an accident."

"No? You must get someone to give you a dictionary for your next birthday. An accident is something fatal that happens without any intent. Unless you're suggesting the old girl meant to put herself under the wheels of the car . . ."

"You know quite well I mean nothing of the sort. She didn't put herself anywhere; she was run down."

"You want to watch it," counseled the young man, looking more dangerous than before, like a vicious ferret or something. "No excuse for not wearing glasses now we've got the National Health. Go ahead and tell me what you think you saw."

"What I know I saw. Your friend made a mad spurt to pass you, instead of dropping back, and in so doing he collided with the old woman and her dog."

Her companion's brow darkened. "It's immoral, that's what it is, letting any old fool own a dog by paying seven and six-pence. They ought to pass a test, the same as motorists. The old fool was on the wrong side of the road anyway. And what's more," he went on, sweeping away her attempts at speech, "she knew it. That's why she suddenly tried to scamper across the road when she saw us coming. Didn't have a chance, poor old trout. Nor did we. And that's what you want to remember. If she'd let go the blasted dog's lead we might have been able to miss her, though it's dubious, very dubious."

"She didn't attempt to cross the road and the evidence will prove it," Sara insisted. "She was trying to pull the dog in . . ."

"These pedestrians seem to think a car's like a vacuum cleaner." Stan Marvyn went on. "Put your foot on the pedal, and it stops. Never allow for the time it takes to come to a halt. Poor old grannie, she never had a chance."

"No," agreed Sara. "You saw to that."

"You want to watch that tongue of yours," warned Stan. "Could get you into bad trouble one of these days."

"And anyway," continued Sara, "why are you here?"

"Well, you know what the police are. They'll ask were there any witnesses, anyone who can give information. Mind you, you'd be giving evidence on oath . . ."

"If I'm dragged into this," retorted Sara, "I can only tell the truth, which is that you were going hell-for-leather down a dangerous hill—there's a warning sign at the top, or were you going so fast you didn't notice that either?—and you didn't attempt to brake when the old woman came around the bend."

"Got it all pat, haven't you? What rate should you say we were doing?"

"About sixty."

Stan began to laugh. "You had me worried for a minute. Honest. I thought you might be going to make trouble for us. You come into any court and tell them we were going down Folly Hill at sixty miles an hour, and they'll send for the trick cyclist."

"I happen to be a driver myself. I don't make mistakes about speed."

"That so? Well, me and Red happen to value our lives, and if we were tired of them we'd choose a more peaceful way of getting out than having ourselves smashed up in a car crash. You ever seen anyone after . . . ?"

She shrank back, her cheeks ashen-pale. "Go away," she said in a low, violent voice, "stop tormenting me. I don't know why you came, but if you think you can intimidate me . . ."

"I'm not tormenting you," protested Stan. "I just asked . . ."

"My husband was killed in a car crash. I had to identify the body. Does that satisfy you?"

He remained unmoved. "Well, then, you'll realize it's not the way any sane man would take, not when a handful of tranquilizers or a coin in the gas meter would do the trick . . ."

"Is she dead?" demanded Sara. The words snapped out like a breaking twig.

Stan looked genuinely astonished. "Are you kidding? You can't walk into a car coming downhill, even if it's in low gear, and get off with a black eye or a sprained ankle."

"Mummy," called Mike impatiently from the kitchen, "*I want my tea.*"

"You'll have to excuse me now," said Sara, abruptly. "I must look after my little boy."

"Your only one?"

"Yes."

Stan nodded. "I suppose you could say you were lucky to have him. Mike," he called. "Do you know any bee that likes chocolate?"

Mike came rushing out, clutching a stuffed tiger called Tigger, a remarkable animal whose ears and tail had been replaced with a material that didn't suit the rest of him; he had one eye but you could tell at a glance it would do the work of two without blinking.

"That's a fearsome brute," Stan suggested. "What's his name?"

"Tigger. Mummy got him in the market. We go every Saturday."

"It looks as though I'm missing something," said Stan, carelessly. He held out a chocolate bar. "Now, don't choke on it or your mum will think I have designs upon you. And, seeing you're all she's got, you want to be careful how you go. It 'ud be just too bad if anything was to happen to you, and you do read *such* stories in the press." He patted the rosy cheek. Mike offered Tigger a piece of the chocolate bar. "Not that I need warn you really," Stan wound up. "Anyone can see you're the apple of your mum's eye."

His own, bright as a robin's, met Sara's. "Well, ta-ta for now. I've enjoyed our little talk." He gave Mike a mock salute and made the child laugh gleefully and throw up his own little fat hand. Off Stan strode through the snow, leaving immense tracks, like an animal—a wild animal, Sara thought. She stood immobile, staring after him. The inference had been too obvious for even a dunderhead to miss and she wasn't quite that.

"Mummy," said Mike patiently for the third time, "I want my tea."

"Of course." She slammed the back door and bolted it, as well as turning the big old-fashioned key. Snow had drifted into the house through the window of the big living room that looked over the woods. Mike pressed his nose against the pane.

"There might be a wolf," he offered, anxiously.

Oh no, thought Sara, hoping she wasn't going to succumb to hysterics, the wolf's gone, anyway for the moment. She ran around the room like a human dynamo, shutting the window and blocking the ill-fitting sashes with wads of newspaper, piling up the fire, lighting the emergency oil stove that glowed like a rose and whose brilliance was reflected in its own chromium frame. She boiled eggs and sliced bread and produced a freshly made banana jelly—Mike's favorite "after," no matter what the temperature—and settled him at the table. She compelled herself to drink tea and nibble a cracker, since Mike liked company, but at last, Wellingtons exchanged for bunny scuffs, hair standing on end with the rough toweling she gave it, he was settled in front of the television set. Then and only then did she slip into the hall and lift the telephone receiver.

In imagination she could hear the station officer at Plowford demanding indignantly why she'd wasted so much time; why she hadn't tried to help, or at least tried to flag a passer-by. Only there'd been Mike and that man and there hadn't been any passers-by. She had seen no one else in the woods until his car had come crawling around the bend; after she turned away he must have alighted to discover the extent of the damage. And then, looking ahead, come stealing through the snowy woods to silence the only witness in a manner both apt and devilish. Tell, and see what happens to your little boy—that was the gist of it; she was surprised to find herself with the receiver in her hand. But the police must be his equal, she reminded herself scornfully.

She was so much obsessed with these considerations that it was a full minute before she realized she was getting no response. The snow, clearly, had brought down the lines. It occurred to her that she hadn't needed to use the telephone during the past thirty-six hours or so; they might have been down yesterday and she not aware. Slowly she hung up. This enforced silence seemed to be the measure of her isolation. And yet in a way it was a relief. It absolved her from taking any further step before morning. No one, not even the police, could expect her to leave a four-year-old child alone in a cottage in a wood, with no very near neighbors and not even a telephone. Darkness was coming down like an indigo curtain; the only sound was the occasional fall of snow that was overloading a neighboring bough. Not even a bird called.

She thought of the old woman lying in the snow—dead, no doubt, or he wouldn't have left her. It seemed a lonely way to die. The snow, now falling faster and faster, might well have covered both bodies by this time, and only a vehicle crazily trying to negotiate Folly Hill under such conditions could hope to discover what had occurred. She might lie there for days, getting more deeply buried with snow. Footprints, tire marks, everything condemnatory to the driver, would have disappeared. There'd be no evidence against the culprits except her word. And even that mightn't go for much. Young men like this one—she didn't even know his name yet—were clever; they'd have a lawyer who wouldn't find it too hard to persuade a court that a young woman engrossed in a little boy and standing some distance from the scene of the crash was a pretty inconclusive sort of witness.

She didn't suppose his conscience would trouble him much. She realized she was taking for granted he was some kind of small-time crook, and it didn't surprise her at all. You couldn't imagine him turning out regularly five days a week to go to work. Chaps of his sort played the dogs, worked a tobacco or fruit machine, were confidence tricksters, a bit more handy than most with a pack of cards. I'm the one who should be the trick cyclist, she thought. Deducing all this from a single meeting.

"Mummy," called Mike, imperiously, "the picture's gone all funny."

She went in and adjusted the set.

"You're wearing your thunder face," Mike accused her.

"It must be the snow."

"Can we go out tomorrow?" he demanded.

"Not if it's going to be like this." As she cleared the table she recognized there was more, something in the general picture she hadn't yet seen. As a child she'd had books with concealed animals on the picture pages; the sharp eyes of youth could discern a kitten curled among the leaves of the trees, a frog behind some stones, chickens in a flower bed. She turned her present picture this way and that, looking for the wild creatures it concealed.

It's more than the old woman, she decided. He didn't care two straws about her, and if he told his story about her trying to bolt across the road he'd most likely get away with it. It was the sort of thing old women were doing every day of the week. He had to make sure how much I'd seen, what I intended to do, and prevent my doing it. She was like someone climbing a very slippery ladder, not knowing what the view might display when she'd mounted the next rung. And yet, if I had told my story, they wouldn't be in any real danger, nothing they couldn't have oiled out of without much difficulty. So—they couldn't afford to come into the limelight. Probably got a record as long as my arm, decided Sara, recklessly. Wanted perhaps. Or afraid of being charged with leaving the scene of a crime. Anyway, resolved to keep out of sight, and not minding what threats they used to make sure I don't come forward, too. She might be an obstacle in their path, as the old woman and the dog had been, because she had seen what had happened to them.

So—there was no choice really. Mike had rights, too. I'm all he's got, and it could be his life at stake. I can't play ducks and drakes with that. And it swept over her with a sense of numbing shock that that smiling charmer would be perfectly capable of putting his implicit threat into action, if he even believed she'd gone to the police.

And, of course, I'm not going, Sara declared. They might offer us protection, but they have to play the game by the rules. If it came to a showdown between him and the police, she knew where her bets would lie.

After Mike was warmly tucked up, with the door open an inch or two so that she would hear him call out if he wanted a drink of water or a wolf came baying at the door, she sat up late, a book on her knee that she couldn't read for more than a paragraph at a time. Both doors were locked and bolted, and she was glad now she had insisted on having wire screens fixed on the outside of the lower windows. The neighbors, what there were of them, had come to stare and gone away amused, at a townswoman's pernickety ways, but she thought they had forgotten the energy and initiative a four-year-old can display. It wasn't to keep wolves and marauders out but to keep Mike in that she'd had the installations made.

All the evening the snow continued to fall. Once Sara started up, thinking she heard a sound outside the cottage, but it was only a great lump of snow breaking through one of the more fragile branches, and she went back to her chair. The next thing she knew the old-fashioned clock was chiming three A. M. and the oil stove had burned itself out. She pulled herself up, stiff as a board, rekindled the stove, made up the fire, put on a kettle for tea. She looked in on Mike as if somehow he might have been spirited away while she slept, but he was safe enough, looking like a mischievous angel, with the disreputable Tigger clutched to his breast.

She went to stand by his window for a moment; the snow had stopped but the world was nothing but a white sheet stretching to the horizon; even the telegraph wires, where they sagged, were heavy with snow. She made the tea, set it on a tray, and at last dragged herself into bed.

2

Arthur Crook, the London lawyer who was known as the criminals' hope and the judges' despair, used to think that going to the country was second only to exploring the polar regions. He was, he would explain, a man with a sense of timing, and though anyone who knew him could have told you that so far as he was concerned clocks need never have been invented, since darkness and light to him were both alike, at least in London you did know the difference between two in the morning and two in the afternoon. But in Sleepy Hollow—his name for Plowford—where one of his slightly odd jobs had taken him, time seemed to stand still. If a love for the metropolis hadn't burned in him as steadily as the blue lamp over an old-time police station, the odds are he would never have tried to get home on that Sunday night. But Monday was always a rush day, with chaps wanting to be hauled out of the pits into which they had fallen during a week end of leisure, and if the

17

road, despite the snow, was good enough for the night trucks, then it was good enough for the Old Superb, his famous ancient Rolls, yellow as a canary and determined as a gatecrasher. But by 6:30 that evening, when he was ready to start, the snow was coming down so furiously he didn't think it right to ask even such a gallant old battle-ax to chance climbing Folly Hill, so he sat lugubriously in the bar of The Live and Let Live drinking something he'd have hesitated to employ to poison a rat. The bar was practically empty, which wasn't surprising, and the landlord looked about as cheerful as the weather but less clean.

At about nine o'clock a confident voice over the air assured anyone who cared to listen that the Meteorological Office didn't anticipate any further snowfall before morning, so "me for the open road" decided Mr. Crook gratefully. He was a shade disconcerted to discover the depths of the snow through which the Superb would have to plow her way, but the notion of spending the night at The Live and Let Live so appalled him that he decided to take a chance. At worst he could find a parking area and spend the night there. But you'll do it, he assured the imperturbable old yellow car, and snugged himself in behind the wheel.

A solitary traveler passed him during the next hour. In spite of the dangers of the road, he noticed the man and wondered what he was doing afoot on such an inclement evening. He decided he'd probably got snowed in and left his car somewhere along the road—he'd already passed three looking like miniature igloos—and was probably making for The Live and Let Live for a night's shelter.

"God have mercy on such as he," caroled Mr. Crook, cautiously approaching Folly Hill. (He belonged to an age when it was respectable and even admirable to quote Rudyard Kipling's lays.)

He proceeded through a silence that became as deep as the snow itself. And indeed the flakes, settling on this and that feature of the landscape, had thrown up some pretty remarkable shapes so that it needed very little imagination to see them as memorials in some unfenced graveyard, and not much odder at that than plenty you could find in ancient cemeteries. He was close to the foot of the hill when, as if to spite the Meteorological Office, the snow suddenly started again, driving in the face of the car, blurring the windshield and blotting out all landmarks. The windshield wipers were of little avail in the face of such malevolence, and he approached the hill at a walking pace. Even the Superb was going to have her work cut out to make it in these conditions, but it never occurred to him to look for an easier way around. He was like Robert Browning's hero who tackled every obstacle breast-forward. Up the first leg he went in low gear, hoping he wouldn't cannon against any abandoned car left carelessly in the middle of the road.

We don't make enough allowances for Eskimos, he decided, and resolved that if ever he were asked to act for one who'd run amok he'd take the job, even if there were forty-four witnesses who had seen the fellow plunge the icy dagger into his victim's throat. Not a bird cheeped—they'd had the good sense to bed down long ago. No vehicle was traveling in the opposite direction. Even the night trucks were making a detour, where they were on the road at all, but most of them had followed the example of the birdies. Still, once up the hill, it should be easier going.

As a rule, Crook enjoyed night traveling, resenting the hours of daylight wasted in getting from point to point. They knew him and served him at all the night cafés, and that was something even royalty couldn't claim, since these are as exclusive as Mayfair clubs, and a lot more suspicious, but they never tried to exclude him. Self-preservation most likely, he would reflect, knowing that one of these days they might need his services. Around the first bend he came, man defying the elements, but a minute later even the Superb had to admit defeat. And it was more than just snow, he decided. Probably half a tree blown down and obstructing the road. He hopped out, crouching like a gnome or a troglodyte, in his bright brown overcoat and saucy checked cap, scrabbling away at the snowy pile with big red hands. It looked like a strange sort of dog, watching the snow fly from beneath its paws. And a dog, in short, was what he unearthed, a dog that hadn't just lain down and died in peace.

"Another motoring casualty not reported to the cops," he told himself, scrabbling away a bit more snow. The dog presently uncovered, or partially uncovered, was revealed as a large bulky creature, bull terrier type, not, Crook supposed, weighing more than about half a ton.

"I should drag you to the side of the road," he told the corpse, dismally, not much relishing the job. Even quite light bodies mysteriously double their weight when they're dead, and this one could never have been an easy armful. There were no stars, of course, but the snow and a fitful, reluctant bit of moonlight gave him some illumination. He scooped away a bit more snow, and then received a shock that paled even his rubicund cheek. Attached to the brute's collar was a leash, drawn tight; the leash had snapped near the loop, and the loop itself was gripped fast in a woolen-gloved hand. The hand itself was as stiff and unyielding as the body of the poor old dog. The snow had turned the woman into a long coffin-shaped hump, and the violence of the impact had flung her against the bank at the side of the road.

Not much snow under the body, he noted, and she was stiff as a board, so the accident had taken place some hours earlier. The snowfall had started, he remembered, soon after four; it was now a quarter to ten, so she had been lying there for the best part of six hours. Only why the devil had she been lying there? One thing was obvious. The police hadn't been informed. Whoever was responsible for the old girl's death—and never tell him the chap responsible didn't know what he'd done —had escaped. A new thought struck him and he flung the light of his flash far and wide, but there was no crashed car in the vicinity, and he hadn't passed one for some time. Fellow must have thought he was safe enough—no witnesses, no proof. It shouldn't happen to a dog, he thought.

When he came to examine the old woman more closely his anger rose to such a pitch it was a wonder the snow didn't begin to melt. The thing that struck her had done some pretty revolting damage, although, miraculously, her face had suffered little injury. His light picked out the rough-lined features. A real last ditcher, he reflected, the kind that said in the war, I don't mean to let that man drive me out of my house, and he never had, except with a direct hit. Crook knew, none better, that these old girls are tough and need to be, the world being the way it is, but there are limits even for them. This one, he adjudged, had been drawing the pension for quite a while. He looked at the arrogant weather-beaten face, the bony nose, the lips close as prison bars, the mousy gray hair escaping from under a woolen cap like a misshapen beehive.

In the affluent society these old girls were being crowded out, and you wouldn't see their like again, more's the pity. They lived in a day when the only rights you had were the ones you fought for, and Crook was such an old shellback himself he mistrusted everything that was handed to you on a plate, with parsley around the edge and a nice ribbon bow for a decoration. Nothing is for free was his gospel, and he'd never be surprised to find a sizeable dose of cyanide under the pretty wrappings. Dead clients aren't exactly profitable, but then and there he resolved that if there was anything he could do to flatten the man responsible for this—"Well," he said aloud, "name it, just name it." Stan hadn't had any idea what he was doing when he got himself mixed up in a jam like this.

Crook had found himself in some pretty weird situations, but few more macabre than this vigil in the snow, cut off from everywhere, with only a dead woman and her dog for company. He looked around for a handbag or any means of identification, but if she'd been carrying one it was buried deep in the snow, and anyway on a Sunday afternoon she was probably only taking the dog for a constitutional and wouldn't need a purse. Then it occurred to him that dogs have to carry identification labels—and in any civilized society the same would apply to humans—so he worked the collar around till he could read the name on the medal. Beverley, he read, and an address at a place called Sursum Parva. Back in the Superb he hauled out his road map, but it didn't show any such place. Probably half a dozen cottages and not even a general store. He wished he could put up a red light in case the world contained one other lunatic as crazy as himself, but had to be content with unwinding a checked brown and gray scarf and tying it on a convenient bit of hedge to mark the spot, since every place looked alike in this weather. Then he coaxed the Superb into reverse, and with the snow behind him now, started the crawl back to Plowford.

Sergeant Richard Probyn of Plowford Police Force replaced his telephone receiver, wearing a look as black as the instrument.

"I don't know," he told his assistant, "whole world's gone balmy. That's the seventh call I've had tonight from some fool whose car is stuck in the snow, and he expects me to do something about it. What do these types think I am? A snowplow?"

He was still fuming over this when the station door was pushed open and an apparition bounced in, who might have stepped out of the music halls of the sergeant's childhood. He was short and agreeably plump and wore clothes that the refined might describe as chestnut, but the outspoken sergeant called ginger. The coat had a draggled look . . . If he's come to complain about a car, thought Probyn balefully, and barked, "What can I do for you?" but not as though he hoped he'd be able to oblige.

"Come to report an accident," said Crook.

"A car?" inquired the sergeant, dangerously.

"Caused by a car—at least some motor-driven vehicle. On Folly Hill." He described what he had found there.

"Must have been lying out the better part of six hours, name of Beverley," he said, helpfully.

"Beverley," repeated the sergeant. "Don't seem to know the name. Did you notice the address on the dog's collar?"

"I wasn't born yesterday, and I don't usually have to point it out," Crook assured him, cheerfully. "Four Market Cottages, Sursum Parva." The local records showed that 4 Market Cottages was occupied by a Miss Agatha Tite. No mention of Beverley.

The police constable, who had been working at the back of the office, looked up to say, "That's the one, Sarge. Beverley's the name of the dog, big white brute, got the staggers. She takes it everywhere, see it sitting outside St. Faith's, while she . . ." He caught the sergeant's eye and prudently stopped.

"Where's St. Faith's?" inquired Crook.

"Bottom of the hill, you mightn't notice it. One of these little churches that squat in the valley."

"What time's their evensong?"

Both men looked surprised.

"She could have been down if it's held at three o'clock, say, the way it sometimes is in a country district. She'd be tigging back up the hill, plus Beverley, wouldn't need a purse, sixpenny bit in her pocket for the collection . . ." He'd got the picture in his mind as clearly as something on a movie screen. Lugging the old dog around the corner, suddenly everything goes up in smoke, might never even have seen what hit her.

"No accident has been reported," snapped the sergeant.

"I'm reporting it now," said Crook. "Mind you, I couldn't see any trace of a submerged car, unless it had flown over the hedge, but there wasn't one dangling in the trees either . . . And don't tell me it might have been a bike, because if so there'd have been a third corpse, to say nothing of the wreckage of the bicycle. And if it had been a truck it would have gone smash through the bank. Anyway, odds are a truck driver would have reported it. They've got their licenses to think about. You want to watch out for some car being taken to a local garage for a bit of a face-lift," he wound up, chattily.

The sergeant said in resentful tones, "You didn't tell me you were in the police, sir."

Crook guffawed. "Well, is it likely? I tell you no lie, the notion of me in a slop's uniform would make the angels split their sides." He yanked a card from the pocket of his suit. His cards erred on the original side, and were mostly meant to reassure the faint-hearted, who had as much to fear from a conventional lawyer as from the law itself.

"What's this? Music hall stuff?" The sergeant pushed the card back.

"Ain't it marvelous?" asked Crook with a sigh. "Don't you deal in proof hereabouts? Still, no skin off my nose." He

23

pushed the card back into his pocket. There'd be plenty of chaps glad enough of the offer. "If you should be sending anyone to the scene of the crime you might get him to rescue my scarf. Tied it to a branch to mark the spot."

"You come by car?" asked the sergeant, and Crook stared.

"How else? She's outside. Come and take a looksee," he added, boastfully, thinking of no better way to cheer this morose and lumpy man. The sergeant came out, saw the Superb and gave a sort of gasp.

"Your calendar's wrong," he pointed out. "This isn't the day for the Old Crocks' Race."

"You pit yourself against the Superb and you'll soon learn which is the old crock," Crook assured him, pleasantly. "Any dosshouse here where I could get a bed for the night? Besides that miserable pub on the corner, I mean?"

The sergeant looked at his watch. "Left it a bit late, haven't you? We keep early hours in Plowford."

"You don't know you're born," Crook assured him. "The things that go on by night . . . Well, The Live and Let Live it'll have to be. I can't let the Superb stand around in this weather." He spoke of her as affectionately as if she'd been a Derby runner. "Unless, of course, you were thinking of offering me a cell here. I wouldn't expect the Ritz."

"You try The Live and Let Live," advised the sergeant, dourly. He was going to have his work cut out, setting things in train, making a report, contacting the hospital—though if the story was right and both victims were dead, it was hard to see the sense of turning everyone out in this weather. Still, if he didn't, Crook looked capable of going back and lugging the body in himself. He glared resentfully at Crook.

"Mr. Beresford's not going to like this," he threatened. "The bar 'ull be shut . . ."

"That makes two of us, doesn't it? I'll tell him you sent me though."

"I'll want a statement," said the sergeant disagreeably, and Crook said, "O.K. What are we waiting for?"

"Tomorrow 'ull do. I've got to get the body brought in."

"What's known about her?" asked Crook, inquisitively. "Before she was dead, I mean. Any relatives? Bags of gold in the cellar?"

"Not to my knowledge," the sergeant assured him. It was a pity, he thought, that road accidents usually happened to the wrong people.

"Still, your knowledge is a bit limited, ain't it? I mean, occurred to you it mightn't be an accident at all?"

Probyn who, at that stage, didn't know Crook even by reputation, and who was later to regret his happy ignorance, couldn't realize it was second nature to the man to suspect dirty work at the crossroads in any emergency.

"You can leave all that side of it to us," the sergeant said. "We're obliged to you for reporting the incident. And we do know a certain amount. She lives alone. In any case the telephone wires are down between Folly Hill and Newtowers—we've had the report—it may be some days before service is restored. Naturally, if there was anyone at the cottage we should send a man up. You'll be informed about the inquest," he added, spitefully.

"You won't want me for that," protested Crook. "I didn't even know who she was, and I ain't a doctor, I just add two and two . . ."

"You found the body," the sergeant pointed out.

Never begin what you can't finish, was one of Crook's maxims. And great oaks from little acorns grow, meaning that you never can tell how the least promising case will develop. So he said, "Don't forget about my scarf, will you?" and took himself off. Even if the chap concerned had had the good sense to take himself out of the neighborhood, there was the car. Unless he abandoned it pro tem, hoping the snow would remove all traces of the accident. All the same, it couldn't have escaped scotfree. The garages were the police's best bet.

It was now 10:40 and there wasn't a light to be seen at The Live and Let Live, but he thundered on the door until an upper window was flung up, and Beresford's voice shouted down, asking him if he didn't know the drinking hours in this part of the country.

Crook cupped his hands around his mouth and made a pretty formidable trumpet.

"Police sent me," he bellowed, and the whole building seemed to shake for a moment—shock tremor, perhaps. "I'm a traveler," he went on.

The landlord declared he had no accommodation, the law couldn't force him to create a nonexistent room.

"I know all about the law," retorted Crook. "It's my profession." And that sobered the chap a bit. When he came down and recognized his visitor his anger rose again.

"Road accident Folly Hill," gabbled Crook. "Not mine. Police setting out to collect the body now. Can't go on, police want statement, but not tonight. Sleep on the couch, sleep on the floor, on the bar or under it. But you can't turn me away. Never heard of the Licensed Victualers Act?"

"What's all this about a body?" demanded Beresford.

"Let me in and I'll tell you. Or nip across and see the sergeant. Very put out he is. Old lady called Tite."

He didn't in the least mind stealing the official thunder, and it worked like a dream. He didn't imagine the police would love him the more, but he'd never regarded it as part of his vocation to make things easy for them, and pretty soon the dour landlord had rustled up some coffee—powdered variety, but probably better than anything the man could have made himself, and infinitely preferable to the good old river mud and water the publican called beer. By the time he was ushered into the least comfortable room he'd seen since coming back from France in 1918 the man had unbent so far as to offer him a small cold pie. "Not for me," said Mr. Crook. "I'm too young to go."

Once he'd shut his door he added up the scraps of information he'd gleaned from one source or another. The old girl was no more than ninepence in the shilling, poor as a church rat. No friends, no enemies, so far as anyone knew. Beresford had said it was fishy, though he couldn't suggest the nature of the fishiness. Crook sensibly didn't try, not having enough facts to go on. So he went to bed. And what a bed! Still, look on the bright side. A bed like this was a good preparation for a coffin. He'd hardly notice the difference . . .

He was up bright and early for greasy bacon and speckled tea, but long ago he'd refused to give his stomach best, so he paid his bill and came bouncing out as jolly as a sunbeam to rescue the Superb. On the whole, she seemed to have had a better night than he had. It was a cheerful morning, though the landscape was sculptured by the snow that had been rapidly frozen as it fell. The air was clear and frosty, and he bounded into the police station to sign his statement and leave an address. "If it's necessary for me to return for the inquest, this'll find me," he said. "I can't stop now, I've got work waiting for me in London, and you can get me day or night at one of those numbers."

When he came out he found a tall dark young man hanging about in front of the pub apparently enjoying the fresh air. He turned with a low respectful whistle as Crook approached.

"Now that really is a car," he said, and there was no doubting the sincerity of his tone. "She wouldn't be balked by a tree, she'd have blown the blooming thing down. And according to Dismal James there, there's not much prospect of digging her out for a couple of days, even if I could wait, which I can't."

"Passing up the breakfast?" asked Crook, kindly. "Well, you haven't missed much." Then he grinned. "I've got it, you're the chap I saw making for Plowford last night. They say life's an inn," he went on cheerfully, "but if there's many like this one it ain't surprising the suicide rate's going up."

"I saw your car," agreed the young man, introducing himself as Denis Carew. "Atalanta conked out in a lane at the foot of Folly Hill, buried her face in the shoulder of a sympathetic tree, and wouldn't be budged."

"I see you and me talk the same language," observed Crook, admiringly. "Can I give you a lift anywhere, or . . . ?"

"That's what I was going to ask. The fact is, I'm supposed to be meeting a V.I.P. at Southampton this morning. Meant to get down there last night—and why these tycoons can't fly over and get met at London Airport like the rest of us I don't know," he added, candidly.

"I have to go into Maidment, which sounds a roundabout way to return to London, but I've got to see someone there," Crook told him. "You might be able to get a connection. If not you're sure to get something from Martindale, always supposing any trains are running at all. One thing," he added consolingly, "the ship won't have docked last night."

"She wasn't due to dock till this morning, but she was promised to come in early." He added that he was a kind of P.R.O. for a business organization working on exports. The man he had to meet was crossing from Canada to attend a trade delegation . . .

"What are we waiting for?" asked Crook.

Denis Carew got into the seat next the driver. "Fact is, I hate leaving her," he confided, "but she'll have to be dug out, and I haven't the time even if I could get the tools."

"One thing," Crook consoled him, "no one can steal her. Come down Folly Hill last night?" he added casually.

"I was warned it would be suicide, and was told about a detour. I must have gone all round the county. This snow makes it difficult to read the signposts and this is virgin ground to me. Anyway, Atalanta signified she'd had enough for one day and ditched me." He laughed ruefully. "Hence my appearance at The Live and Let Live, and if I'd known what the pub was like I'm not sure I wouldn't have started walking to Southampton."

"What time did you get to—wherever this place is where your girl friend stalled?"

Denis looked a bit vague. "Round about nine, I should think."

"Did you persuade mine host to give you a meal? Well no, I needn't have asked. You'd probably be running for the cemetery stakes if you'd eaten there."

"I know something about trying to get food in the English countryside on a Sunday evening," Denis assured him. "I brought a nosebag along with me. It might have been the end of the world that last hour or two. Except for you I don't believe I saw a living creature."

Crook tersely explained the line of his questions, and at Maidment stopped the Superb as near the police station as the law allowed. Miss Tite, he was told, was in the mortuary and he insisted on going to see her. Paying his last respects, he called it. There she was on her marble slab, remote and scornful, a proper old party and just his cup of tea. He thought it would have shown a nice Crusader touch if they'd put the dog at her feet, but the police don't think of these niceties. They leave them to crackpots like Arthur Crook. He collected his scarf, which they'd kindly dried on a radiator, and went out to join his passenger.

"I suppose they didn't ask to see me?" Denis suggested, and Crook answered, "Well, it's not a tea party. Any reason why they should?"

"I couldn't tell them anything, if that's what you mean, but it occurred to me they might want to interview anyone who was in the vicinity last night. Oh well," he added, hastily, "forget it." They didn't speak much till they reached Martindale, where they had been told there was more chance of getting a train to Southampton; here Denis alighted, bought his host a pint—a point in his favor—and accepted Crook's business card.

"Not touting for trade, of course," Crook assured him. "It ain't allowed, but keep it for a souvenir."

He made his way back to London feeling as though he'd been entered for a giant obstacle race. He found himself thinking about the old woman and the young man, and wondering about a possible connection.

"Forget it," Denis had said, impatiently. But in so saying he'd insured that this was the one thing Crook wouldn't do.

3

The inquest on the old woman was held at Maidment on Tuesday. It was a brief affair, adjourned when medical evidence as to the cause of death had been given, and identity fixed, in order that the police could continue inquiries. At that stage the death didn't attract much attention. Most people were too much concerned with their own affairs, the effects of the snow, the freezing of pipes with consequent water shortage, to bother much with an old woman who, in her lifetime, certainly hadn't bothered much about them.

The family was represented by the snooty wife of a snooty cousin living in Canterbury, who thought it typical of the old girl to have got herself knocked off in this sort of weather. She identified the body, listened to an odd person in a vulgarly bright brown suit give evidence of finding it in the snow, looked searchingly at a girl who seemed utterly out of place here and who surely hadn't anything to do with mad old cousin Agatha during her lifetime, and that was all. Really, she thought, why they should have sent for me—but her husband had said they were the only surviving relatives and, so far as he could recall, there were two or three quite nice pieces among the junk in her cabinlike cottage. She heard the coroner say a burial certificate could now be issued, and that was that.

"All this red tape," she said, scornfully, picking up her gloves and not caring who heard her. "All on the taxpayer's money."

The bright brown person turned right around to stare.

"She's entitled to her whack like anyone else," he suggested.

Dorothy Blake scowled in response. "My husband's cousin was an eccentric. She never answered letters, lived in a dream, probably walked under the car without even knowing it was there. Really, I can see no point in keeping the affair open. The verdict must be a foregone conclusion."

"Hasn't occurred to you to wonder what a car was doing on the wrong side of the road?" suggested the vulgar person, who looked no more human in her eyes than a dolled-up chimp in a circus. "If you want my opinion"—and she saw she was going to get it whether she wanted it or not—"she gave her life to save one of these little ones, and of such is the kingdom of heaven."

Dorothy Blake sniffed ostentatiously. Drunk and at this hour of the day, said her pinched aristocratic features. Even a police officer, standing nearby, looked startled at Crook's pronouncement.

"Wouldn't let the dog go, see?" amplified Crook.

"It only proves my original contention"—Dorothy's voice was as crisp as a new-baked biscuit—"that she was peculiar. Any sane person would have let go of the lead and saved her own skin."

"What for?" demanded Crook. "It's like the poet and the primrose. (He was apt to come out with these sudden scraps of culture, confounding his audience.) 'A primrose by the river's brim a yellow primrose was to him, and it was nothing more.' I daresay that dog was just a smelly old brute to you, but to her it was the one who made a house a home. And I know what I'm talking about," he added, threateningly. "I've forgotten more about these old girls than your high-and-mightiness ever knew. She may have been seventy-plus with a face like the back of a taxicab, but she was still a woman, and women can't live on their own." His glance included the shocked police officer. "They have to look after someone or something. Who makes your life, lady? Hubby? Well, maybe. Same way, that old dog made hers."

"I don't know who you are," began Dorothy Blake, and he said, "Crook's the name, Arthur Crook. And old girls like your auntie are my cup of tea. By the way," he added to the police officer, "when you go over the house, don't forget to look under the carpets. She might have paved the floor with five-pound notes. One of my old girls did. Used to boast that she trod on a fortune under her feet."

Coming out of the stuffy little room where the inquest had been held he almost cannoned against a creature so charming, so fresh, so like a flower herself, that he put back his head and began to sniff the air. Then he remembered seeing her in the courtroom, sitting at the back as if she thought no one would notice her there.

"She's got a hope," he reflected, his agile imagination wondering where she fitted in and already resolved to find out.

"Friend of yours, sugar?" he suggested, and she turned in sudden fear. He noted the fear at once and stored the fact in his memory.

"No, no, I never even met her. That is, I've probably seen her about . . ." Her vague voice faded. Then she asked in a nervous burst, "Do you think they'll find whoever was responsible?"

"They'll do their best," returned Crook, solemnly, "and an angel can do no more. You shouldn't have come, sugar," he went on. "Too distressin'. Though, if she should be looking on from anywhere, it 'ud be a treat for her to see something not smelling of death and decay."

He saw she looked faint and he caught her arm and marched her into The Ewe Lamb. She was so much surprised she didn't even protest. She couldn't have told you precisely why she'd come to the inquest; some kind of compulsion—

even a sense of guilt. She didn't examine her motives too closely; she'd left Mike at The Leather Bottle, the social center of her small world, where you picked up the bus on market days, and where the paper boy and the baker and the milkman left their goods to be collected by all those crazy enough to live in a wood like a lot of flopsy bunnies. Mike would be happy enough. He was a favorite with Mrs. Gorton, who kept chickens and rabbits and had a tame budgerigar.

Sara had looked around nervously in case either of the drivers of the Albions were in court, but of course they weren't. It's only the mouse with a nonexistent I.Q. that deliberately puts its head into the unbaited trap. There were a few villagers and a hard-faced handsome woman, who proved to be a cousin, and this man in the bright brown suit who now caught her arm and was ordering a shot of brandy for her despite her protests.

"Feel like declaring an interest?" he was asking, and she started with such violence that the liquid splashed over the edge of the glass.

"I don't know what you mean."

"You can't be thinking. Let's have it. Did you know the old lady?"

"I told you, I never spoke to her. I'm not even sure if I ever saw her. Of course, she might have been at the Saturday Market . . ."

"According to the local P.C., most of the food in the house seems to be for Fido. What made you come then, sugar?"

She said slowly, "My husband was killed in a car crash. I suppose that was the link."

Crook remained looking at her for a full minute, his eyes very bright and skeptical. "You suppose?"

She drained the glass. "If you mean, it was foolish of me you're right. There was nothing to be gained. I must go back now, Mrs. Gorton's looking after my little boy, and about lunchtime he's inclined to get under her feet. It's so hard to keep him out of the bar. He's only four."

"He's starting young," commented Crook. "Still, it's a step in the right direction. Easy to see you've given a hostage to fortune." He asked one or two questions about Mike. Then, just as she was saying thank you and beginning to edge out of the bar, he whipped a card out of his pocket.

"Keep it," he advised her, "you never know when it might come in handy. I mean, if you should change your mind . . ."

"Change my mind?"

"Not got a parrot in your pocket, have you? No, I thought not. I mean, as to why you turned up this morning. I know about your husband, but that's a reason to stay away. Well, don't forget, you can get me all round the clock, and I mean round the clock. Telephone orders welcome," he added.

Dorothy Blake, still shocked by Ginger's lack of respect, had watched the couple move away together; her expression would have soured any milk within a radius of five hundred miles.

"What's he doing here?" she demanded of the sergeant.

"I thought you knew," returned the man, wondering, as don't we all, how it is that these battle-axes are always spared while the flowers of the forest get mown down regardless. "He's the one that found Miss Tite."

"I suppose he isn't also the one who ran her down," suggested Dorothy, spitefully

"Well," returned the sergeant, who had been doing his homework since the discovery of the old lady in the snow, "from what I hear, Mr. Crook might run down you or me and make it look like an accident and win a commendation from the coroner for getting assistance so fast; but he'd crash that precious car of his sooner than scrape the skin of an old lady's knuckles. He has a sort of reputation," he added a shade defensively. "Ask the police in the metropolitan division."

Dorothy remained unimpressed. "What does he do? Persuade old women to take out insurances or subscribe to good causes? I wonder how much money he wheedled out of Cousin Agatha."

"You've got it wrong, ma'am." The sergeant felt it was time for the k.o. "Mr. Crook's a lawyer from London, he never met Miss Tite—not living, that is—and when he found her he turned round in a snowstorm and came back. I wouldn't," he wound up, "care to be the chap who ran the old lady down and left her to die in the snow, not with Mr. Crook on my heels."

Dorothy Blake dismissed Crook as too gross for further consideration. "Who was the girl?"

"I really couldn't say, madam. A friend of Mr. Crook's perhaps. Or of your auntie."

"She was not my aunt," retorted Dorothy Blake, glacially. "She was my husband's cousin, twice removed. What was she doing here—the girl, I mean?"

"The public has a perfect right to attend."

"Ghoulish, I call it."

Shaking the dust of the unsympathetic court off her fashionable shoes, Dorothy had herself driven to Sursum Parva to survey the prospects and labeled the few pieces she intended to keep; presumably everything would come to them. She thrust all the old woman's clothes into a battered trunk—they'd do for the refugees—the rest of the stuff was junk, not worth the price of carting away.

She went on to see the vicar about the funeral, but when she mentioned cremation, which in her view was the only civilized form of committal, she found that here at least the old girl had superseded her.

"Miss Tite bought a plot in the cemetery," Mr. Purvis said. "And she left an appropriate sum to cover the cost of the funeral and the provision of a stone. She wished everything to be very simple. Simply her name and the date of her death."

She couldn't make him arrange the funeral for the next day, which involved a second journey, all very tiresome. Really, the old thing had been nothing but a burden, start to finish.

When, a few days later, she discovered there was a homemade will, but perfectly legal, bequeathing everything to the Royal Society for the Prevention of Cruelty to Animals, she was so furious she could have driven over the corpse herself.

"I certainly shan't go down for any deferred inquest," she assured her husband. "Not that anything fresh is likely to turn up." But as the odious Crook would have been the first to tell her, it's always the unexpected that happens.

If there had been few people at the inquest there were none at the funeral. Neither the ginger-headed man nor the slightly haggard-looking girl turned up. According to the wishes of the deceased, there was no choir and no flowers. The weather didn't encourage hanging about and it was all over by midday. Driving back in her own Rollux this time, Dorothy Blake saw a young man in a duffle coat digging out what he called a car from the snowdrifts near the foot of Folly Hill; he glanced up as she went by and at the thought he might be going to ask for assistance she increased her pace and shot past him. She'd had enough of Plowford and its environs to last her a lifetime.

Denis Carew watched her go. That was something like a car, he reflected, unenviously. When earlier he had inquired about the possibility of getting mechanical assistance to release Atalanta from her gelid prison, he had been told he could abandon any such absurd hope. Too many and too valuable cars were in the same plight as his own for any labor to be available at the moment. The garage at Plowford had merely looked over its shoulder to throw out this information and the same went for the first Maidment garage he approached; but Mr. Gladstone at the Blue Garage in the High Street promised that if her owner could beguile her as far as his premises, he'd see about doing a bit of spit and polish, face-lift, underpinning, the lot. On the other hand, if she was unable to proceed under her own steam, she was as safe with her nose jammed against a treetrunk in Nightingale Lane as anywhere.

Denis, disagreeing but having the wit to keep his mouth shut, got a lift to Nightingale Lane, hired a spade and got to work. He proceeded slowly because he didn't want to scrape any more paint off his darling's complexion than he could help, and she wasn't one of these heavily made up girls at the best of times. Two of her tires seemed to be wedged in a ditch some vandal had half filled with broken glass, rotten tins and various forms of flotsam likely to do a car harm, but though he cut his own hand and, in his own parlance, bled like a pig, the car hadn't suffered. True, she'd need a new bumper and her front looked more like a Pekingese than before, but so far as he could judge without removing all the snow, it could have been a lot worse. The main thing was whether she could be coaxed to amble as far as Maidment under her own steam. Carefully he loosened the snow all around her, working her gently back and forth, throwing up miniature walls of snow as he released her wheels, rubbing the worst of the snow off the roof and windows.

He felt as if he'd worked a personal miracle when, the wheel supple under his hands, he brought her around the corner into the main road. Behind him Folly Hill reared up against the ice-colored sky. Seeing it in daylight, it looked menacing enough with its sharp curve and steep incline. The old girl, Agatha Tite, must have been in possession of unusual physical abilities for her age if she could still negotiate that. The steepness of the hill, the sudden curve and the treacherous nature of the weather—with a shudder he turned his back and set out for Maidment. Surprisingly the engine ran as sweet as spring water. He began to sing, regardless of the surprised looks turned on him and his car by the occasional passer-by. The sun was up now, and a thaw forecast, which meant the roads would be filthy and Atalanta's shampoo would be a waste of money. Still, she'd earned it. For the first time there seemed to be a smell of spring in the air. Denis found himself looking at the little cottage gardens he passed, expectant of a first primrose, the first peal of snowdrop bells.

He passed The Live and Let Live, whose landlord was standing gloomily at the door, thinking up fresh ways of poisoning his customers, without actually being run in, Denis supposed. Or perhaps more simply just contemplating suicide. There was a mess of cars in various stages of deshabille around the garage in the High Street and he was glad he'd had an early word with Mr. Gladstone. When he reached the Blue Garage its proprietor had gone out to look at a second-hand car—he did quite a bit of second-hand deals—but a tallish chap with ginger hair came to meet him, candidly interested in what he saw. The circus must be on the road today, he reflected. He'd already caught sight of an aged yellow Rolls looking rather like a gaudy hearse, that came bowling through the village, and now this.

"Don't tell me," he besought Denis, in the easy way of his kind who know their price is above rubies but are prepared to take rubies if there's nothing better going, "this is the one you had for the Monte Carlo Rally."

"She'd have left 'em all at the post, only we didn't have the time to enter," Denis agreed. "Some of us have to earn our bread, worse luck. Glad you mentioned it all the same. Shows you appreciate her."

"What did she do?" asked the young mechanic, whose name was Stokes. "Try and fly?"

"She'd do better at that than some angels I've heard of," maintained her intrepid owner. "No, she had a disagreement with a tree at the foot of Folly Hill, and the tree took advantage of the weather conditions."

"A copper bitch," agreed young Stokes, who had clearly perpetrated this witticism before.

"You've got your botany wrong," Denis assured him. "A copper beech couldn't have done this. How long?"

"Don't hurry the doctor," said Stokes. "Got to give her an x-ray first, haven't I?"

"She's running like a dream, just wants her face fixed a bit," Denis protested.

"That and half a dozen spare parts, which we may or may not have in stock." Never does to let the customer get away with a single trick. He opened the hood and looked in. "You're a lucky girl," he told her. "Someone looks after you very nice. Married?" he added, casually, closing the hood.

"What did you say?" The words jerked from Denis in sheer amazement.

"Funny," mused Stokes, "when you've been on the job for a while you can tell the cars that belong to the husbands. More gadgets inside and less work on the engine. Unmarried chaps now, they have the time and what's called the singleness of purpose."

"You're not a local chap?" hazarded Denis, and Stokes said, "Too right."

"What do your friends call you?" inquired Denis, amicably.

"The name's Stokes," said the young man pleasantly, "and I can't see that it matters to you what my pals call me."

"Fair enough," agreed Denis. "How long?" He nodded toward the car.

"Look in sometime tomorrow."

"Tomorrow, nuts. I told you, I have to work for my bread. I'll be back at six."

"Please yourself," said Stokes, airily, "but don't say I didn't warn you. There are other cars, you know." He grinned.

"I had a word with your boss," Denis reminded him. "Look!" It went through his mind that an advance payment of a pound, say, that wouldn't appear on the bill, might put Atalanta at the top of the heap. Two pounds would make it a certainty. If he didn't get the car back tonight he'd have to return to London as best he could by train. "Well"—he handed over the money—"here's something to be getting on with. Six o'clock?"

"I'll see what I can do," promised Stokes.

After Denis had gone he stood looking at the car for a minute, a speculative thought in his eye. He saw the pound notes in his hand and grinned again. A shame to take the money, he thought. He had begun to examine the car when his employer came in.

"What have you got there?" he demanded. "What does the owner think this place is? A hospital?"

"He said he'd had a word with you—this is the car that got bogged in the snow in Nightingale Lane." His expression changed, a new warmth came into his voice. "She's a beaut, Mr. Gladstone," he said, simply. "May not be much to look at, but take a gander at her engine. He swears you promised him priority," he added, in extenuating tones. "Can't wait till tomorrow, got to get back to London."

"What's wrong with her?" remarked Gladstone in gloomy tones.

"I'll know more when I've had a chance to give her the once-over. If you want to know what I think . . ."

"I don't," said Gladstone, simply.

"I was just going for my tea," murmured young Stokes.

"It'll have to wait. I've got a chap coming in about this second-hand Bostock, and no one to attend to the pumps." He read the whole situation easily enough. Chap had bought young Stokes—no morality about any more—and if you have to knuckle under to the new generation you don't have to make it too obvious.

Young Stokes grinned and nodded. He knew about Mr. Gladstone's transactions. All open and above-board, of course, but anyone with an angled eye couldn't help noticing new bits of furniture that suddenly appeared and were taken in by the side door, and no invoices presented. And once a whole case of beer. Oh well, decided Stokes, more than one way to kill a cat, and good luck to him. He turned his attention to the job in hand.

He was standing beside her, looking unwontedly grave, when Gladstone came back.

"In and out like a dose of salts," he said rubbing his hands, meaning he'd had quite a profitable deal with the Bostock. "That done, Stokes?"

"Just got to polish her off," said the young man.

"What's up? She's all right, isn't she?"

"I don't know," said Stokes, in a tone so weighted and grave, and therefore so different from his normal near-insolence, that the older man was immediately impressed.

"What do you mean—you don't know?"

"It's not that I don't know what was wrong with her. It wasn't too bad, she'll live to run another day. But . . ."

"Well?" Gladstone sounded impatient.

"This chap who brought her in said she banged up against a tree in Nightingale Lane."

"Didn't she look as if she had?"

"Just a tree," repeated young Stokes. "He didn't say anything about running into a sheep or a cow . . ."

"Why should he, if he didn't? Pull yourself together, Stokes."

"Well," said Stokes, "it's the first time I've heard of a tree bleeding."

Gladstone, who had been about to move off, turned sharply.

"What are you talking about?"

"There was blood on the hood, Mr. Gladstone. At first I thought it was rust, though why there should be rust on the hood and nowhere else is anyone's guess. Then I looked again, and I'll swear it was blood."

"Perhaps he cut himself," suggested Gladstone, rather feebly. From the look in young Stokes's eye he could see he was in for trouble.

"It was on the hood under the snow."

"He could still have cut his hand, couldn't he?"

"Well, yes. Come to think of it he had got a bit of plaster . . ."

"Well then?" Gladstone sounded impatient.

"Only that wouldn't account for the hairs."

"What hairs are these?"

"Like I said—a cow or a sheep—short, white, more like a cow really. Only what would a cow be doing walking up a lane in a snowstorm?"

"It could," suggested Mr. Gladstone, "be trying to get back to its barn."

"And the snow got in its eyes and it walked into the car? All the same, it's odd. I mean, that's not pasture land round there."

"Just what are you getting at?" retorted Gladstone, crisply.

"There was that police message, Mr. Gladstone, went round all the garages . . ."

"To look for a car that might have been involved in the fatality to Miss Tite. Well, but—Stokes, are you saying this car could be it?"

"He doesn't look the sort of chap who'd knock an old woman down and leave her to die, not when he's sober, anyway," Stokes allowed. "Only, if he was sober, would he have run the car against a tree anyway?"

"Which way was the car facing?" inquired Gladstone, abruptly.

That momentarily winded his young companion. "How on earth should I know? I mean, it's hardly the sort of thing you'd ask . . ."

"It's the sort of thing the police will ask."

"The police?"

"Isn't that what you had in mind?"

Young Stokes's lips tightened. "Look, Mr. Gladstone," he declared, "I'm not accusing anyone. But you know what they say. If the police don't bring in a clue within a week, there's a tendency to write a case off as unsolved."

"I don't know who told you that," interrupted Gladstone, "but I shouldn't think it's true."

"Anyway, before they wrote it off, if that's what they do, wouldn't you think they'd come down to the individual garages and make sure there's no information—that's why I told you. I mean, say I wasn't here when a chap came, and you said there wasn't anything suspicious—well," he tailed off rather desperately, "I just thought I'd mention it."

Gladstone stroked his chin; he seemed a bit agitated. "Just suppose they did, Stokes, they'd want proof. Well, can we give them proof? If you'd thought there was something queer about the car why didn't you leave it on one side?"

"I didn't start thinking—well, I've got better things than other chaps' cars to think about"—Stokes defended himself—"not till I came to the hairs. I'd washed her over and she was a bit bashed, and then I started looking closer and—well," he confessed, making the best of a bad job, "at first I thought why say anything? I mean, you can't do the old lady any good, and no one wants to tangle with the police—only that dog was white, remember? And this chap was in a whale of a hurry to get out of the neighborhood."

"I suppose he gave you something for yourself? All right, if chaps are fool enough . . ." But his voice was grim as the day of doom.

"It was two pounds," blurted out Stokes. "That's a bit high, only—well, I thought most likely he runs an expense sheet— nice work if you can get it—but I begin to see you're right, Mr. Gladstone, I don't want to make trouble, and as you say we couldn't prove . . ."

"Less of your we," said Gladstone. It was the first time he'd ever had Stokes at a disadvantage. "This chap's only got to say you made a mistake, you couldn't even prove about the money . . ." He spoke with vigor, but inwardly he was quite upset. He was a man who did everything possible these days to avoid trouble. For years he'd suffered from a nagging wife, had made the mistake of marrying a masterful woman with a little bit of her own, and all through his married life he'd played second fiddle to a brother-in-law who was the senior partner in the business. Now heaven had taken pity on him and he was free of the pair of them, all he asked for was peace. And though he didn't often find himself in agreement with his young assistant, he knew that wise men kept away from the police. "Doesn't occur to you that if this chap had been involved he'd have taken his car for repair right out of the district?" he suggested. "Got her here under her own steam, didn't he?"

Young Stokes suddenly cheered up. "That's a fact, Mr. Gladstone. I hadn't thought."

Gladstone wished the young man had kept his suspicions unvoiced. Nobody could help poor Agatha now. And suppose Stokes was wrong—and he couldn't prove anything, it would be one young man's word against another—it would be pretty rough on the car's owner. Mud sticks. "I don't know what you think we can do now," he burst forth. "I didn't see the car myself, or we might have a case."

"I did wonder"—young Stokes hesitated—"chap's coming back at six, you might have a word."

"Ask him if he's the chap who ran down an old woman and went on his way? You can't have that kind of accident and not know it."

"He could have a perfectly reasonable explanation," urged Stokes. "Oh well, I just thought I should mention it." No gratitude, these old buzzards. Time I thought of moving on, he told himself. The place was about as cheerful as a wet weekend, anyway. These were still the golden days for motor mechanics, they didn't have to worry about the dole or hanging around the Exchange, and whatever Gladstone might think of him personally, he couldn't deny his assistant's competence.

Cost him his immortal soul if he did, reflected young Stokes, bitterly.

4

When Denis returned at six according to schedule, he was pleased to find his car awaiting him, with shining morning face.

"That's what I call service," he said, in appreciative tones.

Mr. Gladstone suddenly appeared like the pantomime witch leaping through a trapdoor.

"That was a nasty collision you had," he offered.

"You know how it is with women." Denis's voice was easy, you'd have said he hadn't a care in the world. "Get an idea into their heads and there's no stopping 'em. Why she chose that particular tree is as much a mystery to me as to you. Still, she took it gently all things considered. Just ambled over like a perfect lady and laid her head against the trunk."

Gladstone frowned. "That wasn't the collision I had in mind."

Denis looked up sharply. "What's that supposed to mean?"

"My chap found some white hairs on the front of the hood."

"I don't believe it," said Denis, scornfully.

"Think of any reason why Stokes should invent it?" Mr. Gladstone's tone was dry, and Denis sobered at once.

"Well, no. But . . ." He paused. "It flummoxes me, too—unless it was the cows," he added, not too helpfully.

"Cows?"

"About five miles out of Burnside. I wasn't going at much more than a crawl, weather being what it was, when some chap came herding cows—back to be milked perhaps. I wouldn't know."

"You couldn't but know if they were ready for milking," Mr. Gladstone assured him, briefly.

"I'm not a countryman, and anyway it was taking me all I knew to steer Atalanta through the waste as it was. You'd think those precious cows had never seen a car before. Came roaring up as if I was the man from Mars. To tell you the truth, I was afraid one of them might spoil Atalanta's beauty. She's not precisely in her first youth . . ."

"It's no joke injuring a valuable beast like a cow." The garagekeeper's voice was a good match for the icy wind. "Not in the country, that is."

"I hope you don't imagine we career down Piccadilly looking for cows to slaughter," Denis pointed out. "Anyway, if farmers are anything like poultrykeepers—knock over an old hen who wouldn't recognize an egg if she saw one, and they're ready to go into the box and swear she was the best layer of the lot."

"And that's your explanation, sir?" Gladstone made it clear he didn't think much of it.

"It might not win the Ellery Queen Award but it's the best I can offer."

"And the blood?" Mr. Gladstone was rather like a human snowplow himself.

"That's simpler. I cut my hand on a bit of broken glass, bled like a pig." He held out his bandaged finger as proof. "As for the hairs"—his voice was suddenly quietly savage—"I can tell you where they didn't come from, and that was an old dog lugging an old woman up a hill."

Gladstone metaphorically drew in his horns. This chap was an awkward customer, and Stokes had made a proper cow of the job. Either he should have left the car the way it was, or kept his big mouth shut. This way he saw to it they got the worst of both worlds.

"Just thought I'd mention it," he mumbled. "Farmers think a lot of their cattle hereabouts."

"When you hear of one reporting a cow that came home minus one foot you can drop me a postcard." Nothing of sunshine and light here. He asked for his bill, checked it and paid.

"There's one I wouldn't want to meet in lonely lane after dark," observed Stokes, who had been listening from a vantage point at the back of the yard. He had doffed his overalls and was buttoning himself into his jacket. Six o'clock was his knocking-off time, and he didn't believe in letting himself be put upon.

"You heard?" asked his employer, looking at his assistant with dislike. "It was most likely a cow."

"And the blood was his own? Well, why shouldn't it be true?" Young Stokes sent him a contemptuous look. "As you say, Mr. Gladstone."

If the old chap saw a man cut his wife's throat he'd cross the road and look into a shop window pretending he hadn't seen a thing. A natural shirker. Oh well, let it ride. He'd said his piece, The Ewe Lamb was open and he had Denis's two quid. Start with The Ewe Lamb, go on to The Flying Fox. It wasn't often he had so much in his pocket on a Thursday night. Easy come, easy go, that was Stokes. Tomorrow was payday, wages were good now, even old skinflints like Gladstone had to shell out; and at the weekend money came easy. Pushing off, followed by Gladstone's disapproving gaze, he thought again, time I was moving on. New jobs, new pubs, new birds.

There was no one he knew in The Ewe Lamb, so he didn't stay long. The Flying Fox looked more promising. He looked around for a mate, so they could pair up, pick up a couple of girls and go along to the pictures. Maidment was a dead hole, not much to do. He used the phone at The Flying Fox to call a friend, but no soap. He didn't mind much, just chattered on for a bit preventing a man old enough to be his father from using the line, then went to the bar. He recognized someone there, bit of a wet fish really, who worked on the *Maidment Record*. No future there, though. The paper was said to be dying on its feet. From his appearance old Hardie—must be every day of thirty-five—was dying with it. He used to hang about the Fox and The Jolly Tars in the hope of picking up a squib or two. Young Stokes, who couldn't stand his own company for long, but would have been shocked to know that anyone on earth agreed with him, ranged up alongside.

"What's yours?" he asked.

Hardie nearly fell off his stool with shock.

"Give it a name," encouraged young Stokes. A little imp of malice gleamed in his eyes. "Looking for a scoop?" he went on, when he'd given the order. "Maybe I can help."

These young chaps! thought Hardie in much the same way as Gladstone had done. But, like Gladstone, he knew you couldn't afford to disregard them. They were the kings of creation these days and they knew it. Hardie was a disappointed man; starting with the usual high hopes he'd expected to be in Fleet Street long before this, but here he was running hither and thither for titbits like some measly little lapdog. He eyed young Stokes morosely. Hold him up by the heels and the money 'ud come rattling out of his pockets. He took his pint and said, "Cheers!" adding, "Things must be booming in your line these days."

"Got a bit for you," offered young Stokes. "The cow that loved cars. How's that for a headline?"

"Go on," said Hardie, not half sure he wasn't having his leg pulled.

"See your boss is running a safety first campaign," continued Stokes, unabashed. "Warning drivers to look out for kids, old-age pensioners, cyclists, motorcyclists, stray dogs, errand boys and acts of God. How you can see where you're going if you have to keep your eye on that lot he doesn't explain. And he's forgotten something. Cows." He banged his empty glass on the counter and ordered same again. Hardie quickly drained his also, in order to be included in the refill.

"Which cow was this?" he asked.

"One of old Oliver's herd—we think." Chuckling, he retailed the story of Atalanta.

"Might do," acknowledged Hardie. "Have to be handled carefully though. We don't want this chap bringing an action against the paper."

"He won't do that," retorted Stokes, elaborately scornful. "If he'd meant to make a stink he'd have dotted old Gladstone's i's for him." He paused for an instant—such a witty chap and didn't he know it? Hardie smiled mechanically. "But he just paid up and made off like the wind. What d'you make of that?"

Hardie shrugged. "Maybe he was having a butting match with his grandmother." Suddenly his whole face sharpened, he tilted up a nose as bony as a bird's bill. "What night was this?"

"Night of the snow—Sunday that 'ud be."

"Sunday! Didn't say where—oh yes, Burnside."

"Car buckled up in Nightingale Lane. What's up?"

"Nightingale Lane—and white hairs. Sunday's the day that old dog died on Folly Hill."

Stokes glanced around. A couple of nubile young females had drifted in while they were talking, with spider-leg coiffures, huge round eyes. He gave them a casual glance, and they put their heads together as if he didn't exist. He turned back to Hardie.

"What's that you were saying about a dog?"

"Miss Tite's dog. That was white. But that was killed Folly Hill. This chap came round by Burnside."

"Now, look," Stokes expostulated, "that's police talk. What do we pay 'em for but to sort out trouble?"

"Who said anything about the police?"

"Leave me out, I was just doing you a good turn. Bit of a giggle. I've already had old man Gladstone on at me," he added, gloomily. If I'd had any suspicions, I should have left the car as it was for the authorities to see. And given my two pounds to the Police Orphan Fund, I suppose. That's what the chap gave me to make it a rush job," he explained. "Anyhow, the old girl's gone, no sense crying over spilt milk, and Gladstone doesn't want the cops brought in. Funny, that!" he added, speculatively. "Makes you wonder what he's got to hide."

The door opened again and a chap called Percy Baynes strolled in. He recognized Stokes and saluted him. "You see what I see?" he inquired casually, indicating the nubile females. Five minutes later the two pairs had coalesced; Hardie might have vanished like a puff of smoke for all the notice any of them took of him. And that suited him, too.

Like the invisible man, Tom Hardie walked out of the bar, along the passage and up four stairs to the pay phone on a half-landing. He telephoned Mr. Oliver.

"*Maidment Record* here," he said. "There's a story going round about one of your cows being damaged by a car last Sunday, and, since we're running a motorists' safety week . . ."

"Someone pulling your leg," said Oliver, brief and inelegant.

"You mean it wasn't one of yours?"

"If it was it's the first I've heard of it, and I'm not one of those fools who leave all the spadework to the cowman. And if it had been one of mine the world would have known about it before this."

"Sunday afternoon," pleaded Hardie, sounding a bit desperate.

"What gives you the idea?"

"Chap at a local garage found a car that was abandoned on Sunday with white hairs and some blood on the hood. Driver says he cannoned into a cow . . ."

"Then *he's* pulling your leg. Here, half a minute. Did you say Sunday?"

"That's right."

"Blood and hair?"

"Yes."

"White hair?"

"Well, yes, he said a sort of white."

"You take my tip," said Oliver somberly, "it's not an injured cow you're looking for. Other animals besides cows have white hair. You want to think about that. Sunday," he repeated with some emphasis.

49

"You're thinking—a white dog. Anyway, this chap says he wasn't on Folly Hill."

He was talking to himself. Oliver had rung off. Hardie came slowly back and oiled out of The Flying Fox. That made two of them—them being the blooming public—whose thoughts had instantly sprung to the Tite tragedy, as it had been christened. Might be worth a try, no knowing, and he'd nothing else to offer. He made his way to the offices of the *Record*.

Geoff Saunders, the *Record*'s present editor, was in his way nearly as disillusioned as his reporter. The *Record* had been a sound little paper once, not a nation-wide or even country-wide circulation, but creditable figures and some contributors who had later made their name in Fleet Street. That was when Maidment was a cozy market town with people coming in from miles around. But when they put up the glass factory at Martindale, Maidment soon became no more than a suburb. The housing estates went up near the factory, the television aerials were like harbor masts, all the young chaps had motor scooters. Maidment was like a sedate maiden aunt in a party of rambunctious matrons. And the paper suffered, well, of course it did. For one thing, with TV and radio and these tape recorders that started selling like hotcakes, the reading public dropped. The proprietor had warned Saunders they couldn't go on losing money and if he valued his job he'd better do something about it. But what? The fact was, things didn't happen in Maidment any more. (Nonsense, Crook would have said, things happen everywhere, all the time. It's just a matter of keeping your peepers on the ball.) In Fleet Street, perhaps, news could be manufactured, but not here, where everybody knew everybody else's business anyway. Martindale had its own organ, the *Martindale and Harrowford Gazette*, and that was shooting like a hollyhock in spring. He looked gloomily at his scraps, like things out of a ragbag. That old woman on Folly Hill now—could he make anything of that? Police were foxed, relatives uninterested, body interred. He was brooding along these lines when Hardie came in.

"What have you got?" he demanded harshly.

Hardie told him. Saunders stroked his chin. Shocking, the way bristles came up—worse than bills these days.

"Could do," he said at last. "God knows we need something. What kind of a car?"

"Regency."

The editor nodded. "That's something. Don't see many of them about these days. This chap—what's his name?"

"Stokes?"

"That's the one—couldn't be selling you a pup, I suppose?"

"Why?" asked Hardie, simply. "Nothing in it for him."

"You'd need to play it down," said Saunders. "Feature the cow rather than the car. And don't mention the dog. Anything known about the owner?"

"Londoner, Stokes says. Just passing through. Gave him two pounds to make a rush job of it."

"That doesn't signify. Chaps with the dough 'ull buy time as easy as they buy drinks. Not that we can mention him directly, anyhow. Whose cow?"

"Should be one of Oliver's, but he says no."

"Unidentified cow, unidentified driver—best keep it that way. *Somewhere in the county there is a cow with a passion for cars.* Color?"

Car? Hardie thought. Had Stokes said? He recalled a phrase. She'd got a nice tan on her, Stokes had observed in his facetious way. Asked if she'd been in the Monte Carlo Rally.

"We might use it," agreed Saunders, grudgingly. "But go easy on the details. It's safety week, remember."

So the ball began to roll.

51

5

From the time of Agatha Tite's death to the day of the funeral Sara lived like someone with an exposed nerve. The sound of a knock on the door, a tap on the window—these primitive announcements still exist in the country—was enough to send the blood rushing to her head. Her heart would start thumping.

"Mummy, you do look funny," Mike observed.

She could even be grateful that the telephone remained dumb; the second heavy snowfall had brought down yet more lines, and subscribers were warned that in the outlying districts it might be some time before service could be restored. In a way it was a comfort that the weather remained too bad for Mike to go far from the cottage; she could scarcely let him go outside by himself, fearing disaster.

"I'm not a baby any more," Mike yelled. "I can go to the bathroom by myself."

She listened to the local news on the radio, but no one came forward with information about a red car that had knocked down and killed an insignificant old woman. She had compelled herself to attend the inquest for the satisfaction of hearing the coroner announce a verdict of death by misadventure, which would mean the end of the inquiry. The adjournment came to her as a horrid shock. It meant the affair would drag on and on, not be smartly folded up and put away on the shelf—and forgotten. She brooded a lot these days—that bumbling old chap she'd met at the inquest, who had insisted on buying her a drink. A queer card he'd seemed, but you could never be sure. Her husband Michael would have enjoyed him, she thought.

She thought, too, about the red car; after such a collision it must need some professional attention, but no one had taken a statement to the police. Of course, chaps like that don't have to come into the limelight when they get into a bit of trouble. There's always a buddy tucked away in a back street somewhere who will do the necessary and keep quiet about it, provided the price is right. And, without her evidence, the police hadn't really got a case. Even if they discovered the existence of the red car, they couldn't so much as pin a manslaughter charge on the driver. And that evidence she'd no intention of giving. It was too late to help old Miss Tite, and anyway what's an aged witch's death compared with a little boy's safety? It was part of the nightmare that she'd realized from the start he wouldn't have a qualm about putting his implicit threat into effect. Under the surface charm and good looks, the "Know any bee that likes chocolate?" camaraderie, he was as ruthless as a machine. And even if he knew there was no advantage to be reaped for himself he was capable of acting from sheer, thwarted malice. Don't ask her how she knew—she knew.

By Saturday morning, though, her mood had begun to lighten. Agatha Tite was dead and buried, there'd been no further threat, and anyway Saturday was the highlight of the week, the day of the market at Maidment. Practically everyone went in—Plowford shops were as miserable as Plowford beer, and you couldn't say more than that. Mike adored the market, though Sara often wished she had a third eye and a third ear for the occasion. Mike was like quicksilver, darting this way and that; an independent child, his attention was perpetually caught by some new thing or other, some strange voice, a man selling from a stall, a lady offering lucky charms. He didn't appear to know the meaning of shyness or reserve; he took after his father in that.

They never took the car to Maidment on a Saturday; parking difficulties were virtually insuperable; no matter how early you arrived the CAR PARK FULL notices were always in place. Anyway, Mike wouldn't have foregone the delight of the bus ride for the world. They picked it up at The Leather Bottle, where it arrived from Martindale more than half-full. This inn was Sara's nearest link to civilization.

There were a few cottages dotted around in the woods, occupied by a selection of humanity that would have enchanted Crook—two aged sisters who'd locked their door years ago and were reputed not to be sure if the war was over or not; old Mrs. Clarke who walked about with streaming white hair and open sandals on enormous bare feet; a brace of artists whose work was too rare ever to be shown. Mrs. Foster and her two little girls lived about a mile away, but the young marrieds (Mrs. F. was a divorcee) were farther along the Martindale Road, nearer the schools and the churches and the public park. But they all met—all those who didn't live on berries and leaves, that is—at the Bottle on Saturday mornings.

Sara was well known there. Plowford tradesmen wouldn't deliver at the cottage, so each day she and Mike went down to collect the milk and the newspaper and the mail, and any parcels that might have accumulated there. Twice a week they brought back the empty oil drums and collected the full ones. And kind Mrs. Gorton acted as baby-sitter for Mike on the few occasions when Sara couldn't take him on errands.

This particular Saturday was a bright day with a merry wind blowing, though the snow was still lying in hummocks and oases at the foot of trees and in the half-concealed hollows. Mike was in the best of spirits, discussing the personalities of dwellers, animal and fairy, who lived in the woods. Tigger

always came to the market and served as a means of identification if Mike strayed too far. A little boy—four years old—carrying a stuffed tiger with ears and tail that don't match. At the
Bottle, Sara handed over her plastic milk-bottle carrier and
glanced at the morning paper that had arrived a little earlier.
The weekly edition of the *Record* was there, too, but she never
opened that till Saturday afternoon. There were two or three
letters, but after a quick glance her heart subsided. Nothing
unusual, nothing mysterious, no cheap white envelope with her
name in printed capitals. The cloud that never hovered far
away moved off a little.

Mike's hand slipped into hers. "You're wearing your storm
face," he accused her.

Two or three people smiled. She knew what they were thinking. Shocking to lose your husband like that, but she'd drawn a
lucky prize out of the bran pie when she got Mike. The little
boy was holding the field, telling everyone he was going to
have his hair cut. One of the women asked, a bit shocked,
"Doesn't your mummy cut your hair?"

"Women," confided Mike, "don't understand about cutting
hair." And the way he tossed his head, with his confidential
smile, bestowed on them all equally, suddenly brought the
dead Michael back with a poignancy his widow could hardly
bear.

"Oh well," she said, recovering herself quickly, "he's a man
now." Besides, a haircut at Tredgold's was a treat in itself. Mike
insisted on going early so as to get a ride on the rocking-horse,
a fierce creature with scarlet nostrils and a tossing mane; and
then a turn in the swing chairs. In the long run, Sara had
expostulated once, it would be cheaper to buy a toupee. But he
didn't have much fun, except what he made for himself, and
he was going to feel the loss of a father more and more as the
years went by. She knew, of course, what people said about
widows marrying again, but she'd never met anyone she could
even contemplate in Michael's shoes.

Anyway, Mike's sojourn at Tredgold's gave her a chance to
order the groceries and get on with some essential jobs, like
buying a new girdle or a pair of shoes. Afterward they lunched

at the Cloverleaf Café, where the food was approved by the children and loathed by the adults. There were always some other mums and children there and casual market friendships were set up. She alighted at The Sceptre and joined the line at the cake shop. The sort of cakes children like were sold here, and she waited nearly fifteen minutes to collect an order given some days before, and choose some rye bread that you couldn't buy from the baker. Mike was given a cheesecake to eat to keep him quiet, and as usual, when she turned from the counter he was holding his own audience.

"Mummy sees things," he was announcing proudly. "She saw a big dog on the road. And there wasn't any dog there."

Sara smiled uncertainly at two women standing by; she sensed that while they might be sympathetic it was more likely they thought her child no more than ninepence in the shilling. Dolts, she reflected scornfully. Mike could run rings around all their brats.

"But then they probably think the same of me," she decided recklessly. Young, passably attractive, living from choice in a wood, pumping water in the nineteen-sixties. They weren't really country folk—most of them had married into farming families, or bought little houses outside the towns—but they were all accustomed to the amenities of civilization, and would have thought it dismal to pump your own water and have outside sanitation.

Progress down the street was as slow as always, with Mike saluting his many friends, stopping to admire pavement artists and peddlers, and only hustled on by Sara's reminder (a) that if he didn't get to Tredgold's on time he wouldn't get his ride, and (b) they were going to the market after lunch, before catching the 4:10 bus home, and he'd get better value for his money there. She saw him installed at the hairdresser, then ran down to the Bolton's for groceries, waited there in another line, went to the public library to get books for them both, collected her weekly woman's magazine, then went into the post office for National Health stamps. Here she met Mrs. Foster with her two little girls and invited them to come to tea with Mike on Monday. Finding a phone booth free she hurried into that to try and engage another mother with two children to complete the party, but the operator told her the number was still out of commission, so she decided she and Mike would walk over next day and leave the invitation in person. She wanted to call her dentist and make an appointment for a check-up, but looking over her shoulder she saw several people waiting impatiently—time was money on Market Day, and with so many lines out of action there was a run on the public booth.

Dr. Carter must wait, she decided.

"Hullo again!" said a voice as she pushed clear of the line and she looked up and found herself face to face with Stan Marvyn. The encounter was such a shock that for an instant the world really did darken, and she must have stumbled, because he put out a hand and held her arm. Instantly she shook it off, as if it were a spider or some horrible insect.

"Ups-a-daisy," said Stan. "How's the little feller?"

She said impulsively, "Oh, I can't bring him marketing, he spends the time with a friend. I'll collect him on my way back."

"Heard they've found the chap who may have charged into the old girl," offered Stan, casually.

"But—you mean Red?"

"Red? Who's she?"

"The man in the red car, I mean."

"You've got it wrong," he said. "I don't know who you're talking about."

"But you can't," she panted, "let an innocent man . . ." She hadn't thought of this.

"If he's innocent he'll be able to show where he was with no help from us, won't he?" Stan offered. "You know, it's a mistake to go barging into things. Just thought I'd tip you the wink."

"You'd let him be accused, wouldn't you?" she said slowly. "Even though you knew he had nothing to do with it."

"Where did you get this idea from that I know anything? Oh well, be seeing you—maybe."

He'd gone with a cheery wave, and after an instant she went

after him, but he'd disappeared. Not that she'd anything more to say to him.

"Don't panic," she told herself. "It was sheer chance his seeing you. Of course he isn't keeping tabs on your movements, why should he be? He knows you couldn't prove anything. Anyway, Mike's safe. You didn't tell him where he was, and in any case Miss Vane would never hand him over to a stranger."

All the same, she recklessly abandoned the remainder of her shopping. It would wait till next week, or the phone would come back and she could call up. Horrible stories read in magazines or heard on the radio rushed back into her mind. Sedate elderly women calling at schools for a small pupil whose mother had sustained some shocking accident and been taken to hospital, personable young men representing themselves as doctors or emissaries . . . She set out for Tredgold's at a determined trot, the nylon bag swinging uncomfortably against her calves, the basket bruising her hip. But when she got there she fortunately caught sight of herself in a glass, and forced herself to stop for a minute before going in. She knew her son; to see her in this state would elicit one of his most candid comments. She waited long enough to collect her breath, let her cheeks cool. She glanced, apparently casually, up and down the street; she didn't see a soul she recognized.

When she entered the salon Mike was impatiently awaiting her.

"You have been a long time," he said.

"I had a lot to do," she began; then stopped in dismay. "But you've taken off all his hair," she cried. "He's as cropped as a convict—or a soldier."

"I didn't want all those curls," stormed Mike. "I'm not a girl."

For a minute she could not speak. For the first time she saw her son not as a little boy, childish, dependent, but as the young man he would presently become.

"There's one thing," she remarked at last. "You're going to be too handsome for your own good."

She paid the bill and gave the girl a box of chocolates she

had bought in the town, caught Mike's hand and off they went up the street to the Cloverleaf. The place seemed packed; they were a little later than usual, and it had filled up. Mike, with the conservatism of his years, strongly opposed going anywhere else, but luckily in a corner she spied two other mothers with a child apiece, who were signaling to her. Thankfully she sank into a chair.

"Why don't we all live on lozenges or something?" she wondered.

"Wouldn't be much pleasure left to life if we did," said Mrs. Nash promptly. "Curry's off already."

"I've had my hair cut off," announced Mike.

"Quite the little man," agreed the second mother, whose name was Brewer. "Very nice, too. Still, it's a bit of a shock when you get them shorn for the first time. I had a brooch made out of our Artie's hair," she added.

"I wouldn't dare," murmured Sara. "Mike would never stand for it."

A waitress arrived to take their order. Mike demanded liver and bacon with onions, as he always did, regardless of whether it was on the menu or not. Sara said vaguely, "Oh, anything—roast lamb would do." For a few minutes they discussed the usual domestic matters, a bargain line in this or that, a change in the staff of Burgoyne's. Then Mrs. Nash remarked, "I see they've found the man who ran down old Miss Tite. In the Record—haven't you seen it?"

"Not yet," said Sara, feeling herself going white. "I don't pick it up till I get back. How can they be sure?"

"Traces of the dog's hairs. Mind you, they don't tell you who it is. Chap in the car says it was a cow. I ask you, a cow! Townee, of course," she added, as though it was hardly necessary to explain.

"Why couldn't it have been a cow as he says?" Sara asked.

"Because no one's had a cow injured. Besides, it was the day Miss Tite was killed and she had a big white dog, remember?"

"If they don't know the driver . . . ?"

"They'll find out. My boy, Harold (one of the latest recruits to the County force) says when they do, this chap 'ull have to answer some very awkward questions. Young chap at the garage noticed it when he was washing the car down, remembers the make—oh, they'll trace it all right."

"I should hope so," agreed Mrs. Brewer.

"But—can they prove—I mean, suppose he's speaking the truth?"

Truth, Crook used to aver, is what you can make the other chap believe. But if it had been a cow, surely the animal could be found. A cow isn't like a stray cat, it's a valuable animal, you can't go about running cows down—more important than old women, really.

"Anyway, it's not a criminal offense," she heard herself say, and blushed for the folly of the words.

Mrs. Nash opened enormous nostrils and sniffed as though she'd sniff up the ocean.

"Not criminal? To knock over an old woman and leave her to die? We don't even know when she died. That lawyer from London didn't find her till hours later. I hope they give him ten years," she added, vindictively.

"He can't be found guilty because someone has found a few animal hairs on his car," Sara protested.

"It won't do him any good whichever way it goes," pronounced Mrs. Brewer with immense satisfaction. "I mean, who's going to give a job to a man like that? Put up at The Live and Let Live that night and never said a word."

"Can't you realize it could be because he hadn't a word to say?"

"Funny he didn't mention the cow."

"He might have been afraid he'd injured it . . ."

"Any man who'd leave a wounded cow in the road would do the same for a human being," pontificated Mrs. Nash. "You don't know him, do you, dear?"

"I don't even know his name," Sara protested. "Does he say he came down Folly Hill?"

"Well, of course he doesn't. But you're not going to get me to believe a young man makes a wide detour just because there's a steep slope ahead. It's against nature. Silly really not to report it. But that's townsfolk all over, never think country folk can add two and two."

Fortunately at this stage the children began to clamor for meringues, and after the usual argument won, naturally and also as usual, by the children, there was only just time to swallow a cup of coffee, get the children tidied up and go. The Cloverleaf shut down at 2:30, closing its doors against new-comers at 2:15. This gave the staff a chance of a rushed meal, after which they reset the tables and opened at 3:15 for tea.

"I've got rather a headache," murmured Sara. "Suppose, Mike, we took the 2:40 back for once? We can just do it, if we hurry, and it's never full. We don't want to stand with all these parcels."

Mike turned in incredulous rage. "You mean, go home *now?* Not go to the *market?*"

"Just this once." She smiled. "I really have got a headache."

He gave her a most unchildlike look. "Going to the market would take your mind off the headache," he prophesied darkly.

Once again Sara recognized the maddening Mrs. Carter. Mike picked up what she said as agilely as a parrot. Mrs. Carter, a self-confessed martyr to migraines, used to whirl around the cottage declaring "When you've got a headache it takes your mind off it to be at work."

"We've got an awful lot to carry," Sara pleaded.

"You could leave it with Mr. Nichols. You always do."

"But we don't want to buy anything."

He looked at her as though he couldn't believe his charming pink ears. Of course, they didn't want to buy anything; the fun of the market was to look, and occasionally, when no one was noticing you, cautiously to handle.

"You *said* we could go to the market," he insisted. "We always go to the market. Tigger wants to go to the market." And then, as a final stroke of genius, "I have to buy him a birthday present."

Sara gave in. They left their parcels with Mr. Nichols, where she bought a bottle of gin of a brand she couldn't get at the Bottle, and promised to return within the hour. Then she and Mike set forth, Tigger naturally accompanying them.

The crowd was not so bad after lunch. Indeed, the food stalls were rapidly emptying, and one or two of the stall holders were beginning to pack up their props. The cars, vans and carts were assembled in a parking lot on the north of the square, and those who could get away early had the advantage. But the food didn't interest Mike. To him food was something that appeared on your plate at regular intervals—not for him to bother how it got there. What he liked were the old-clothes stalls, Sara couldn't imagine why; he could be seen beaming at an ancient evening dress of purple velvet—who on earth had bought *that* in the first place?—a beaded sweater, a hat with a brilliant feather. He was his father's son all right—the best is good enough for me, Michael used to say. What Mike enjoyed was texture and color, the finished article meant nothing to him. They went by stalls of silver, bric-a-brac, furniture—and that gave Sara an idea. They could do with an extra chest of drawers now that Mike's possessions seemed to be perpetually and permanently on the increase. There was nothing to be seen here, but at the far end of the market a shrewd little woman had a stall where, though the goods might be shabby and not particularly a bargain, you never saw anything shoddy or badly made. It was she who had told Sara that the test of a good chest of drawers was an ability to insert the two small drawers upside down and still push them in. Mike stopped to admire some appalling plastic flowers and an immense china frog. In a minute she knew he'd be suggesting Froggy might like to live in a wood, but ruthlessly she pulled him on.

"I was only thinking," he said in offended tones, "Tigger gets lonely sometimes. And it is his birthday."

"Tigger shouldn't be so exclusive. There are plenty of other animals for him to hobnob with."

Gloom hung about her today like a miasma, although the weather was cheerful and she had managed to get most of the things she'd come out for.

Let us have a quiet hour,
Let us hob and nob with Death.

Who wrote that? She couldn't remember.

"Oh, nonsense," she adjured herself.

"What's nonsense?" demanded the little boy, turning to her with an injured stare.

"Not you, lovely. Oh look, that might be just the thing to put your belongings in."

She indicated a Victorian yellow wooden chest with white china handles and round wooden feet. She ran the drawers in and out experimentally; they ran smoothly, and the shelves themselves were made of solid wood, not the orange-box variety you found only too often in cheap modern stuff. I could decorate the handles, she told herself, paint the chest—blue or green or any color Mike liked—it would be useful wherever we went.

She asked the price. It was commonly accepted you did a bit of bargaining in the market, it was part of the fun. Anyone mad enough to pay the exact sum demanded without a bit of haggling would be marked for life. She offered two pounds less than she was prepared to pay and four pounds less than the price asked. Both women enjoyed the transaction, and when the bargain was closed each felt she had the better of the other.

"I haven't got my car with me, and I'm not sure I could strap it on the top even if I had," Sara said. "Will you be sending it over to the Bottle by the carrier during the week?"

"George could bring it Tuesday," said Mrs. West at once. "He'd want two shillings."

And a drink, reflected Sara, but the chest was sturdy and of a convenient size and she hadn't paid too much for it, so she closed with that and paid in cash. This left her rather short of money, but she was sufficiently well known now to be able to cash a check at the Bottle, and, if not, she could always go in to Plowford, where she had an arrangement with the local bank.

"You'll be able to get it home from there?" suggested Mrs. West.

"We can bring the cart along. It's a porter's cart actually; we bought it in the market for about five shillings and

Mike adores it. Between us we should be able to manage."

"How is the little boy?" asked Mrs. West, making change. "I see you haven't brought him today."

"What?" Sara whirled around. "Of course he's here. He was trailing at my heels a minute ago; at least when I saw the chest he was there."

"Are you certain?" Mrs. West looked startled, then recovered herself. "That was a silly thing to say. Of course you know if you had him or not. He must have wandered over to one of the other stalls. You know what children are."

Sara looked about her, her heart racing. Pull yourself together, you fool, she adjured herself. At this rate you'll be going to the doctor for a National Health tonic. You know what Mike is.

The market had continued to empty while she bargained for her little chest. It was after three o'clock and some of the shoppers were anxious to snatch a cup of tea before making for home. They came from the out-lying villages for miles around, mainly to shop, of course, but also for the social interchange and the pleasure of seeing more than the half-dozen neighbors they met every day. Life could be pretty solitary around here, as Sara herself knew. The market was a kind of Saturday club, you never knew who you might run into, what delicious snippets of gossip might be retailed. But after three o'clock the crowds started to disperse. A little boy as striking as Mike shouldn't be hard to spot.

Sara ran from stall to stall. She began to ask questions—my little boy—she described him carrying a toy tiger. The stall holders were prepared for the most part to call it a day. Stands were coming down, barrows and vans being loaded, unsold goods noted and repacked. They were reasonably polite, glanced up to shake their heads and go back to the job. Their voices clanged in her ear, making no sense at all. "Not here, missis. A little boy in a fur hat? Try the Golden Bough." That was the fantastic name of a stall that sold books and used toys and oddments of china, flotsam and jetsam from a hundred households. All the children loved it. Yes, she panted, he might be there. But when she had sped across the cobbles it was the same story. Behind her back Mrs. Lewis was saying to a neighbor, "Shouldn't be surprised if we had more snow. Not much point waiting, we shan't do any more business today."

At the Golden Bough the woman in charge was remarking, "Funny I didn't get an offer for that baby carriage. I quite thought . . . Yes, dear?" This to Sara, whose words seemed to be forced between clenched teeth.

"Mike. My little boy. You must have seen him. He always comes . . ."

"I daresay I did, then. What was he like?"

Inadequately she tried to describe him. "Well, I don't remember him in particular," the woman acknowledged, "but then you'd hardly expect it, would you? I mean, they come all shapes and sizes, so unless he had two heads or something . . ." She laughed to show it was a joke.

"It's not that funny," cried Sara, fiercely. "He's four years old and he's lost. He was carrying a toy tiger," she pleaded. "You must . . ."

"I told you, if there wasn't something special."

"But there is something special."

"What then?" The woman began to sound impatient.

"Well—just being Mike. I mean, people who've seen him once never forget him. He's special." She could find no alternative to express her feelings.

Mrs. Andrews smiled. "My dear, aren't they all, to their parents? I know when my children were kids I'd be downright offended if people didn't stop in the street to notice them. And now they're married with kids of their own, they're just the same about them."

In Sara's heart a furious voice shouted, "I don't want to hear about your horrible children. I don't want to hear about anyone but Mike."

"Perhaps he went off with a friend," offered Mrs. Andrews, still miraculously untroubled, but now making it clear she wanted to get on with the job of dismantling her stall and reach home before dark.

"No. He wouldn't do that. I mean he wouldn't go off with them. He knows we have to catch the four o'clock bus."

"I thought you said he was only four years old."

"He is, but he's not a moron." She checked her too-hasty tongue. There was no help to be had there. She looked around desperately. There were still a few stalls left standing, a few people gathering around cheap jewelry, china and glass, a stall with fluttering gauzy petticoats in vivid colors.

Beside this stall a few girls were standing. Perhaps Mike was concealed there. She ran across. The instant she mentioned her son the girls began to giggle.

"He's four years old," shouted Sara furiously, and there was an uneasy pause.

"Now don't take on, dear," said the stall holder. "If he's strayed the police will have him."

"The police!" cried Sara, scornfully. "You don't know Mike. It would take the whole C.I.D. to keep him quiet."

"I'll tell you what it is, he's wandered off and he couldn't see you and he thought you'd gone without him. Why not look in the car lot?"

"We didn't come by car. We came by bus."

"Well, there you are. He'll have gone to look for you at the bus station."

"At four years old? It's more than ten minutes' walk."

"He may have said to someone he'd lost his mum and they had to catch a bus, and whoever it was has taken him along. Probably crying his eyes out at this minute, wondering what's happened to you."

"Mike doesn't cry," said Sara coldly. He was the most independent child she had ever known. When it finally got through to him that Michael wasn't coming back, he had accepted the situation philosophically. He had been about three. I'll take care of you, he promised. Well, she'd lost Michael and now it looked as if she'd lost her son as well.

"You've never heard of a happy medium," her husband used to tease her. "If a friend of yours has flu you go out the same morning to order a wreath."

And it was true. Probably this woman was right. Mike wouldn't have wanted to go with a stranger, but if that stranger said, "We're going to meet Mummy," it wouldn't occur to him he was being deceived. Deception was something foreign to his experience. And it wouldn't occur to him that she could let him down. She was still to him what presumably the Almighty was to the saints of old, the rock that cannot be moved.

She turned back to say, "Thank you for taking so much trouble, let's hope you're right," and back she went across the market, her eyes on sticks as Arthur Crook would have said, for the gleam of a blue suit, a fur hat, a sudden triumphant shout as the mischiefmaker pounced from behind a dismantled stall or a heap of orange boxes. But there was no sign of him, and she made her way out of the market, where the light was beginning to fade already, and a sky, burdened with unshed snow, lowered above the roofs and treetops. She even called his name softly—Mike—Mike—Mike, we shall miss the bus. But nobody answered.

It was like a nightmare that had tormented her for weeks after Michael's funeral. In this appalling dream she had known her husband to be in deadly danger, but she could save him if she could reach a given destination within a stated time. The road was empty, there were no obvious obstacles, no one hung on her arm, there was no reason at all why she shouldn't get there in time, but her feet were made of lead, they wouldn't allow her to progress. Each time she put them down they marked the identical spot where she had been standing, and the minutes streamed by and the destination was as far away as ever, until a clock chimed and the darkness came down and it was too late—too late.

Now she felt herself the cynosure of all eyes, though actually there were few people in the streets. Those there were probably thought she'd have been having a drink or two. The road to the station stretched on forever, no kindly car offered her a lift; her eyes pierced the gathering shadows for a sight of a small familiar figure, her heart seemed to be screaming though no one but she could hear the sound; and though, now and again, a child did come dancing or idling down the street, it was never Mike.

6

At the bus station the lines were long and growing impatient. "You'd think they'd let us rest our feet," cried one exhausted housewife, her arms full of parcels. Too late Sara remembered the bag and the basket she had left with Mr. Nichols. Still, if Mike should be here, as of course he must be, they could hire a car—it was an enormous expense, but she didn't care, she'd spend a whole month's income to get him safely home. Their bus went from Bay 4 and she hurried up the line. Someone who didn't recognize her said abruptly, "The end of the line's over there."

"I'm not looking for the end of the line," retorted Sara. "It's my little boy—he must have run on ahead."

The woman stared, as if she were an idiot. Sara pushed past to the head of the line. There were some women there with young children and she forced herself to speak to each in turn.

68

"A little boy in a blue wind breaker and a fur hat, like a Russian," she implored, "carrying a striped tiger."

"A striped tiger?" One of the other children tittered. Sara could have hit him.

"Well, a toy naturally."

"He's not here," said a little boy's mother in distant tones.

"How old is he, love?" said the second, sympathetically, but when Sara said four the expression changed. As she turned away she heard one woman confide to the other, "These women can't keep an eye on their own kids, don't deserve to have them."

"Four years old," repeated the other. "Poor little thing."

Sara was so shaken with fury that for a moment it almost extinguished fear. She wished she had the laden bag so that she could bring it down on that wicked, lying head. She started to run crazily up and down the other lines in the bay, asking, asking . . . A little boy—four years old—a toy tiger —a fur hat . . .

Suddenly the awful blackness broke.

"A little boy carrying a toy tiger? Was his name Mike?"

"Yes. Yes." She could have dropped on her knees on the dirty ground and kissed the woman's shoes.

"Fancy them not telling you," marveled her informant. "But that's men all over. It's all right, dear," she added quickly. "Your husband's got him."

"My—husband?"

"Well, that's what I thought. I heard him say, 'Come on, Mike, Mummy wants us to go now. We're going in a car.' "

"A car? Where was this?"

"In the market, of course." The woman stared in turn. "That's where you were, isn't it?" She sounded puzzled. "Are you sure you're feeling all right?"

Sara felt like someone who's been wound up with a key, a toy of some monstrous kind, having to perform certain motions, make prescribed gestures, enunciate certain lines. She wasn't an individual any more, just a cog in a diabolical machine.

"A cog," she said aloud. And they all stared more than ever.

"I haven't got a husband," she explained, marveling at herself. Because the Sara Drew she knew would never have said that to a pack of strangers, and it only proved how little control she had over the robot Sara Drew who had taken her place. She pushed her hands into the pockets of her coat, feeling for the handkerchief she carried for emergencies; she could feel the sweat breaking out all over her, sure prelude to a faint in her youthful days, but that was all to the good since it showed she was still human. Her fingers felt something besides the folded handkerchief—a card, the sort shop assistants give you for reference, in case you want to telephone later. Only it wasn't that neat, more like something torn off a card. She pulled it out and there it was, the message, neatly printed, impersonal, the one she'd been expecting through the mail all week:

He's paying us a little visit, he'll be quite all right. He's a big boy now. No names, no pack drill. Remember, silence is golden.

The ridiculous melodramatic message didn't seem true; even in a film it would have sounded inept—but it was there, she wasn't dreaming, and she knew, of course, who'd put it there. Thrust it into her pocket in the press without her even knowing. But then in the crowd, with everybody rubbing against you and other people's shopping baskets catching your coat and bumping your arm, it wasn't surprising she had felt nothing. She never had any doubt, of course, who was responsible. It was that man—she didn't know his name yet; it was funny, she stifled a crazy inclination to laugh; he had her son and she didn't even know his name.

She realized how easily he had lured Mike. "Why, it's the Bunny-suckle," he'd say. "Come on, Mike, Mummy's waiting. We're going home in my car." Mike would surely have protested at being cheated of his bus ride. Perhaps he'd decided to raise his outcry when he met his mother face to face. But even if he protested no one would notice. The market was packed with children who didn't want to go home, and twisted and whined and shouted. No one cared. Everyone knew what kids were like. Only—when he reached the car and she wasn't there, wouldn't he set up a yell then? Not if the man said, "She's doing a bit of shopping in the town." Mike would remember Mr. Nichols, they always visited him on their way back to the bus station, and once in the car it wouldn't matter. She'd seen the pace of the driver; and no doubt he had his own methods of quieting a tiresome four-year-old.

She felt as though she were standing on the rim of the world looking down into the abyss.

"What is it?" asked the woman to whom she had been speaking. The line began to stream forward, the bus having arrived without either of them noticing it. Sara looked up. She saw the glance and recognized it. She'd only got to say, "It's wrong, it's a kidnaping" and she'd find herself hustled off to the police station, statements made, descriptions given—and she remembered what she'd known about him from that first afternoon. Play the game his way if you want to see Mike again, insisted a small voice in her head.

To her everlasting credit she achieved a laugh, the sort of laugh a skeleton might produce; her smile, that followed, was a skeleton's smile, too.

"You said it yourself," she murmured. "Men are the end." She whisked the card in front of the other woman's nose without letting her see what was written on it. "He must have slipped this into my pocket while I was bargaining for the chest of drawers. Mike's godfather," she explained. "We saw him earlier in the day, now he's taken him home, leaving me to come on by bus.

"Well, that's a relief," agreed the woman, but her voice sounded doubtful. "You'd think they'd wait for you, though."

She looked wildly around. The bus had arrived in Bay No. 4, and people were pushing forward to get seats.

"You'll miss your bus if you're not careful," Sara said. "And thank you—for the minute I was quite alarmed."

"Who wouldn't be? I hope you'll give that young man a piece of your mind when you get back. Did you say your bus was No. 4? You'll just catch it, won't you?"

"I left my parcels down in the market, I seem to have

lost my head completely." Oh that false, false voice and the false laugh that accompanied it. "Never mind, it'll give me a chance to get a cup of tea."

She doesn't believe me, at least she's not sure, Sara decided, watching the other move away at last to take the last seat in the crowded bus.

All the bays were emptying now. The No. 5 went off last, crowded like the rest, luggage racks jammed with parcels. Only a few people remained in the bus station, waiting for the long-distance buses that weren't council-operated. There was a cafeteria here, and Sara longed to sit down, have a cup of tea but she didn't dare. Someone might have noticed her talking, might try to open a conversation. Someone might remember seeing her arrive with a little boy and wonder what she'd done with him. In vain she counseled herself to be her age, who was going to notice one particular mother and child? But she couldn't believe anyone could fail to notice Mike.

She walked away from the darkening bus terminus back to the market, because there didn't seem anywhere else to go. And there were the goods she'd left at Mr. Nichols's. If she didn't pick those up he'd start asking questions, too. In her mind was a crazy hope that the young man had only intended to teach her a sharp lesson and would be waiting back on the cobbles. If only that's true, she thought, and this mindless hope lent wings to her feet. She didn't care now about the innocent owner of the tan car, he was a grown man, he could look after himself. Mike was helpless, a little boy of four, her own . . .

The market was like a theater when the play's over. All the make-up and greasepaint, so to speak, were being taken off, stalls were all coming down, the last shoppers were walking away with their eleventh-hour bargains. She crossed the cobblestones, greasy and soiled now with empty cigarette cartons, chocolate papers, crumpled bags, and went into the car lot. Not many cars remained, and there wasn't a man with a little boy standing by a blue car picked out with a darker trim, though she sought everywhere. Sometimes, when the parking lot was full, drivers put their vehicles on a bit of waste ground beyond. But now even this space was empty. A dark snowy cloud was crossing the sky, which seemed to be crouching lower and lower over the earth.

She didn't dare hang about for fear of being questioned—there were always police near the market on the lookout for petty thieves and bag snatchers—and, of course, for lost children—only naturally they hadn't supposed Mike was lost. She remembered Mr. Nichols and ran back to find him putting up the shutters.

"Thought you'd forgotten, Mrs. Drew," he said, cheerfully, and went behind the counter to collect her goods. "Where's Mike?" he added. "I had a little something for him."

"Oh, we met his godfather and he took him home. It makes it easier to get on the bus without a child."

Ananias, she thought, was struck dead for less than that, and yet it was true—it was easier. I don't kno.v the difference between truth and falsity any more, she thought.

She took the chocolate bar and hurried away as fast as she could, though why—why? The next and last bus didn't go till six o'clock, nearly an hour and a half to wait. Back she went to the market, though it was no good, and she'd only attract attention. But as though the violence of her feeling could compel Mike's presence she loitered on the dirty stones looking despairingly at the dirty sky.

"Looking for anyone?"

She swung around, her heart beating wildly, but it was only a policeman who had strolled across the market.

"I missed my bus," she gabbled. "There won't be another for more than an hour. I was thinking—I might get a taxi."

They both looked disbelievingly at the empty rank. He was a new man, she thought, not one of those who knew Mike.

"There's only a stand for three," he told her in a deep voice. "They go quickly market days. Might do better to try the Cross."

She sent an explanatory glance at the parcels grouped at her feet.

"It's uphill. Perhaps if I wait . . ." But it wasn't likely a taxi would come back here now.

"You'd do better at the Cross," he said, but when he realized

73

the silly creature wasn't going to take his advice he moved away.

"Go, go," her mind was screaming. "Don't ask me any more questions."

She watched him, bored, impersonal; once he looked over his shoulder.

"Keeping an eye on me. Suppose he did see me with Mike? Suppose Mike spoke to him? That's my mummy."

But he didn't come back and she stood in a sort of desperate reverie till the toot of a horn made her turn again. One of the taxis, against all probability, had returned.

She stumbled toward it. "Where to, missis?"

She told him and he frowned. He'd never heard of Fell Cottage. When she told him where it was he shook his head. "Outside the radius," he explained. "And I wouldn't get a fare coming back, not that far, not this time of the evening."

Taxis going outside the radius were entitled to make their own prices, she reminded him. He quoted his, and she staggered. It was outrageous, and they both knew it. They both knew, though, she was going to accept. The policeman had turned and was watching them. The driver didn't offer to help with the parcels—why should he? She wouldn't give him any extra—but she fumbled open the door of the cab and got them inside, and they moved off. As they left Maidment behind them she wanted to scream, "Stop, stop! Let me out. Mike's still here somewhere." She had a vision of two of them watching her go, concealed by a wall, the man's hand over the little boy's mouth, perhaps, to stop him from screaming. There's your mummy, gone off without you. Now will you be a good boy?

But it wouldn't be like that. Mike wasn't there, and whether she ever saw him again, alive, depended on herself. Once more she thought of Michael. How could you let this happen to me? she panted. She must have spoken aloud, for the driver turned his head and looked curiously through the window glass separating them. He slid it back.

"You say anything?"

"Doing accounts," she lied quickly. She made herself lean back and appear relaxed.

The drive seemed to go on forever. It was strange—in the bus it never seemed particularly long—but then she'd never been alone in the bus. When the car reached The Leather Bottle the driver stopped.

"Can't go any further," he announced briefly. "Didn't tell me you lived in the wilderness. I have to think of my tires and springs."

But he unbent sufficiently to help her with her parcels. She remembered the milk and bread and papers she had to collect, as she watched the taxi go rapidly away.

Mrs. Gorton, attracted by the sound of the cab stopping and then driving off, came to the side door of the inn. When she spied Sara she exclaimed, "Why, Mrs. Drew! This is a surprise. I thought you'd gone by an hour ago."

Sara steeled herself for the inevitable question, What's happened to Mike? but it didn't come.

"No wonder you didn't come in for your things," the garrulous good-hearted woman ran on. "Mind you, I tapped on the window when I saw Mike . . ."

"You—saw—Mike?"

The earth at Sara's feet gaped, she would have sworn she looked directly into a black pit.

"So I thought you'd missed the bus and decided to hire a car sooner than wait for the next one. Should have known, I suppose. Don't often see a hire-car pale blue . . ."

"So they are back!" Her powers of speech returned. "Mike's godfather said he'd bring him, I hadn't finished the marketing —and then I missed the bus."

"You'd think they'd come to meet you, help with the parcels . . ." Mrs. Gorton sounded disapproving.

"They expected me back on the six o'clock," pointed out Sara, who, for the moment, knew all the answers. "We won't come down again tonight, though. I'll just take what I can carry and fetch the rest on the cart tomorrow."

Her heart had begun to sing. She'd been right the first time, he meant to teach her a lesson. Of course he would be there when she arrived, to dictate terms, and whatever agreement he forced upon her she'd accept. And tomorrow, well, in a few days, she'd pack up and they'd both leave the county, settle somewhere miles from a hillside where a harmless old woman had been ridden down, where even her name wouldn't register. As for the man the police suspected, let him look out for himself. She knew at that moment that even if he was faced with a manslaughter charge and she knew he'd be found guilty, she wouldn't speak.

She took the gin and the milk and the bread and the perishable goods and stumbled along the treacherous road to the cottage. Now she could even feel for the merciless driver who'd stopped at the Bottle. Not reasonable really to expect him to bring her down here. She made all the haste she could, tripping over stones and roots still concealed by snow. She could only think of one thing—Mike would be there. Mrs. Gorton wouldn't have made a mistake. Besides, she'd mentioned a blue car. She didn't think he would be hurt, because Mike hurt would be no use to a blackmailer. And that, of course, was what he was. At the back of her mind a certain pattern was forming, but she wouldn't look at it, wouldn't consider it, wouldn't think of anything but Mike. The road seemed endless and the weather was as heavy as a winding sheet. Suddenly through the dark she saw a light gleam ahead. It came from the cottage, it had to come from the cottage, there was nowhere else. That meant they were there. She knew then she hadn't been certain until this instant. He can do anything to me, she thought, anything, just so long as Mike is safe.

But as she drew nearer she realized something else, something that sent her heart rushing into her throat again. There was only one light burning, and that wasn't inside the cottage. It was the light on the porch, the interior was still dark. Of course, she had locked the house when they left that morning, but Mike knew where they kept the key, on the ledge above the door, so why hadn't he told him? There seemed only one answer. Mike hadn't told him where to find the key because he couldn't. And then for the first time it occurred to her as strange that he hadn't called out to Mrs. Gorton as the car bowled past. Mike was great at these impromptu greetings, would yell at a bus driver or any casual acquaintance. But he'd sat there without a word. She tried to remember what Mrs. Gorton had said while she repacked her basket with the things they'd need most. Just sat there, holding his tiger; she hadn't noticed the driver.

Sara reached the gate at last, opened it and stumbled up the little path. On the wooden seat in the porch there sat a striped stuffed tiger with ears and tail that didn't quite match. There was a bit of paper pinned to his chest, with a neatly printed message:

> *I guess you realize I mean business.*
> *It's up to you.*

And, underneath, the three words that had been printed on the card she found in her pocket:

> *Silence is golden.*

Inside, the cottage was dark and cold. There was an oil stove against one wall that never went out, night or day, so the atmosphere must have been warm, but she didn't feel it. Yet the main impression of the interior was not so much cold as silence, a black, dragging silence that might go on for all eternity. Silence—the golden mean, she thought. She put her parcels blindly on the table, and walked from room to room, but there was no hope left in her heart. She knew Mike wouldn't be here; all she could do was wait for the next message. Only patience had never been her strong suit. It couldn't have been easy to persuade the little boy to leave his beloved Tigger on the porch. "Tigger likes company," he used to say. "Tigger's one of us, isn't he, Mummy?" What, then, had he told him? Leave Tigger here to let Mummy know we arrived safely, and we'll go and build a snowman? But it was too dark. A drive in the woods? The same applied. Remembering the woods, she shuddered afresh. They sloped for a long, long way, were full of hollows and ditches and thickets; she had seen pictures in newspapers of searches for other women's lost children, the men spread out, the police beating the tangled branches, ponds and canals being dragged, dogs nosing their way over rough country. Her eye fell on the telephone. Go on, she told herself, pick it up, do something, don't just sit there and let them torment you. She lifted the receiver at last, but the line was still dead.

Go down to the Bottle then, take your messages, tell Mrs. Gorton the truth. Tom Gorton would go down to the police station on his cherished motorbike. She could describe the man, the car, give them Mike's photo. And when they asked why she was so sure then—well, then she'd have to tell them about Miss Tite and what she'd seen on Sunday. They'd move then all right. In her imagination she heard the voices of announcers— Home Service, Light Program, B.B.C. Television, Independent Networks, all chanting the same thing . . . Lured away by a young man (with a description of him that would fit about forty thousand others), driving a light blue car picked out with dark blue—an Albion, though, that should help—Michael Drew, aged four, known as Mike, wearing a fur hat . . . and pictures of him flashed on the screen. And in her too-fervent imagination the doorbell rang, the windows shook as the press came thundering through the woods, up the path, cameras snapping, pencils poised, picture of the house, picture of Sara, picture of Tigger—she heard the eager voices demanding a human story, saw the records of her husband's death sprawled across the papers—WIDOW'S DOUBLE TRAGEDY. And the next thing would be the discovery, not of the kidnaper, who would have been warned by the publicity and gone to ground—but a small body, thrust into a bush, buried in a ditch, rolled into a quarry . . .

"I can't do it," she cried. She picked up Tigger and shook him as if he had been pushing her all this while. "I've got to wait. Don't you understand? I've got to wait. They won't hurt him so long as I say nothing."

But let her make one false move, and out of sheer inhuman malice they would see to it she never saw her little boy again. Or only as she'd seen Michael more than two years ago. It was strange how she knew this—but anyone who would run down an old woman and follow that up by threatening a four-year-old boy was someone to fear. Once the hoo-ha about Miss Tite had died down (and they wouldn't be able to prove a case against this unknown man), people would soon forget, then the child would be brought back. If they ask for money, she assured Tigger, they can have everything, though everything wasn't much. Michael hadn't been the saving kind and she wasn't either. But she had one or two pieces of jewelry, she had a few bonds and shares—the future didn't worry her. She could get a job, housekeeper, caretaker, dishwasher, anything that wouldn't separate her from Mike . . . Of course, if anything should go wrong, she'd be held responsible, both by the police and the general public.

"Why didn't you notify us at once?" she could perceive a granite-faced officer demanding. "Why did you tell so many and such spontaneous lies—to the woman at the bus station, the policeman, Mrs. Gorton?" The answer would always be the same. Because I wanted him back alive. Let them all point at her, call her a coward, dolt, traitor, it didn't matter. She just wanted her little boy back alive.

Presently, like an automaton, she rose and started putting things away in cupboards. But she opened the bottle of gin, poured it into a glass, drank it like water; and like water it seemed to make no difference at all. If anything, it appeared to sharpen her wits, so that she began to realize this incident of Mike was only part of a much larger pattern. Of course, it's never pleasant to be brought into court and asked why you saw an old woman run down and never reported it, sat through the inquest with your mouth closed as a trap, but that hadn't been deliberate, not the way the stealing of Mike had been. And after all she'd been some way off; that yarn of the old woman trying to cross the road might have held water, particularly since the old thing was known to be a bit peculiar. So there's more to it than that, Sara decided. The drivers of the red and blue cars wouldn't take this risk if they had nothing but her to fear. Miss Tite was Chapter Two. Mike was Chapter Three. What mattered now were the contents of Chapter Four, and that depended on the contents of Chapter One.

"Help me, help me," she cried to the ghost of Michael. "He's your son, too."

But, of course, only a madwoman would appeal to someone who's been lying in the churchyard for twenty-six months.

And yet—and yet—after that frantic insane plea, her intelligence started to function. It seemed clear that what her persecutors were after, and for which they were prepared to pay a heavy price, was obscurity. She knew they couldn't afford to have their names linked with any police proceedings, and to avoid that they would go even to the ghastly lengths of kidnaping a child. Why then? There must be a reason, and if there was a reason she should be able to find it. It seemed to her that Mike's life depended on her being able to do this very thing. Perhaps, then, they were wanted by the police for some unsolved crime, were afraid of venturing into the limelight. It would be a serious crime, something carrying a heavy sentence. She shied away from the word murder, but it was in her mind, recurring like a decimal. She poured herself another shot of gin.

If there was an unsolved crime in the county—it didn't have to be this particular neighborhood—who would know—besides the police? And could she, Sara Drew, unskilled in such matters, supremely uninterested in the subject of crime—she never even read a detective story—discover what it was? It would be something, presumably, that had been reported in the press. In the *local* press, assuming it was a county matter. Michael used to say that daily national papers were a waste of time and money, except for the sports pages, since the radio picked out all the walnuts of the news. But local organs were a different affair. Local papers were concerned with individuals and their problems; X was barely a name to the country as a whole, but X living in the next street to you became a person.

Michael had annoyed Sara sometimes by his insistence on keeping the local paper for weeks, months sometimes, in an ever growing pile in a house that threatened to be overwhelmed by all the flotsam and jetsam neither of them wanted to throw away. After his death she'd let it all go, of course. But the one habit had remained. Week after week she neatly filed the local papers, and they were all in what they called the garden room, a little stone-paved back room where she did the flowers and Mike potted plants and generally could make as much mess as he pleased. She rose stiff and unsteady—how much of that was due to the gin?—and hauled the piles for the previous three months into the living room. The clock ticked, unnoticed; time dissolved. Tigger sat drunkenly on the window seat. She pored over the papers that shook in her hands, turning them page by page, demanding some clue.

And after what seemed hours but was actually quite a short period of time she found it. Two men, she read, had broken into a tobacco warehouse by night and escaped with a considerable haul of booty. They had, she discovered, been interrupted by a night watchman, whom they had mercilessly clobbered and left seriously injured on the ground. He wasn't found for some hours—Miss Tite again, Sara noted—and had been taken to a hospital in grave condition. He had recovered consciousness sufficiently to tell the police the marauders were young men with stockings over their faces; he couldn't identify either positively, but he had heard one call to his companion something that sounded like "Let him have it, Fred." He told the story, said the paper, between gasps and with long silences. He hadn't seen the car, but that was no matter because the police followed up a report on a stolen Vauxhall, which was subsequently found some distance from the warehouse. Police found a fingerprint in the storeroom, but this had never been identified; it didn't match up with any fingerprint in the possession of the police.

Sara put back her head. I wish Michael was here, he knows about these things. Didn't I read somewhere that even if your prints are taken as a suspected person you can insist on having them destroyed later if you aren't convicted? She couldn't be sure. But if that print belonged to one of the criminals, then they wouldn't dare take the hazard of being fingerprinted now. Because forty-eight hours after he was found on the floor of the warehouse the man, William Lake, had died. Which made the case one of capital murder.

She sat there on the floor, getting colder and colder and quite unaware of it. She couldn't see herself going to the police with this story.

"And have you any proof, Mrs. Drew?"

"Of course not. Just feminine intuition. Because there has to be some answer and I can't think of any other. Because they don't give two straws about Mike, either way, but they can't afford to let me tell my story about what I saw on the Ridge. And, since no jury would convict on my unsupported word, they wouldn't be taking much risk in coming forward. So there has to be something else . . ."

Round and round in her head it went. Now she felt in greater danger than before. No one could call Miss Tite's death murder. But William Lake—a swinging matter, she thought—and for something like that there'd be no holds barred. And they wouldn't care. That's what was so incomprehensible. Just as some people get born with only one arm or a humpback or absolutely devoid of sight, so some people seem born without a grain of moral sense. Say sin to them and it isn't even a word. Morally color-blind, she exclaimed, as if she'd made some great discovery. And in a way she had. She'd discovered that Mike's danger was even greater than she had hitherto realized.

7

The Sunday papers didn't reach The Leather Bottle until about eleven o'clock, so Sara, who had drugged herself with sleeping tablets she hadn't needed for more than a year, did not arrive until nearly midday. She had waked with a dark feeling, as though the ceiling were only a few inches above her head and might fall at any instant. For one blessed minute she moved in a dark circle of unknowing, then the whole situation became clear. She found she had propped Tigger at the foot of her bed, and he gave the scene a macabre air. For a moment she almost persuaded herself it was all a nightmare, and Mike was asleep in the next room, but when she opened the door there was his little bed, smooth as a rose petal, with his blue sleeping-suit folded on the pillow and his bunny-scuffs on the carpet.

She had forgotten to make up the boiler the previous night, and, as she knew from experience, it was the devil to relight.

By the time she got it going and the kitchen cleaned up she felt black and exhausted, and had to boil a kettle on a Calor burner before she could wash the soot off her hands. She took some aspirin, pulled her bed together, and set out for the Bottle.

Her appearance without Mike was bound to occasion comment, but if she stayed away altogether Mrs. Gorton, who was as kind as she was curious, might send her son, Tom, over to make inquiries. I daren't have anyone calling at the house, she thought, in panic. For all I know I'm being watched as it is. The thought was unnerving; as she made her way along the rough lane to the Bottle she imagined faces peeping from behind gnarled trunks, turned the corner with her heart in her mouth, started at the least sound. No one seemed to be out this morning, though. Sunday was a day of hibernation for many, who only came alive at teatime and trudged down to the warmth of the Bottle about opening time.

"I was beginning to wonder what had happened to you," declared Mrs. Gorton in her friendly way as Sara pushed open the door. "Where's Mike?"

Sara said rashly, "He's got a bit of a cold and the wind's so keen, I thought he'd better stay in. His—his godfather's with him," she added hurriedly, realizing that everyone must know she never left her son alone at the cottage.

"I didn't think he looked quite himself yesterday," Mrs. Gorton agreed. "He's such a bright little boy as a rule, but he seemed—well, lackadaisical, just sitting and staring . . ."

"How could you see all that?" cried Sara, flinging tact and discretion to the winds. "He was whirled past the window, you said they didn't stop. I'm surprised you could recognize him at all. Unless, of course, he waved."

"I told you yesterday, Mrs. Drew, he didn't wave, and that's what seemed so odd. I mean, Mike would wave at a cow or a bird or a telegraph wire. 'You'll be a railway guard when you grow up,' I always tell him, though I dare say by that time all the trains will go by themselves and we shan't need guards at all."

"I suppose he was talking to his godfather and didn't think. We had a heavy day at the market," she added, "and he'd had his hair cut very short—too short, I think, but he was very pleased about it."

She realized that she was talking about him in the past tense, and stopped, appalled.

"Mind you," Mrs. Gorton plowed on, "it never does to disregard a cold. My sister's little girl started with a cold and where did it end? Polio. Of course, one doesn't think . . ."

Sara blew up. "Mike has not got polio, he's just got a little cold, and it's not as though he were alone. I've just come to fetch the other things and the paper—the car's outside—and then I must be getting back. I've got to pack his things," she added, in what she hoped sounded like a casual voice. "He may be going to stay with his godfather for a day or two."

"All the same, you want to watch that cold. You mustn't think I'm interfering, Mrs. Drew, but Mike's such an unusual child. If anything was to happen to him we'd all feel it."

Ho! ho! thought Sara disagreeably. Trying to take out shares in my son now, are you? Well, Mike belongs to me. I don't want any advice and I don't want sympathy. All I want . . . and here she stopped, feeling the treacherous tears begin to start. All she wanted was to walk into the cottage and find Mike sitting there talking to Tigger, teaching him how to wave a paw at passers-by.

Is it too much to ask? she thought. My own child in my own house? Evidently it was too much for her.

"Your paper's on the table over there," Mrs. Gorton went on. "You know, Dr. Callender's always ready to come out even on a Sunday, in an emergency."

Sara felt her control splintering like glass under a sharp blow.

"You can't imagine, if I thought he needed a doctor, I wouldn't bring him in if I had to crawl on my hands and knees through a snowstorm," she exploded.

"Yes, my dear, I believe you would. You're going to miss him while he's away, aren't you? Couldn't you have gone, too?"

"It'll only be two or three days."

"Well, perhaps you've got a friend coming to stay. It's lonely on your own in those woods."

Sara thought, I know why it is that perfectly decent men suddenly pick up a hatchet and murder faithful, loving wives. Kindness isn't enough, service isn't enough, the human creature has a right to privacy. Only, of course, that kind of thing might be all right for townsfolk; it didn't work with country people, who know there's a natural reason for everything, and miracles are pretty fairy stories for children.

When Mrs. Gorton had helped to load the cart it was five minutes to twelve, and in five minutes the bar would be open. Mrs. Gorton beckoned Sara into her sitting room, produced a bottle and glass and said, "On the house. You're not breaking the law, having it here with me."

It's another trick to keep me here, pump me further, thought Sara, who by this time would have suspected the Archangel Gabriel. But Mrs. Gorton didn't speak of Mike again. What she did say was almost as paralyzing.

"I see they've got a line on the car that ran down old Miss Tite," she said. "I hear the owner talks about running into a cow, but Mr. Rokes says his cows weren't out at all that day, and Mr. Oliver says none of his came to any harm. Fellow should have thought up a better story, but I suppose he was caught off balance. Pity that young Stokes didn't keep his wits about him," she added in a jolly voice. "Might ha' bin a reward. Chap's a foreigner," she added.

It didn't matter where you looked, thought Sara, danger came on from all sides. It was easy to say he's a grown man, he can look after himself, and they say even prison is an experience, though of course it wouldn't come to that. (Why it shouldn't come to that she couldn't have told you.) But the fact remained he was innocent and she knew it and she wasn't going to say. Through all the turmoil and anguish of the hour, she clung to that one certainty. She wasn't going to say.

I shouldn't have told Mrs. Gorton Mike had a cold, she scolded herself, wheeling the laden cart over the rutted ground. Now she'll ask how he is, and of course everyone will know I haven't sent for Dr. Callender. It would be well to map out a plan for Mike's mythical godfather, because someone was sure to ask, "Where does he live? How big a family has he got? Why haven't we heard about him before?" She hoped no one would remember about the child with a cold that turned into polio. Within twenty-four hours the whole place would know it had happened to Mike; or else he'd have smallpox or something. Only those who have lived in a village have any notion how rumor travels.

She wheeled the cart around to the back door of the cottage and forced herself to put everything neatly away before mixing herself a drink. She washed the breakfast dishes—one cup and a coffeepot—cleaned the sink, polished the taps and sponged some of Mike's fingerprints off the paint. Too late she thought, One day, perhaps quite soon, the police might ask for those, but once the police came into the case nothing would matter any more. At least she could no longer postpone the moment when she must return to the sitting room and confront Tigger's dumb reproach from his tipsy stance on the window seat. Lunch was gin and a few crackers; later in the afternoon, because she couldn't endure the emptiness of the house and also because she feared someone who was as curious as Mrs. Gorton might "drop in" for another inquisition about Mike, she put on her snowboots and tramped aimlessly around the desolate woods. The dwellings here were slapped down hugger-mugger, like a child dropping his toys in the least expected places; they might have a quaint appearance, but they were solidly built with some notion of comfort, and had grown up before a Town and Country Planning Bill had been put on the statute book. She thought, someone may have seen them together, perhaps he'll take Mike for a walk, I might turn a corner—only, of course, she knew that was wishful thinking. No one who wasn't a moron would take that sort of risk. Mike knew everyone locally and everyone would recognize him. She began to wonder who was looking after him—you couldn't imagine the man married, and still less could you imagine him nurse-maiding a little boy. He could be locked in a room somewhere, left alone—he wasn't a coward, but he was only four.

She walked herself so exhausted that even thought grew dull. When she got back to the cottage she found she'd had a visitor in her absence. The same plain bit of paper, the same neat capitals, and even if it was gone over with a microscope you could be sure there'd be no telltale fingerprints. He was too clever for that.

> *Mike sends his love, he's very well, he says*
> *look after Tigger. And remember Bluebeard's*
> *wife.*

He must be feeling very cock-a-hoop. It was the first time he'd used Mike's name, thereby identifying himself with the kidnaper. Disagreeably, she realized that her first suspicion was probably right, someone was keeping watch, someone who knew she'd be out and chose that period to leave the note. It was an hour later when she remembered that she had used the back door both on her return from the Bottle and when she went out this afternoon. Possibly the note had been waiting for her since midday.

The light paled quickly from the sky, the threat of snow returned. Sara sat idly by the dead telephone, removing the receiver from time to time in case service had been restored. She couldn't quite make up her mind whether to be relieved or no when the line remained dead. Of course, there was nothing to stop her taking the car into Plowford, going to the station there, producing the three messages—only would Stan allow her to get that far? She'd seen their dealings with a defenseless old woman; her little car wasn't much more than an assembly of boxes, an Albion would ride right over it.

And again she battled with the conviction that to bring in the police meant signing Mike's death warrant. Besides, it was such an improbable story at this stage. If she'd gone to them right away, next morning at latest, her story might have carried some weight, since they would understand she couldn't leave a little boy alone in the cottage at night. And surely it wasn't her fault that the telephone was out of order. But now she was entangled in a choking web of her own falsehoods and concealments, and you could be sure they would trace the woman at the bus station, the young policeman, Mr. Nichols, Mrs. Gorton, and anyone to whom any of these had passed on her story.

"What would you do?" she implored her dead husband.

She knew very well what he wouldn't do. He wouldn't sit here supinely with his son in enemy hands. He'd go out with a gun—she remembered with a start the revolver he had owned, and for which he had been granted a license, during the first year of their married life, when they lived like Hansel and Gretel in the middle of a wood. Where was it now, she wondered? Stored, with the rest of her possessions, she supposed. She had left the donkey work to the lawyer, who had made all the arrangements. It was months after the disaster before she began to become alive again; if it hadn't been for Mike she wouldn't have bothered. She began to scheme. Use your wits, she said. This note was left when you weren't in the house. The front gate creaked, giving warning of any approach; whatever you were doing you'd hear it. Mike had made the experiment again and again. So—Stan had known she wouldn't be there, and it followed—didn't it? —that he was keeping an eye on her movements.

In which case, she argued, he must be quite near. Suppose I went out as if I were making for the Bottle, then round the curve before he could get me into view again; I might slip through the trees and double back. He'd be bound to return and I should catch a glimpse of him. And then I'd know—know what his accomplice looked like, she meant. Because clearly there must be at least two of them in the plot. She wouldn't allow herself to consider the possibility that they'd leave Mike tied up, gagged even, in some remote hiding place. She found herself wishing she had Michael's gun, though she'd never have the nerve to pull the trigger. Not because she felt any pity for the conspirators, but they were the only people who knew where Mike was. Next day, she decided, she would fasten both gates with a bit of black sewing cotton, it would be invisible but that way she'd know if anyone called while she was out. Although she had no reason to congratulate herself, since knowing that the criminals had entered her house didn't really advance matters in the least, she felt eased when at last she went up to bed.

Next morning she didn't think so well of the idea, but the only alternative seemed to be to go to Plowford and report the whole affair to the police; then she thought of another plan. She would go to The Leather Bottle, where the telephone might be working, and telephone from there.

I could warn them that probably they'll be watched, she thought, confusedly. After all, if there were only two of them they couldn't be in more than one place at once, and if one was spying on her and the other was guarding Mike . . . of course they would see a police officer approaching the house, but even they wouldn't attack one openly. It involved facing Mrs. Gorton again, and somehow someone would overhear her conversation—there wasn't much privacy about the Bottle—but the fat was bound to be in the fire anyway. She kept on reassuring herself all the way to the Bottle, but when she got there Mrs. Gorton said, "Oh, ours isn't working either, dear. If it's a message—the doctor, say—I'll get Tom." Tom was only seventeen and so couldn't help in the bar, and was still, in fact, making up his mind what he wanted to do.

"Oh, it's not important," said Sara, carelessly. "No, it's not the doctor. I'd have gone down in my car if that's what it was. Anyway, Mike's away just for a day or two. Didn't I tell you?"

When she got back she found the cotton was unbroken, and there was no sign of a message. She hadn't been back long when she heard a sound that half paralyzed her. It was the clatter of a telephone bell. She looked around, anticipating some form of trick, but the bell rang shrilly on and on until, unbelievingly, she picked up the receiver. Immediately a voice she thought she would recognize even in the grave, observed, "You should complain. You pay your bills, don't you? You've a right to demand service. The number of times I've tried to get through . . ."

"Where's my son?" she cried.

"Well, that's just it—what I'm trying to tell you. He . . ."

There was a noise as if eagles screamed through the room, windows blew in, curtains ripped; her head throbbed, his voice went away.

"Are you there?" she asked. She didn't know she was screaming, too.

"Where's the fire?" asked the voice; and suddenly everything went quiet again.

"Mike wants a word," he went on. "I've told him you're in hospital, but not to worry, we'll look after him, and he quite understands about not being able to come and see you, not till you're out of the wood. Now, listen, Mrs. Drew. Don't try and upset the kid or get a message through to him. Just say the usual things—'How are you? Being a good boy? Is Uncle Stan kind? Tigger sends love.' You know the kind of thing. Reassure him."

"You mean he's frightened?" She was onto that like a knife.

"He's only a little chap, it's strange here. But he's O.K."

"How long . . . ?" began Sara, between set teeth.

"The police 'ull soon lose interest, can't be too soon for us."

"Don't you know they suspect an innocent man?"

"That young fool at the garage—I'd like to have him here. Still, it's the chap's own caper, isn't it? Says it was a cow." She heard the hearty, conscienceless laugh. "Matter of fact we're planning a little journey, me and my friend, and it won't be convenient to take Mike along, so—keep your chin up. Not been to the police, I take it?"

"Not yet," she said. "But if this goes on much longer I could."

"Mightn't be such a bad idea at that."

Her senses reeled. "You're telling me to go to the police?"

"You were an eyewitness," he reminded her, smoothly.

"You want me to tell them I saw you . . ."

"Not me. Just a chap in a sort of tan-colored car—you weren't close enough to see what he was like, can't tell the make of car, but . . ."

She cried, "Stop, Stop! Of course I shan't tell them anything of the kind. If—when—I go to the police I shall tell them the truth, that there were two cars, Albions; yours, pale blue picked out with Oxford, and a red car . . ."

"It sounds as though you should see an eye doctor," Stan said. "Or maybe you're color-blind. No, it was a tan-colored car . . ."

"He's probably got an alibi," cried Sara, recklessly.

"Then he's in the clear, isn't he? That's why I say play it dodgy. Don't say what he looked like, you couldn't tell anyway, or the sort of car. No jury 'ud expect more detail than that, not in a snowstorm, and you had your little boy, too."

"If you suppose they'd clinch a case against him on that story . . ."

"You learn slow, don't you?" suggested Stan in the same easy voice. "Who wants to clinch a case? It's just that it 'ud make the slops call off the hunt, and when that happens me and my friend 'ull go off like I said, and Mike can come back to you. Simple really, isn't it?"

"Everything's simple if you don't object to lies and cheating," she said, recklessly. "But this man's got a life, too."

"Oh well!" She could almost see the casual shrug over the line. "If that's more important to you than young Mike . . ."

"You know it isn't. But what you're asking me to do is perjury . . ."

"It wouldn't come to court," explained Stan, patiently. "You think it over. I'll give you another ring tomorrow, say. Now have a word with Mike."

There was an instant's sickening pause, then Stan's voice said, "Stand by to receive" and instantly she heard her son's voice, clear as a bell.

"Hullo, Mummy."

"Hullo, darling." (Don't let your voice shake.) "Lovely to hear from you. How are you?"

"All right, thank you. Uncle Stan took me for a ride in his car."

"That must have been nice. Where did you go?"

"He says when I'm older I can have a car, too."

"Well, one of these days, perhaps. I missed you going down to the Bottle, I had to take the cart myself."

"I'm sorry you're ill, Mummy. I wanted to come and see you but Uncle Stan says they wouldn't let me in."

"I'll ask them if you can come tomorrow, shall I? Uncle Stan could bring you."

"How's Tigger, Mummy?"

"He sends his love. Oh, and where's his red jersey? He says he feels the cold."

There was a brief break in the conversation. She called, "Mike, are you still there? Mike?"

"I've got to go now," said Mike. "Good-bye."

"But you haven't told me anything. Is there a garden? Who looks after you? Oh—and isn't it silly of me?—I can't remember Auntie's name."

He didn't reply to that; there was a small sharp sound—it couldn't be a slap, surely? She cried in fury, "What's going on? What are you doing to my son?"

Stan answered her. "I told you not to try any funny business. If you try and upset the applecart now you won't be able to speak to him again." He didn't say "ever" but his tone said it for him. "It's up to you now," he reminded her.

"Do you suppose they'd believe me, after all this time?" Her voice was scornful, and rapid with fear.

"Oh, you'd think your way through that. Say you didn't think at first the evidence was worth taking—not seeing the man or knowing the number of the car or even the make. Then reading that piece in the paper got you thinking again. I hear you were at the inquest," he added, abruptly.

"Who told you that?"

"It's no secret, darling."

"Don't call me . . ."

"Who was that chap you were with?"

"I wasn't with anyone."

"Don't give me that. Why, you went into the pub together. You were seen."

"By you, I suppose?" But of course he meant by himself. The driver of the other car wouldn't recognize her if they came face to face. It all went to show that Stan was keeping tabs on her, himself keeping out of view.

"A lawyer," she said, answering his question. "Not Miss Tite's. He found the body," she added. "He comes from London."

"Say anything to him?"

"If I was going to talk to anyone it would be the police."

"You do that," Stan advised and rang off.

Like a mechanical figure she got up, and measured coffee and water. When the coffee was made she sat warming her hands on the cup, drinking the strong dark brew. She didn't doubt that if she told the police Stan's version of what had occurred and they believed her, she'd get Mike back. If they believed her. Those were the operative words. And, after all, mightn't it be a case of the ends justifying the means? Once Mike came back she could coax a lot of stray bits of information out of him, piece them together, build up a background for Stan that might eventually identify the pair of them.

I'm one step further on, I know his name's Stan, she reflected, but that wasn't much help, because he could have told Mike to call him Uncle Stan, it was no proof that it was his own name. Then another thought struck her. The call had been made direct, hadn't come through the exchange, which meant it was a local call. It followed, then, that Mike was within a certain radius, hadn't been removed from the district. But if he was alive someone must have noticed him. You can't suddenly import a four-year-old, and particularly not such a striking one as Mike, without someone being curious. And if Mike got the chance he'd talk the hind leg off a goat. Stan and Stan's girl friend—she was assuming a woman mixed up in the plot—couldn't censor every word he spoke. Unless, of course, he was a prisoner. Her thought always came back to that.

But he sounded cheerful enough, she assured herself. Not frightened, no tears, no "please Mummy, I want to come home." Could he have been drugged? But she negatived that. The voice had been far too clear. All the same, there was something, something not quite right—it had troubled her even while they were talking—a curious hesitation, almost as if he were waiting for a cue. And he hadn't answered her question about Tigger; when she said she'd gone alone to the Bottle with the cart he hadn't cried jealously, "Why didn't you wait for me?" although the cart was, next to Tigger, his most treasured possession. Instead he'd said, "I'm sorry you're ill, Mummy . . ."

Thought came to a dead stop, so suddenly it almost turned a somersault. She repeated the words. "I missed you going down to the Bottle, I had to take the cart by myself." And Mike said, "I'm sorry you're ill, Mummy. I wanted to come and see you but Uncle Stan says they wouldn't let me in." And then the truth hit her with a blow that almost knocked her out. Mike was only four but he had his wits about him. When she spoke about the cart his cue was to say, "But how can you be wheeling the cart if you're in hospital?" And he hadn't answered a single question; it was as though his side of the conversation had been made up for him, and he was obediently reading his answers off a card. What persuasion were they using to make him do that? And then a last consideration came into her mind. When they had lived for a short time with Michael's sister, after the funeral, before she moved out on her own with the child, Millicent had always ended a telephone conversation with "God bless" just before she hung up the receiver. Mike, young as he was, had been impressed by this mannerism.

"God bless who?" he demanded.

And Sara said lightly, "You, of course."

After that he had always ended a telephone conversation with "God bless me." And what earthly reason was there for him to abandon this normal procedure this afternoon? There hadn't been any sound of a scuffle, a cry, tears, anything to indicate a struggle, or a telephone receiver being dragged out of a little boy's hand.

But it was Mike's voice, I couldn't mistake it. Then the sinister thought intruded—the voice was the only genuine part of it. It wasn't like Mike to stand meekly by while Stan gave her her instructions about the driver of the tan car; then perhaps he wasn't in the room. Stan had called "Now!" and then the voice had come. Only guarded, considering, with pauses—and he hadn't taken her up on the matter of Tigger's red cardigan.

The truth seemed so obvious she wondered she hadn't

thought of it before. She hadn't been talking to Mike, only to Mike's voice on a tape-recorder. Everything he'd said had been prepared beforehand, had been impersonal, noncommittal. The real Mike would have asked, "What's wrong with you? Have you got Tigger in the hospital?" He'd have chattered away about his surroundings. And there had been the occasional hesitation where the tapes had been joined. So—what did that imply? That Mike was dead? Possibly. Only she would not let herself believe that. A dead child arouses such wrath in a community as might halt Attila himself. Most likely they had him under sedation, he could even be in another county. She picked up the receiver, she no longer had any excuse not to call the police, but she didn't make the call. The police weren't fools, they'd detect her lie, would bring the facts from her, and then the search for Stan would be on. They might find him— oh yes, they might do that and trace his companion and bring them both to justice, but it wouldn't save Mike. She waited like someone in limbo, where time has ceased to exist, waited for something she couldn't name to happen.

Two hours later Stan telephoned again.

"Well, what did they say?"

"What did who say?"

"The police, of course."

"I haven't rung them yet."

"You crazy or something? What sort of mother are you?"

"It didn't occur to you they mightn't believe me."

"That 'ud be up to you, wouldn't it?"

"But they'd realize I had been there and seen a car. Suppose they got the truth out of me? How would that help anyone?"

"You tell me," said Stan.

"And this man isn't responsible. You know he isn't."

"Fancy that! Well if you don't like that notion, how about saying it was you?"

"Now I know you're mad. Have you seen my car? It would have crumpled—and the simplest policeman isn't going to believe I could be involved in that sort of crash and not leave a trace on either of us."

"I'm only trying to be helpful," snapped Stan. "You won't

involve this chap, you won't involve yourself. Have you any better ideas?"

She said helplessly, "Only the truth."

"And when I say it's all a mistake, I wasn't there, never set eyes on the kid, wouldn't know him again if I met him—what then? Try to get it into your noddle I'm not in the picture at all. I'm just a—what's the word?—a figment of your imagination. I don't exist. Just you try and prove I do."

Something like an explosion occurred in Sara's brain. She began to laugh helplessly; it was the beginning of hysteria, though she didn't recognize it as such.

"What's so funny?" snapped Stan.

"You are. Though you don't know it yet. You're acting on a premise, an assumption, that nobody saw you with Mike—but you're wrong."

"So you say!"

"Mrs. Gorton saw you. And she saw the car. She'd come forward and testify. An army wouldn't alarm her, and she hasn't got a little boy to hold as a hostage."

"You must think me dumb to fall for that," scoffed Stan. "I mean, you should have brought it up a bit earlier."

"I didn't think of it before."

"I guessed it could be like that."

"She was surprised to see me come up in a hire car because she'd seen Mike go past sometime before with a man driving a pale blue car with a darker trim. So when I arrived she came out . . ."

"Been opening your trap, have you?"

"I told her," returned Sara, steadfastly, "that you were Mike's godfather. Everyone thinks that's where he is now."

"If I was his godfather that 'ud be the truth. Well, that accounts for her."

"No. She suspects something's queer, I've known that all along. She saw that Mike wasn't himself, didn't call out, didn't wave. She wouldn't be afraid to come into court and testify, and the police would believe her. If you had her and the Archangel Gabriel giving witness on opposite sides you'd hesitate to back the Archangel Gabriel."

"Oh, pipe down," said Stan, disgustedly. "Who do you think you're kidding? An old girl looks out of a bedroom window . . ."

"Not a bedroom window, and she's not an old girl. She's the licensee of The Leather Bottle, everyone knows her, and everyone would take her word. You wouldn't stand much chance with her if anything happened to Mike. Anything I left of you she'd mince up for the dog's dinner."

"Very nice," agreed Stan. "Now you tell me how that helps Mike?"

He laughed and rang off.

8

When she put down the receiver she found she was shaking so she could scarcely replace it on the rest. And yet surely she should feel reassured, she had spiked Stan's guns, he wouldn't dare do anything—dreadful—to Mike now, not with a witness to contend with. Mike is safe, she said, without believing it, and wondered why she didn't feel more satisfaction. She refused to examine the dregs of her mind where the appalled suspicion hid that Mike was only safe from further despoliation because he wasn't part of the human scene anymore.

Of course, she decided, trying to whip herself into activity, I must tell the police at once, now, in case Stan tries to make a bolt for it. They must be warned.

They wouldn't approve of her, of course—you were always hearing about public noncoöperation with the authorities—would think her craven, sitting right through the inquest and not making a sign. She went into her bedroom and began to change her shoes, she didn't quite know why. But she had the fixed idea that she would have to go down to the station. As she smoothed her hair and tied a scarf around it she began to rehearse what she was going to say.

A voice would answer her call—Plowford Police Station— and she'd say, "My name is Sara Drew. I live at Fell Cottage, Sursum Magna. I'm telephoning about my little boy, Mike. He was lured away at the market on Saturday by a man called Stan, who is holding him as hostage because I know it was his friend who ran down Miss Tite on Folly Hill. And I've every reason to think these are the two men concerned in the warehouse murder . . ."

She had been murmuring aloud, and now the insolence of her own words brought her to a halt. Reason—what reason had she? She wanted it to be that way because it would explain so much that was at present dark, she hadn't an iota of proof, and now that Lake—Lark—Larkin—what was his name?—was dead, she couldn't look for anyone. The fingerprint, she said, it has to be the fingerprint.

She came back into the living room; it looked dusty, unkempt, though not precisely untidy. Rooms are untidy when there are things lying about, if, say, you have a small boy rushing through them like a miniature cyclone. No, this room wasn't untidy, it was worse, it was dead. Even the air had a used feeling as if it had been devitalized and puffed back by people who'd no further use for it.

Two things happened simultaneously; the chiming clock struck the half-hour, and the front doorbell rang.

She looked at the clock first. Half past three. What had happened to the day? It had just oozed out like milk from a leaking can. As for the bell—it might be Stan, returning Mike now he knew the game was up. He'd have the wit to realize that once Mike was home she'd make no further move; she wouldn't accuse him or the driver of the red car, but she wouldn't lift a finger to help the other man, Carew, either. All the same, her heart misgave her. It wasn't like Mike to stand quietly at a door, without a sound. What have they done to him? she cried fiercely, yanking the door open.

A short, rather plump woman with a little girl on either side of her stood on the step.

The anticlimax was so tremendous that for an instant she couldn't speak, and it was Amy Foster who had the first word.

"You were expecting us?" she inquired, in a suspicious voice. "You asked us to tea on Saturday—remember?"

"Of course." Numbly she stood back to let them in. "Oh dear, I should have told you."

"Told me? What?" Amy's eyes, small and black, like little shining beetles, ran over the room's deshabille. She saw what Sara in her hasty glance had overlooked. The dirty glass, the bottle of gin two-thirds empty—a nice upbringing for Mike. She could have eaten a meal off the floor of her own house at any time of the day or night.

"That Mike isn't here," Sara was explaining. "He went at very short notice to stay with his godfather." She stopped short, horrified. Why was she keeping up this ridiculous fantasy now, when she'd made up her mind to tell the police the truth?

"He's a bit young to stay away by himself, isn't he?" Amy suggested. Her manner suggested other things, that he'd been removed from the guardianship of a woman who was only a lush in secret. "You've never spoken of his godfather before," she said.

The two little girls, having realized that Mike was away, had made a simultaneous dive upon Tigger, and were now fighting for possession.

"Put that down," Sara cried, wrenching the toy away.

"Isn't that his precious tiger?" Amy said in wondering tones. "I thought they were inseparable."

"He left him for me in case I was lonely," Sara explained. "Wasn't it charming of him?"

It was like hearing a robot use her voice, make her gestures; she still couldn't understand what she was about. Had she then been fooling herself all along the line? Hadn't she meant to go to the station after all?

"Why can't we play with him?" demanded one of the little girls. Amy should have had something done about her adenoids, Sara thought. Both of them were staring jealously at the comic shabby figure. Mike had always carried him from room to room, and Sara had insensibly done the same thing.

"When did he go?" Amy continued.

"Yesterday. His godfather came for him."

"Just like that? Out of the blue? I mean, you didn't know on Saturday or you wouldn't have asked us."

"I didn't know a thing about it then," Sara agreed.

"Just like a man. Why didn't you go, too?"

"Perhaps I wasn't invited. He rang up a little while ago," Sara ran on. "He seems to be enjoying himself, but, of course, I am counting the days till he gets back. We must have a real party then."

"Oh?" Amy's brows lifted. "Isn't anyone else . . . ?

"I was going to ask some others, but—I do apologize, Amy, I ought to have let you know."

Amy recalled something else. "Did you say he rang up?"

"Yes."

"So your telephone's working." There was a world of injury in the slightly nasal voice. Perhaps adenoidal tones ran in the family, Sara thought.

"It came back today. Isn't yours . . . ?"

"Not a peep. Do you mind if I use yours to report to the exchange?"

"Help yourself," said Sara, blindly.

She turned to the little girls—Phyllida and Dolly, of all the silly names for two small creatures who looked like Yorkshire puddings—as their mother greedily snatched up the receiver. "What would you like to do?"

"Why can't we play with Tigger?" Dolly demanded.

Behind her, her mother's voice was declaring she was going to deduct a portion of the quarterly fee for nonservice. "And don't give me that about Act of God," she threatened. What on earth made me ask her at all? Sara wondered. But, of course, the country isn't like London. You can't pick and choose; your friends and your neighbors have to coincide, unless you're going to live in a vacuum.

Amy slammed the receiver down. "Really," she observed in wrathful tones, "there are times when I long for the good old days when you could grind the faces of the poor. Now we're the poor . . . Come, Philly, Dolly, we're going home."

The little girls burst into a storm of protest. "Aunt Sara said we could stay and play."

"But Mike isn't here."

"We can play without him. We can play Hide and Seek."

"You can play that at home."

"No, we can't," they assured her. "There's nowhere to hide at home, unless we can go out-of-doors, and you never let us."

"There are just as many places to hide at home as there are here."

Two indignant voices assured her that wasn't so. "Here there's cupboards and an attic . . ."

"And a workshop . . ."

"And funny corners under the stairs . . ."

"And the glory hole."

"Aunt Sara won't want you turning her house upside down."

"But she *asked* us to stay."

"She wasn't expecting us, she'd forgotten we were coming."

Sara snatched at this excuse for postponing further immediate action.

"Why shouldn't they, Amy? I can easily mix up a few scones . . ."

"Can we have them hot from the oven?"

"Why not?"

"Too indigestible," declared their mother.

"We never have indigestion. "

"Did you walk here?" asked Sara, idiotically.

"Well, what do you suppose? Our road's still blocked. Apparently it's no one's responsibility, though we pay taxes like everyone else. It's not surprising the girls were counting on today's party. We've been shut off . . . Has Mike's godfather got any children?"

"There's one little boy there," returned Sara evasively. "He lives in Kent," she added on the spur of the moment.

"Can we go into Mike's room?" asked Phyllida, and Sara reared up at once.

"I don't think he'd like that when he isn't here. There are plenty of other places."

"There's a tree outside the window," Dolly explained. "You can climb out." They were both older than Mike, six and rising eight, but when they were together Mike invariably took the lead.

"Not in your party frocks," Amy objected. "Anyway, you don't really climb out, do you?"

"It's quite safe," said Sara. "I've got an idea, though. Why don't you practice on the typewriter? I'll put out some paper . . ."

She had a big ancient machine in a room at the back of the cottage, on a solid wooden table rescued from someone's kitchen and bought by herself in the market when she first came here. It was too big, too old-fashioned, too stained for the dainty housewives of today. She had no patience with people who couldn't stand anyone else using their machines. Mike hammered away on hers whenever the mood took him, and if he couldn't put it out of order it was unlikely that the little girls would. She saw them settled, explained about shift keys and space bar, and left them composing a letter to Mike. They were arguing fiercely whether they should say dearest or darling.

When she came back Amy Foster was thoughtfully handling Tigger. No reason why she shouldn't, of course, but Sara wanted to clout her over the head.

"They'll be quiet for a while now," she observed, pacifically, making for the kitchen.

Amy put Tigger back on the window seat and followed her.

"What's really happened to Mike?" she said.

Sara, who had just opened the refrigerator, almost dropped the milk bottle. "Happened? I told you."

"I know. I thought that was because of the kids. But it does strike me as odd that in more than six months you've never before mentioned this godfather. And why wouldn't you let the children go into his room?"

"You know what Mike's like. He likes to do the honors on his own premises."

"I suppose it wouldn't be because he's actually *there?*"

"Have you gone out of your mind?" Sara inquired.

"I'm not quite a fool. I can see there's some mystery about him, something that so preys on your mind you didn't even remember you'd asked us this afternoon, though it was only Saturday . . . Is it something contagious, because, if so . . ."

"Mike—is—not—ill," insisted Sara. "Nor is he in his room. He is not in the house, he's staying away. Well, really, Amy, is there nothing I can say that will convince you?"

"In that case you won't mind my just taking a peep, will you?"

"What's come over? I've told you—Mike's staying . . ."

"With his godfather in Kent. I know." Amy giggled, a horrid ill-bred sound. "I suppose you're not hiding a man there?"

Sara was so furious she flung caution to the winds; without another word, she marched upstairs and flung open the door of the little boy's room.

"Come and see for yourself."

In her rage she tore open the door of the blue painted wardrobe to show the little suits and rompers on decorated blue and green hangers. Not pink, Mike insisted. Pink's for girls. "Don't forget to look under the bed," she reminded her visitor.

But Mrs. Foster wasn't in the least disconcerted; she walked slowly to the bedside and stood staring at the pajama case, shaped like a spaniel; she prodded it experimentally.

"Gone away?" she inquired softly. "Without his pajamas, his hairbrush, robe"—this was hanging on the back of the door. On the shelf of the wardrobe stood a blue traveling case. "You'll have to think up something better than that, Sara."

Sara's face was so white she looked as if she might faint. "Something's wrong, isn't it?" Amy insisted. "Have you told the police?"

"What have I got to tell them?"

"What's happened to Mike."

"I've told you . . ."

"And I've told you I don't accept your explanation."

"I told you he spoke to me on the telephone this morning, he wants me to find Tigger's red cardigan, as he's afraid he may catch cold."

This piece of nonsense seemed to shake Amy Foster for a moment. Then she said, "You told Mrs. Gorton he'd had a cold, but you didn't send for Dr. Callender."

"You don't send for a doctor every time Philly or Dolly has a cold."

This was becoming dangerously like a nursery slanging match.

"And if the service only came back this morning," continued Amy, boring away like a little beetle, "how did his godfather know he could get through?"

"He tried several times, and the last time he was successful. It's the first incoming call I've had since the lines came down."

"I see." But what she saw was anyone's guess.

Sara flared up. "Really, Amy, what is all this in aid of? Why shouldn't you believe me when I say that Mike talked to me this morning? But if you're so suspicious, why don't you check with the operator? Oh no," she corrected herself, "I was forgetting. You can't check local calls."

The moment the words had left her lips she knew she had said something fatal. "Local? I thought you said his godfather lived in Kent."

She spoke so loudly that the little girls looked up wisely from the typewriter to observe, "Mummy's in a stew. Should you think it was about Mike?"

"I expect it was Aunt Sara not remembering she was coming. Let's put in a bit about Tigger." Casually they dismissed their elders and returned to the work in hand.

"Where have you put him, Sara?" Amy Foster persisted.

"I've put him nowhere, and if I had it would be nobody's affair but my own. He's my son, remember."

"Is he in hospital?"

"No. He's not ill, and this is not a contagious house."

"And yet he's gone away without any luggage and without his toys."

"He doesn't need a suitcase for a few days. And he's got

other toys besides Tigger. I told you why he was left behind . . ." But she didn't think she could keep this up much
longer.

"He hasn't run away, I suppose."

"Oh, don't be a fool. He's four years old. If he'd done anything so silly I should have had the whole neighborhood out.
Oh bother, all this talking has made me forget to light the
oven."

"I'm sure you'd rather we didn't stay. Besides, I expect
you're going to the Institute Gala this evening. I mean, with
Mike away you're a perfectly free agent."

"The gala? Oh, of course." The Countrywomen's Institute
played a great part in the rather remote lives of the neighborhood. Its annual "do" was a great affair; singing, food, dancing
for the young women who brought their husbands or boy
friends. The refreshments and the band were so good no one
stayed away who could come. The Leather Bottle was closed
for the evening and would have done precious little business if
it had been open. Not quite legal for a licensed house, perhaps,
but no one complained.

"Of course," Amy continued, "I don't get down, I can't leave
the girls. No one here will sacrifice an evening to baby-sit."

"I suppose you can't blame them," Sara murmured. "No, I
don't think I shall be going down. I'm sorry about the sham-
bles this afternoon. As soon as Mike's back we'll really have a
party and try to make it up to the girls. He went into Maidment on Saturday," she added, "and Miss Vane at Tredgold's
cut off nearly all his hair. Of course, he's as proud as Punch."

To her horror she heard her voice beginning to shake. Amy
waited; it wasn't till later that Sara realized she was waiting to
be pressed to stay. When the anticipated pressing didn't mate-
rialize she prized away her two little girls, who howled with
rage. "You promised, Aunt Sara promised." Dolly actually
kicked her mother; she'd pay for that when she got back, Sara
thought. Pray heaven her telephone doesn't come on tonight,
she added to herself, spreading a cloth over the scone mixture
—she'd as soon have tried to eat cement as solid food now—and
thank goodness, everyone will be too busy with the gala to

pay her any attention. Amy Foster wasn't very popular locally. She thought herself a shade better than her neighbors, and expected them to realize it.

But first thing in the morning she'll be down in the village spreading the glad news, Sara reflected shrewdly. I wouldn't even put it past her to drop in at the police station. Sergeant Probyn wouldn't have much time for her, but as a matter of routine he would probably ring Fell Cottage and make inquiries. And then all the fat will be in the fire, she decided.

She didn't know what she could do now; only she couldn't stay alone in the cottage any longer. If she was being watched, if anyone saw her go out, he'd only think she was one of the early birds who were going into Maidment to put things in readiness at the hall for tonight's festivities. She pulled on a leather coat, found flat-heeled stumpies and pushed her hand into her pocket for the gloves she always kept there. There was more in the pocket than the gloves—another card, just the same as before. And again she thought, But when? When? Had Stan crept up, unbeknownst, for the second time—or Stan's friend, whom she would not recognize? This, she recalled, was the coat she had worn at the inquest. She pulled out the card reluctantly. It was inscribed: ARTHUR CROOK. *Your trouble our opportunity. The firm that works all round the clock.*

It was the craziest card she had ever seen, outside a circus. But she didn't really think about that aspect of it. It was like a message, an arrow pointing the way. She hadn't been able to think where to go, whom to consult, and here was the arrow. It never occurred to her to hesitate. This Arthur Crook, this great bumbling gingerbread man, this inspired lunatic, was the answer to her problem. She couldn't have told you what she expected him to do for her, except that whatever it was it would have to be a miracle. Ultimately, she supposed, she expected him to find Mike and restore him safe and sound. She got her car out of the garage and checked gas and oil.

She saw some posters in a corner advertising tonight's event, and on the spur of the moment she slammed one of these against a window, as if to advertise her destination. Then, if

Stan or his ally were watching, he might swallow the bait. She left a lamp burning in the living room behind drawn curtains. Anyone passing would expect her to be there, assuming, of course, he hadn't seen her drive away. She put on the little transistor radio, that would burn itself out in due course, but it would enhance the impression she wanted to produce. Then she tightened the scarf around her bright hair and set out.

There was a light burning in an upper window at The Leather Bottle, but the notice announcing its closure for that evening was prominently displayed. For a moment she thought of stopping and enlisting Mrs. Gorton's help, but after another moment's reflection she decided the time wasn't yet ripe. Anyway, Mrs. Gorton was one of the pillars of the Countrywomen, all her thoughts would be with them, it wasn't fair to barge in with her troubles about Mike. And it wasn't, she discovered, going to be too easy to make the woman understand why she'd been so cagey, so mysterious. No, leave that problem to Mr. Crook when the time came.

She sailed past and along the Plowford road. Already a few stalwarts were on their way to the gala. There were a lot of preparations to be made, stalls to be set up, refreshments to be laid out. One woman, Miss Dacre, hearing the car behind her, turned, paused and waved. Confidently she expected a lift, but Sara called, "Not going your way" and sped on. She had forgotten already about the telltale poster in the window. Miss Dacre stood staring after the little car.

"Well, really," she ejaculated to no one in particular. "Who does she think she is?"

Sara glanced at her wristwatch. Nearly half past five. The clock was playing tricks with her again, it couldn't surely be so late. She could hardly hope to reach London much before eight. She would encounter the home-going traffic which was liable to be heavy. But once she was past the peak hour she would make good progress. On the main roads all the snow had been cleared away and there wouldn't be many pleasure seekers out in this cold weather.

In Maidment she almost met disaster. A much larger and heavier car suddenly shot past on the wrong side, causing her to swerve dangerously. The driver never even looked back. Sara braked and paused, her heart thumping. She hadn't allowed for possible accident, no one knew whither she was bent, and she had the conviction that Mike's life now depended on her reaching Mr. Crook all in one piece. Young Stokes from the Blue Garage saw the incident; he was returning from delivering a car to a favored customer. He knew Sara slightly, she had turned up once when the Plowford garage was too busy to undertake a speedy repair. Drifting up alongside he asked sympathetically, "Everything all right, Mrs. Drew?"

She turned her head sharply. "Did you see that?" she demanded. "He might have crushed me like an eggshell."

"You want to be careful, some of these chaps never heard of patience," counseled young Stokes—a clear case of the pot calling the kettle black, but you have to butter up the customers. "Going to the gala, then?"

"No. No, I have to go to London." Well, now someone knew. If her car should be forced off the road and herself injured, this young man would remember meeting her.

"Someone looking after the little boy?" asked young Stokes, and she said hastily, too hastily, "Yes. I shall only be away the one night."

Then the lights changed and she drove on. She felt nervous tonight, didn't drive with her normal fluid ease. You must have been born at the wheel, Michael used to say, though she didn't often drive him. Like most good drivers, he hated anyone else to be in control. Young Stokes watched her go. Something in the wind, he thought, and fell to wondering whether she'd make it all in one piece. The roads got crowded and there were plenty of bad drivers even in the country. When he got back to the garage old Gladstone wanted him to put in a bit of overtime on a rush job.

"I'm taking my bird out tonight," he protested.

"Won't take you above an hour. Can't she wait?"

"You must have forgotten what it's like, being a married man," ejaculated young Stokes. "Why, the birds think we were only born to be at their beck and call."

But, when he'd made his official protest, he agreed to telephone her. He was away some time. When he came back he said, "I hope the chap this car belongs to understands I'm jeopardizing my whole future to do him a favor."

"Oh, get on with it," said Mr. Gladstone ungratefully. These young chaps expected you to lick their boots before they'd put themselves out in the smallest degree; and then they'd stand out for double pay and probably look for a bit on the side from the car's owner.

"These birds are fussy," said his young assistant. "They don't like being stood up. I've promised mine everything, bar a wedding ring, to hang on for me tonight."

As he got to work he added casually, "Remember that Mrs. Drew—little green-blue Waterbury—lives out on the blasted heath beyond the Bottle? There's one whose name is going to be on a casualty list before morning, if she doesn't watch her step. Parked her kid and off for the bright lights. Driving all over the road and saying it was the other chap's fault. Women drivers!"

He got down to the job, but he went on thinking about Sara.

Sara in the meantime was making steadily for the metropolis. A certain Mrs. Wallace had told her years ago, "If ever you're in a hole and need a bed, come to me. I can fix you up, if it means sleeping in the bath and bedding Mike down in a bottom drawer." The address was Cromwell Road, only a stone's throw from Crook's home address. She had brought a small case and all the money she had in the house. At one time it seemed as if fate, having provided Mr. Crook, was now taking a malicious interest in postponing their encounter; at one crossroads a car had broken down and police were slowly directing the traffic. At another light something had gone wrong with the mechanism and they waited five minutes before the driver of the front car grimly released his brake and went forward into the traffic. And to top everything she just reached the level crossing at Deadman's Point as the gates closed.

Still, she made town by eight o'clock, which was pretty good going, and drove straight to Mrs. Wallace in Cromwell Road.

But when she got there a hard-faced young woman told her Mrs. Wallace had been gone for more than twelve months; the house was now let out as furnished flatlets, with communal bathrooms and cooking facilities. She pointed to a note on the door: no vacancies. Anyway she didn't rent under a month, and in any event, she continued, piling up the agony, she was full for months to come.

Sara decided to let the matter ride for the moment. So off she tooled to Brandon Street, where Crook had a top-floor flat. Only when she pressed the bell of the top flat did it occur to her that he might have someone with him already.

When Mr. Crook heard his buzzer sound, it didn't bother him at all that it should be after eight o'clock. People came to see him at all hours. He simply pressed the catch that released the front door and went out to meet his visitor. He never wasted time asking for a declaration of identity that might be inconvenient to give from a doorstep with a possible cop over the way. He pulled heavy hideous curtains across the window, since this was a populous neighborhood and nothing's going to stop people getting any free thrills that come their way, and some of the dramas and melodramas that were enacted in that shabby top room were worth twelve months' viewing on TV. From the head of the stairway he called hospitably, "Does the road wind uphill all the way?" answering his own question, "Yes, to the very end."

He didn't recognize the female figure who came lightly around the curve of the staircase; mostly it was men who called after dark, but now we've got comparative equality between the sexes there's no reason why women shouldn't time their visits after the pubs open. He only hoped her business wouldn't take too long, he'd got a thirst on him all wool and a yard wide.

"Mr. Crook," said the girl, coming up the last few stairs, "you told me to call if I needed help."

"And very nice to be taken at your word," said Crook, heartily. "Come in. Why," he recognized her warmly, "it's the solitary mourner. Sit down, sugar."

She looked as if she might collapse at any moment, and though he could cope with most situations, he shrank from the notion of a tête-à-tête with a young and attractive corpse. Sara sank into what was probably the least comfortable chair in the borough and found a glass being put into her hand.

"I've been here before," she exclaimed, and he took her meaning at once.

"Best introduction I know," he said, indicating the glass. "Drink up."

She swallowed automatically—and started to choke.

"It's firewater," she protested.

Crook looked apologetic. "The grateful client who gave it me called it Irish whiskey. I doubt it's poisoned." He beamed. "What gives, sugar?"

She said uncontrollably, "I know the man in the tan car didn't run down that old woman on Folly Hill."

When she had said the words she stared at him incredulously. She hadn't even intended to mention him, not at this stage, anyway. Crook looked a bit startled, too, but gratified at the same time.

"That makes two of us. As well as Carew himself."

"Oh, is that his name? But how could you be so sure?"

"He's my client," Crook explained. "And I only work for the innocent."

"I didn't know you knew him," she stammered.

"More people know Tom Fool than Tom Fool knows. Fact is, I gave him a lift morning after the crime. His car was jammed in the snow and he had a date with a V.I.P. Gave him a card on parting, same as you."

"Do you give them to everyone?" asked Sara, who really wanted to know.

"I get hunches—well, not everyone of course. What makes you so sure? Nice of you to come and tell me," he added.

"I didn't really come about him at all. It was my son. The men responsible have got him as a hostage to make sure I don't go to the police."

"I was never any good at crosswords," Crook assured her.

"Say we start at Chapter One. Why should they think you know anything?"

"Because I was there. And of course it's against the law to suppress evidence, but I couldn't tell them because of Mike."

He might look like a great red bear, but where women were concerned, young, old or in between, he could convey a depth of understanding a confessor might have envied. Now he proceeded to draw her story from her, letting her tell it in her own way, deftly sorting the pieces in his mind as he went along.

"You see," she wound up, "I know I've done this man, Carew, a great injustice, because it can't be much fun having people point at you as the sort of man who'd leave an old woman to die in the snow, but you don't know Stan. He'd have no more compunction about—destroying Mike than—than
. . ."

"You or me would have slicing the top off an egg," finished Mr. Crook, helpfully. "Belt up, sugar. I've been meeting Stan's twin brother for more than forty years—well, thirty anyway," he added, hurriedly, remembering his official age was fifty-five, and goodness knows he'd had plenty of time to realize that. "And he's been putting paid to little kids and knocking over old women and tripping up cripples and robbing blind men's tins, the lot. You can't teach me anything about your friend Stan."

"Mr. Crook, I'm nearly out of my mind," she told him. "I've got to get Mike back, I don't care what I pay."

"Only," Crook reminded her, gently, "it's part of the rules that you pay out of your own purse, not some other chap's. And if it was true, what you just said, you wouldn't be here now, but down at the local nick spreading the glad news that you saw my client, and know he's the sort of chap that would think it a good joke to run down an old girl and her dog and do nothing about it."

"I keep telling myself that if he wasn't there, and I know he wasn't, then he's in the clear. I mean, his conscience . . ."

"Dames have a way of saying that sort of thing, as if a good conscience paid the rent and filled the bread basket." He patted his own comfortable stomach. "Didn't occur to you, I suppose, this story might put him in dutch with his boss, and he has to eat like the rest of us?"

She said simply, "But, Mr. Crook, I don't really care, I only care about getting my son back. And I don't know whether it's too late for that. Still, the balloon's bound to go up tomorrow, and if Amy Foster's phone wasn't out of order or she had a baby-sitter it would go up tonight."

"Police?" pantomimed Mr. Crook.

"She wouldn't have to go any further than The Leather Bottle. A word in Mrs. Gorton's ear, and the whole neighborhood would know within the hour. There's a sort of invisible tom-tom, what they call a grapevine, that operates in villages—and everyone will think I'm no better than a murderer not to have come forward before."

"And if you had they'd have said couldn't you put a little child first? Don't worry, sugar. You can't win. Not with her kind. You took your time coming to see me," he added. "How long did you kid yourself that Stan would wait? Patience ain't their virtue, that's their weakness."

She felt control slipping out of her grasp. "I don't know," she cried, "I don't know. Every way I looked the danger came on, it was like a trap, and Mike's only four and he may be terrified, and he'd expect me to look after him, and what use am I? If Michael hadn't got himself killed—how dare men be so careless, when they're husbands and fathers? Didn't he realize I wasn't fit to look after a child . . . ?"

"Often get your face slapped, sugar?" demanded Crook, with sudden grimness, and at his tone she stopped abruptly.

"I'm getting hysterical. I know. But I keep thinking of him, such a little boy, he doesn't know how to be afraid, and they could do anything with him. Anything."

"Had anything to eat today?" Crook inquired, "I'm just going to ring up a friend of mine, so you powder up or whatever it is dames do after a crisis, and we'll go along to The Two Chairmen and get us some food. I don't think so well when I'm a vacuum myself.

He drifted off, and she could hear him talking on the telephone. She produced a powder puff and lipstick and did a few repairs, and they had the same effect on her appearance as young Stokes's ministrations on Atalanta. Then she looked around the square, uncomfortable room, whose furniture all looked as if it had been picked up in a junkyard, and mysteriously her terrors began to subside.

He'll do something, she thought. They say angels come in mysterious disguises, so why shouldn't they wear bright brown suits and checked caps in place of a halo?

It was such a relief to be able to tell anyone; all these days of bottling up the truth, putting on an act, had almost driven her round the bend.

9

Mr. Crook came back. "And thick and fast they come at last. And more and more and more," he quoted. "You look a treat, sugar, and you're going to need it. In, say, fifteen minutes, you're going to have a chance to explain to an angry young man why you held your tongue when you could have cleared him in thirty seconds.

"I've told you," cried Sara, dismayed. "It was Mike."

"Let's hope he's one of these chaps who put women and children first," Crook agreed. "One thing, him having a personal interest in the problem might put him on our side."

"If I could take the responsibility for Miss Tite on myself, I wouldn't hesitate. You must believe that, Mr. Crook."

"Oh, I believe it," said Crook. "I'd believe any madness of your sex. Ever stood up to a police examination, sugar?" He assumed an official, hectoring tone. "Mrs. Drew, you say you were driving your car when it went out of control and collided with the deceased. What sort of car is it anyway?"

"It's a Waterbury—you know."

"What's known in the trade as a hotsy-totsy. Well, it don't take the cleverest brains at the Yard to see that if you'd run into the dog, let alone the old woman, neither you nor the car would have survived to tell the tale. Never mind, though. Let's carry on with our examination. Mrs. Drew, was your son with you? Well, come on, you must remember. Was he?"

She put her hands over her face. "I came to you for help," she reminded him.

"Well, I am helping you. I'm stopping you making an almighty fool of yourself."

"Mr. Crook, couldn't they get Stan on that other charge, the murder of the night watchman?"

"You hop about like a flea in a gale of wind. Which night watchman?"

"It was in the same county, about a fortnight—no, nearly three weeks earlier, and the police haven't got anyone. I did think the fingerprint might be Stan's reason for wanting to stay out of the limelight."

She was hardly surprised to realize he knew the details of the case. "How come you fixed on Stan, though?"

"Didn't you say you had hunches? And there must be some reason behind all this cops-and-robbers business with Mike. If—when—the truth comes out, they won't get any sympathy —don't they say there are two crimes even convicted prisoners won't condone, and one, I know, is violence against a child."

"You know," said Crook, and his voice was full of sheer admiration, "you may have something there. Mind you, only a dame"—or himself possibly, though he didn't say as much— "would make the jump from the factory to old Miss Tite, but— it's a funny thing how often dames manage to be right. Must throw all the mathematicians with their law of averages and whatnot. But it's an undeniable fact that when you know a thing about yourself it's hard to believe other chaps don't know it, too. That's why criminals find themselves in the dock as often as they do. It ain't the brains, it's chaps signing their own warrants. So anxious to wear a white sheet they can't let well alone. Mind you there's always the chance the same bright idea has occurred to the boys in blue." But his voice said they needn't waste much time on that one.

"There was another point," Sara urged. "You remember that night watchman said one of the young men told the other, 'Let him have it, Fred.' Well, that first afternoon, when he followed us to the cottage, Stan said, Me and Red like something or other—I've forgotten what. Well, I did think the night watchman might have got it wrong, and it should have been 'Let him have it, Red.'"

"I couldn't do it better myself," Crook congratulated her. "Drive a coach and horses through the evidence, I mean. One thing I will say for you, sugar, you're a trier. All the same, if there was a cop gutsy enough to stick his neck out and try and pin this crime on this precious pair, you'd find they had alibis a yard long."

"Oh, alibis!" retorted Sara, scornfully, as if alibis were no more than the bits of dust she flicked out of her typewriter. "You don't have to believe them."

"Still, it's always helpful if you can disprove them. As for the loot—about a thousand pound's worth, if my memory don't deceive me—that'll have been distributed a long while ago. You'd wonder they took the chance, all the same. They have to dispose of the stuff through a fence, lucky if they get a third of its value. And you still swing for murder if it occurs during a felony, specially if you use a gun. Judges are so unaccommodatin'—they will ask silly questions like, 'Why did you tote it along if you weren't prepared to use it?'"

"There's the car, wouldn't that help to identify them? I don't mean that night, because they didn't use their own, did they? But there aren't so many Albions about, particularly pale blue with darker trimmings."

"You can bet your bottom dollar it won't be blue any more," Crook assured. "Probably won't have the same license plate or even the same owner."

The front door buzzer sounded. "That'll be our wandering boy," Crook warned, rising to welcome his visitor in.

Sara began to shake again—it was becoming a habit and a tiresome one at that—so Crook said, "Why, you didn't suppose it was Stan, did you? If he'd known you were on the way, the odds are you wouldn't have got here tonight. And even Stan has to draw the line somewhere. I know all about the weaned child putting his hand on the cockatrice's den, but the twentieth-century ditto knows that's a sure way of losing a mitt." He flung open the front door and a tall young man with an expression of vivid curiosity came marching in.

"This," beamed Crook, "is Sara Drew, and your savior. They tell us they come in all sizes, but you've drawn a lucky number all right. Y'see, she knows Miss T. was run down by a chap called Red driving an Albion, ditto."

"And she's come all this way to tell you? I do appreciate that, Sara, really I do." He held out his hand. "Carew, Denis Carew," he added. "Most people would have thought they'd have done their duty if they'd dropped in at the local police station. I take it you are a native of—of—" He looked at her questioningly.

"Sursum Magna."

"What fun they had naming their potholes in those days."

"And Mrs. D. couldn't call on them because she's given a hostage to fortune," Crook continued.

"I'm sure that'll be a great help," offered Denis.

"Where's your gratitude?" Crook demanded. "Mrs. D. has given us the first clues there are, and she's given us priority. We shan't have a lot of Bobbies planting their great feet all over the shop. What we have to do," he went on comfortably, "is run this chap, Stan, to ground. Once we've got him, well, it's like the thread the princess carried through the labyrinth. Follow it up and you're bound to reach the heart of the maze in the end."

"You make it so clear," murmured Denis. "This Stan, has he got another name?"

"Two for all I know," returned Sara, recklessly. "I mean, he refers to himself as Stan—he rang up, he's got my little boy—that's what Mr. Crook meant by a hostage."

"Good grief!" exclaimed Denis. "Why didn't you say so before? I say, what's behind all this? It's more than running an old woman down—unless, of course, she was carrying the family jewels in her reticule, and they vamoosed with them."

"You do it almost as good as me," said Crook.

"This Stan," Denis continued. "How often have you met him?"

"Twice. That first afternoon and then in the market. And each time he threatened me—with Mike. The second time was after you floated into the picture, and I suppose he wanted to make sure I didn't go direct to the police, and ask for protection—once I'd told my story, I mean—so he took the one means that would keep me dumb."

"Did you tell anyone else about him?"

Sara thought, *en passant*, He doesn't seem to be worrying about himself, only Mike. Mr. Crook's right, he is a women-and-children-first man.

"No. No, of course not."

"So no one knows of the threats?"

"There were two anonymous messages, printed on bits of card. Mr. Crook's got them."

"Written by him?"

"Well, who else?"

Mr. Crook, with the resigned air of a man who sees another member of the cast getting all the fat, opened a cupboard and produced an immense bottle of beer. Even that didn't distract them.

"That's the point I'm trying to make," said Denis. "I mean, the police do look for proof. And that's just what you can't give them."

"Isn't Mike's disappearance proof enough?"

"It's proof that he's disappeared. It's not proof that Stan's got him. Unless you can prove he wrote the anonymous messages."

"Won't there be fingerprints?" She turned eagerly to Crook.

"There could be," Crook acknowledged, "but I doubt if there'll be any that can be brought home to him. Well, look how those cards have been handled. You've probably read 'em a dozen times, you've shoved 'em in your bag, I've read 'em—

and if Stan is as smart as you think, he won't have left his dabs on them in the first place. No, Carew's right. All you can prove is that they exist. No one with you when you found them, of course?"

"No. Oh, there was that woman in the bus station when I pulled the first card out of my pocket."

"Happen to mention it to her?"

"I said—I said it was a note from Mike's godfather, to say he was taking Mike home."

"Talk of scattering pearls before swine. You have that one beat a mile. Don't you see the construction anyone who don't believe in Stan could put on that?"

She thought. While she was thinking Crook proceeded to improve the shining hour.

"That conversation you had with him . . ."

"It was a tape-recorder."

"You can be sure that won't exist any more, not that particular tape. There's nothing about the messages to indicate a particular handwriting, paper could have come from anywhere. Come to, sugar. So far you haven't given us an atom of proof that Stan exists at all, or even if he does, that he's got Mike. That's the first thing the police 'ull want to know. Oh, yes, there's the car, but like I said, that'll have gone the same way as the record. And even if you could pick him out, how do you show he's got your boy, if he says he hasn't, and you can come and see for yourself."

She leaned back, aghast at the implications that had at last been driven home; if she'd been pale when she arrived, now she looked utterly burned out.

"Oh no," she whispered. "No one could believe that I—I'm in any way responsible for Mike's disappearance. Why, he's my whole life. Without him I don't exist."

"You've built up a house of cards," Crook told her inexorably. "That silly story about him going to his godfather—you see, you had half a dozen chances of telling the truth—the woman in the market, the policeman, this woman at The Leather Bottle, your lady friend with the little girls, and you stuck to your story like glue. By the way, has he got a godfather?"

"Of course he has. At the moment, I think he's in the Persian Gulf."

Crook threw up his big hands. "Well, you do see, sugar, it's not exactly the sort of place you'd go to for a long weekend if you were a little kid of four. Your trouble is, sugar, you don't trust anyone."

"But I do," cried Sara. "I trust you."

"Well, that's something to be going on with."

"You do believe me, don't you?"

"It's part of my job to believe the impossible. It's proving that's the difficulty. And it's one thing for you to be backed by me and Sir Galahad here, but the police are another cup of tea. They ain't allowed to have faith. Tough, I know, but there it is. And you have to remember you've been conniving at a crime ever since old Miss Tite got her quietus."

"But I'm not an absolute moron; I'd know I couldn't go on covering up Mike's absence forever. Country people are chatty; if something happens they all crowd to look; they're not like the priest and the Levite who went by on the other side, because they didn't want to be involved. They like being involved. They might accept Mike's absence for a few days, but not for weeks."

"You haven't got there yet," Crook told her. "They wouldn't have to accept it for weeks. You could decide to go and join Mike, couldn't you? Cottage too isolated, damp for the little chap, half a dozen reasons. Then you pack and fly, all in the open, all aboveboard. Who's going to start asking questions? Any relatives?"

"Michael had a sister; she's in the States at the moment, husband's got a scientific job there."

"See? Everything's playing into your hands. And if, say, some time ahead she gets a letter breakin' the sad news—now, honey, don't dive right in off the deep end, I'm just trying to make you see young Mike's not the only one in a spot."

"But there must be some way out," she insisted.

"Of course there is," said Denis. "I could go to the police and say, it's true, it was my car on the hill. I knew I'd run down a dog, but it was snowing at the time. I never even saw the old woman, didn't know a thing till I read about it in the press. And then I lost my nerve. How about that? Wouldn't that satisfy the police? And if they're satisfied that should be good enough for Master Stan, and he can send the boy back, and it's honors even."

"I don't know where the honor comes in," snapped Crook. "And even if it satisfied the police and Stan, it don't satisfy me. And I'd be surprised if it satisfied sugar here, either."

"What a ridiculous thing to say!" marveled Sara. "I'm a mother, not a moral principle. It would be all right by me if Mr. Carew was to murder Stan and burn the body on a bonfire. But you're wrong about there not being any witnesses, because there was the woman at Maidment who saw Mike being hustled into a car by a man."

"Would you know her again?"

"Well, I shouldn't think so, but . . ."

"She'd come forward, you mean. And there's your story about the man being Mike's godfather. And then again, she mightn't want to get mixed up in the affair. It's surprising how many folk with clear consciences prefer to steer clear of the police."

"If you could produce one reliable witness," said Denis, groaning. "Someone—what is it?"

"I suppose all this anxiety has numbed my brain. Because that's the thing I realized only a few hours ago, when I was talking to Stan on the telephone. There is a witness, an unimpeachable witness who wouldn't be afraid to come forward. She didn't only see Mike, she recognized him, and she noticed the car, not perhaps that it was an Albion, but she noticed it was a pale blue, and she thought what a strange color for a hire car. And she remembered that Mike was carrying Tigger, but seemed very quiet and lackadaisical, not like himself at all."

"You're getting me mixed up now," said Denis. "If he had Tigger, how is it you've got him now?"

"Because Stan brought him back as proof that he had Mike. I did tell you . . ."

"The picture had reached the second reel before he came in," Crook reminded her. "Who's this paragon who's going to save all our bacon?"

"Mrs. Gorton at The Leather Bottle. I know she can only repeat what I told her, but she did see Mike and she knows I wasn't in the car. And if—if there's anyone mad enough to suppose that I would be mixed up in a plot against my own son, surely I'd choose some way back where he wouldn't be recognized."

"On the other hand," put in Denis, "if he was foxing Mike, that he was taking him home, I mean, he'd have to go by a familiar way."

"I haven't had a girl friend for so long I'd overlooked the fact that when you get a letter from same the first thing to read is the postscript," murmured Crook. "All the same, it ain't going to be a walk-over. You got any proof this chap didn't just drive the boy home and leave him, plus the tiger, on your porch? Well, of course you haven't. And then you didn't confide in the lady at the Bottle—yes, I know your reasons, only reason don't get much of a look-in in cases like these."

"Any judge . . ." began Sara hotly, but Crook intervened. "Your judge, sugar, is going to be the man in the street, and he's the one who makes the rules. This Mrs.—what did you say her name was?"

"Gorton."

"She likely to have confied in a buddy?"

"Probably told all and sundry. I haven't been down there except on Sunday to collect my groceries, etc."

"Stan a supporter of the Bottle?"

"I've never seen him there."

"So he don't know she saw him. Where ignorance is—well, not precisely bliss, but a form of insurance—it's our best bet."

"Well, he knows now," Sara cried. "I told him."

The two men turned like a single figure. "You told him?" breathed Crook.

"Of course. I wanted him to know there was a witness . . ."

125

"*Was* could be the operative word."

"You don't know Mrs. Gorton. No threats could silence her; anyway, her son's seventeen and a bit wild, quite a different proposition from a child of four."

"What she said ain't evidence within the meaning of the act. And if Stan can see his way to putting the silencer on Mrs. G. . . ."

"He couldn't," declared Sara, confidently. "Nothing short of murder . . ."

"And what makes you think he'd stop short of that?" inquired Crook in tones that were dangerously bland. "If you're right and this is the bright couple who put out old Larkin's light, they can't afford to be squeamish. What time do they close in your part of the world?"

"The pubs? Ten-thirty. But the Bottle won't be open tonight because of the Countrywomen's Gala. Mrs. Gorton would'n't miss that for a week's takings."

"Meaning the whole town will be there?"

"Well, a good proportion of them."

"That's something to be thankful for. Where's this fiesta held?"

"In Maidment Town Hall."

"Mrs. G. likely to go on her own?"

"Oh no. Someone's certain to give her a lift down."

"And back?"

"I should think so."

"And even Stan's not going to chuck a hand grenade into the Town Hall. No, it's going home, after she leaves the car. Live alone?"

"There's Tom, but you can't count on when he'll turn up."

"Handed it to Stan on a plate, haven't you?" Crook suggested. "This Leather Bottle—stand flush with the road, back in a shrubbery, down a lane—where?"

"It stands a little back from the road. It's a bus stop for the local buses. Oh, if you mean could someone hide and jump out on her and no one know, they could."

"And then do a melting act. Mind you, it don't have to be Stan. There's the driver of the red Albion. If we could get our hands on either we'd soon have the missing link. Is it true," he added, turning to Denis, "that if you put out a dead rattler its living mate comes up alongside? Well, that's what we've got to do. Spot one and we'll have our hands on the other."

"Rather a lot of if's," suggested Denis. "What you could call building castles in the sand."

But Crook retorted that what the ancients had done with a sizeable supply of sand was still amazing posterity, and what the hell were they waiting for?

"I suppose I can leave my car here—we shan't be gone long," suggested Sara, recalling Crook's earlier invitation to dinner or what-have-you at The Two Chairmen.

"I do like an optimistic nature," said Crook. "If we're all lucky we might be back some time tomorrow, but again we might not. Still, not to worry about Hotsy-Totsy, she'll be safe there. Neat little thing, isn't she?" he added. In some mysterious way they had left the flat and were now standing on the curb. "All the same, if I was an insurance company I wouldn't give you a policy for all the tea in China. An Albion would make no more of running over that than it would a beetle."

"Where are we going?" asked Sara, bewildered

"We're going to try and prevent another crime of violence. You don't seem to have got Stan's measure yet, sugar. If anything gets in his path, he don't politely ask it to move out, and it never goes through his mind that he might step around it. No, he goes over it like a juggernaut. You saw it for yourself with Agatha Tite. Now it's Mrs. G.'s turn."

"You mean, you think he'll attack her, too?"

"Well, what would you do in his shoes? Wake up, sugar. Tonight could be just the job for him. Hang around the darkened Bottle, no chaps staggering home, drunk or otherwise, place as silent as the grave, so why not make it one? And if Tom should get in his road so much the worse for Tom."

"He carries a flick knife," said Sara, suddenly. "Tom, I mean."

"Good for Tom. Your part of the world sounds a place where any chap who wasn't missing his marbles would do likewise. How long did it take you to come up in Hotsy-Totsy?"

"A little under three hours, I should think. I hit peak hour, of course."

"The Superb should get us down in, say, two—two and a quarter, maybe. What time does this Gala close?"

"I've never been to one, of course, but I gather no one will leave before eleven."

"Regular Cinderellas, aren't they?" said Crook. He hauled out his big turnip watch. "Don't do to take risks," he said. "We'll leave word on our way. Nice to provide a Reception Committee for Stan and Co."

He seemed cheerful enough, but Sara was overwhelmed by a vision of kindly comfortable Mrs. Gorton lying out in her own grounds under cover of darkness, tripped by a bit of wire perhaps and knocked on the head before she could rise, caught and twisted and silenced almost before she knew what had struck her—they wouldn't try poison even if opportunity offered, poison wouldn't be amusing enough. It was the concealment, the pounce, the thrill of the actual engagement that Stan would enjoy.

"But will he actually take such a risk?" she cried. "I mean, I could give evidence."

"You could have given evidence in the Tite affair but somehow you didn't," said Crook, unkindly. "How should he guess you'd come forward this time either? Still, no harm spreading the good news."

"You're not going to warn him?" cried Sara, appalled. "That we're coming, I mean? It's Mike's life."

Denis's hand caught her arm. "This has got to stop somewhere," he said. "Mrs. Gorton has a life, too."

"But if you do anything to warn Stan we're coming . . ."

"Oh no," Crook promised, "I shan't do that. No need. You've done the job for me."

He bundled them into the car. "Don't bother about Hotsy-Totsy," he besought Sara. "If you're in no shape to pick it up in the morning I'll pack it up and return it by registered post."

He stopped outside Earl's Court Police Station. "We're promised that one day, if we play our cards right, we'll find ourselves in a world where there ain't no time," he explained, "only we ain't there yet, and while we're still in the mortal coil we can't afford to ease off for twenty seconds. It 'ud make Old Nick himself split his sides to see Arthur Crook goin' hat in hand to the cops, but they say everyone has to eat a peck of dirt before he dies, so here goes."

"What does all that mean?" Sara demanded of Denis.

"I take it he's going to put out a message for the Maidment police on Mrs. Gorton's behalf. But I'll be surprised if the Old Superb doesn't live up to her name."

He patted the high yellow car with a real affection. "For she never yet came in too late to fight," he quoted.

Crook came shooting out again and climbed in behind the wheel.

"Hold your hats!" he said.

So the long desperate race against time began.

10

At Plowford Sergeant Richard Probyn was having a real evening of it. So far as he could see, the whole local world had gone whacky. First of all, there had been an anonymous call in a woman's voice, that said, "Ask Mrs. Drew what she has done with her son."

This had startled him so much he didn't at first think to ask the caller's name.

"What was that you said?"

"Mrs. Drew of Fell Cottage. Her little boy, Mike, has disappeared. And she knows where he is."

"So what?" asked Sergeant Probyn.

"She pretends he's gone to stay with his godfather, but it's the first time we ever heard he had one; and he hasn't taken any luggage or clothes or even his special toy, and Mrs. Drew is so cagey . . ."

The voice forgot its disguise, but even so he couldn't place it.

Not a "country" voice, but then a lot of outsiders had seeped in since the war. Someone who knew Sara Drew, or else someone who wanted to make trouble for her. There were the usual old witches and warlocks in the neighborhood, people who weren't commitable, but were certainly not up to snuff. Old women like Miss Tite were frequently credited with supernatural powers—living alone with a dog or cat was no way for a Christian, said the villagers.

Probyn tried to remember when he'd last seen Sara and Mike. Not for a few days, he thought. And he couldn't recall noticing the little turquoise-colored car flashing around like a dragonfly. Though the Drews had been such a short time in the neighborhood they had impressed their personalities wherever they went. Sara by herself wouldn't have done it, not to this extent, for all her charm and beauty; Mike alone would have been another little evacuee; but the pair together—they seemed inseparable, like bread and cheese, eggs and bacon. He'd heard she was at the inquest on old Miss Tite; she hadn't had the boy then, of course, but that was only to be expected.

He puzzled over the mystery voice. He remembered hearing the tinkle of coins as he lifted his receiver, but that didn't really help, because with so many instruments out of order dozens of regular subscribers were being driven to use phone booths. Short of trying to identify everyone local who'd been noticed leaving one of these booths, he couldn't imagine how he could identify his caller. Sergeant Probyn began to tap with his pencil. Who was Sara's enemy, since only an enemy could be responsible? She didn't seem the type to make trouble, a helpful sort, really. Not likely to remain a widow forever, you'd say, not with her looks and vivacity. Husband killed in a road accident, he'd heard. Had his picture on a side table at the cottage, according to Constable Trent, who had once called there on an official matter.

Trent came in while the sergeant was still brooding.

"Mike?" said Trent. "Get along, Sarge. She might put her own head in the gas oven, but she'd put yours and mine there if she thought we'd hurt a hair of that boy's head. Another crackpot, I expect," he added.

131

Wonder if she's got her line back, Probyn reflected. He lifted the receiver; when he dialed the number he could hear the bell ringing away in the cottage. But though he waited some time no one answered.

"Must be out," he decided. "The Countrywomen's Gala, perhaps."

Trent pulled a long clown's face. "She couldn't take Mike, and she wouldn't leave him alone," he protested.

"Then perhaps someone else has him." It was strange how eager they both were to believe that nothing was wrong with the child. "Who's her nearest neighbor?"

They thought and fixed on Mrs. Foster. "Might try her," said Probyn in rather despondent tones, but her line was still out of order.

"I'll tell you something," offered Trent. "I saw Miss Dacre earlier on, and she was full of some yarn about Mrs. Drew going to the gala and pretending she wasn't. Not going your way, she called, though there was a dirty great poster stuck in the window."

"The day that woman isn't complaining of someone I'll know she's sickening for the tomb," said Probyn, feelingly. "No sign of Mike, I suppose?"

"She says Mrs. Drew was alone in the car."

"Come to think of it, it could have been her on the line," mused Probyn. "It was someone from a phone booth."

Trent looked dubious. "She'd be at the Town Hall," he objected. "There's no pay phone there."

"Where you constables pick up your American slang!" Probyn looked disgusted. "I don't reckon we need worry. If all the mothers looked after their kids the way Mrs. Drew does, the N.S.P.C.C. could shut up shop."

"Why should Mrs. Drew say she wasn't going to the gala if she was?" persisted Trent, who was as resistant as a brick wall. Bounce and bounce against that wall, and the ball 'ud always come back to you. The sergeant took up the phone and rang his wife, a public-spirited lady who would one day cause the Archangel Gabriel to tremble.

"Who's that?" Her voice, as fluting as a buzzard, came powerfully over the line. "I'm just going off to the gala."

"Just take a look round and see if Mrs. Drew's there," her husband told her. "Some lunatic sent a message about Mike having gone missing, and—if Mrs. Drew's with you tonight we'll know it's the work of some maniac. You know what the village grapevine is," he added in placatory tones, sensing that his wife was going to ask a lot of questions he couldn't answer.

"And suppose she's not there?" demanded Mabel.

"Let's cross that bridge when we get to it," her husband offered. "She was seen driving down. Anyway, I don't want this lunatic on the line again."

He knew Mabel wasn't satisfied, but he hung up hurriedly, pretending someone had come in. A little later there was a call regarding a car smash at Chervey Halt and he had to take the necessary action. One man had to notify a wife that her husband was on the danger list, and another chap had to go to the scene of the accident, the hospital had to be alerted; for a while he could forget all about Sara. Then Mabel rang through to say there was no sign of Sara, and what was she supposed to do about it? Miss Dacre had seen her careering through the streets with a poster slapped on one window. Perhaps she'd run into a bus—had he checked with the hospital?

"What did I do to get married to a ghoul?" Dick Probyn groaned.

One way and another he was fairly busy until the call came through from London around about nine P.M. An official voice said they'd had a call from a man called Crook . . . At once Probyn's blood began to chill. Since their first meeting he'd done his homework, and he now knew a good deal more about that intrepid and unconventional figure—enough, anyway, to realize that this call meant trouble.

"Mrs. Gorton?" he said. "Where does she come in?"

"He's got the idea that someone's gunning for her, some gang he's got his knife into. When you know Crook as we know Crook, you'll realize he doesn't call in the police just for fun."

"I don't get it," said Probyn bluntly. "Why should anyone have it in for Mrs. Gorton? There's not a better-liked woman in the county."

"It all ties up with Mrs. Drew and this missing boy. Did you say something?" For the unprepared sergeant had let out an exclamation that surprised his colleague in the metropolis.

"So there is something screwy there." He repeated the anonymous message. "And Mrs. Drew isn't at the gala," he wound up.

"We know where Mrs. Drew is," said the London policeman, whose name was Parker. "She's careering round the country with Mr. Crook. She's not our concern. But it looks as though, without meaning to, your Mrs. Gorton's got herself tied up in the same tangle. Mind you, this isn't London's job, and Mr. Crook knows it. But he put on his modesty act—and that's when he's most to be feared—and said he wouldn't carry enough heavy guns to make any impression in the country."

Probyn groaned. "I knew that man spelled trouble," he said.

"He's been spelling trouble for us for years, but we survive." Parker sounded tart. "And if you want to get any quiet sleep for the next six months you'll see to it that nothing happens to your Mrs. Gorton."

Mabel Probyn was enjoying herself, slapping down the gentry in the person of a certain Honorable Mrs. Abercrombie, when she was approached by one Miss Deedes—and had she suffered from her unfortunate nomenclature?—who told her she was wanted on the telephone. The gala was being held in the Town Hall and Miss Deedes held a clerical position in the tax department. This gave her a sense of importance and when the telephone rang she moved to answer it, as of right.

"Telephone?" snapped Mrs. Probyn. "Nonsense. Can't you see I'm judging the potted plants?"

Miss Deedes came closer and sputtered in Mabel's ear. "Police station?" repeated Mabel, seeing no need for secrecy. "Oh, that'll be Dick. I've told him she's not here."

"She?"

"He was asking for Mrs. Drew."

"He said it was official," repeated Miss Deedes, obstinately.

It occurred to Mabel she might be missing something sensational, so she excused herself and swept away.

"You must be out of your mind," was her first remark, as she picked up the receiver. "I'm judging the potted plants."

"Mabel! Will you try and realize this is the police speaking to you, not your henpecked husband?"

She was so startled she actually shut up.

"I've had a call from London . . ."

"If it's Mrs. Drew, I told you she's not here."

"I told you—no, I didn't, you didn't give me the chance. We know where Mrs. Drew is. It's Mrs. Gorton."

"What on earth has *she* done?"

"Is she there?"

"Well, of course she's there. Leopards don't change their spots overnight, and you can't imagine any festival taking place without her."

"Well, then," snapped Probyn, "see she stays there."

"Is this a murder plot?" demanded Mabel.

The sergeant nearly dropped the receiver.

"What on earth makes you say . . . ? Well, never mind. Just keep an eye on her. We don't want her going home alone. Maidment . . ."

"You don't want her going home with the murderer either, I suppose. Do you know who it is?"

"No one said anything about murder. Just see she doesn't slip off by herself . . ."

He was sending a man to watch The Leather Bottle, and Maidment would have a man outside the Town Hall.

He only wished he knew what it was all about. Shrewdly he suspected London knew rather less than they would let on. If this was Mr. Arthur Crook's notion of a joke—only there had been the telephone call about young Mike . . . He realized his wife was still talking.

"She won't go till the last light's started to flicker."

And by that time this Crook creature should have arrived, the sergeant thought. Anyway, he'd done all he could.

"Don't go spreading doubt and depression," he warned Mabel, knowing there's a perverse pleasure in spreading bad news. "And don't go alarming Mrs. Gorton." Though *she* was a sensible woman, with her head screwed on the right way. He wished he could say as much for Mabel. It was making the best of a bad job having to confide in her at all. Still, it seemed improbable that the villain, whoever he might be, would take a stab at that popular figure in a crowded hall. He rang off.

After all this rush and flurry a great silence descended. The telephone didn't ring, no one came in, even to ask the way. Quiet as the grave, he thought. And shivered. He wished he hadn't put it quite like that.

Later Mabel looked around for Mrs. Gorton, but she was judging fancy cakes. Mabel couldn't very well go over now, because she had entered a cake herself, and anyway with that crowd around her she must be all right. Sara Drew and now Elsie Gorton—very funny business afoot. It even passed through her mind that her hubby was having his leg pulled, which showed how little she knew of Arthur Crook.

She scribbled a note on a bit of paper—See you at supper, something to tell you. And she got someone to pass it along. She knew that 'ud hold Elsie. She couldn't bear to miss anything, if it was only the first fly of the year walking on the ceiling. Then the tables started forming for whist, and Elsie sat down with the air of someone who knows she's likely to win.

Mrs. Probyn went into the next room where they were dancing to the Maidment band, and very good it was, too. Mabel danced with the grace and lightness of many large women; she enjoyed herself immensely, Elsie was off her conscience, and during the next hour she was never without a partner.

Mrs. Gorton glanced at Mabel's note and pushed it into her bag. She didn't, of course, know what her friend was referring to, but any little tinge of mystery added excitement to the day. She settled down to whist at about the time that Mabel moved into the dance hall, and that was the last they saw of one another that night.

She was doing pretty well when Miss Deedes came prowling up like a cat unsure of its welcome and bent to mutter in her ear.

"Not now, Maudie," said Mrs. Gorton. "Can't you see . . . ?"

"Telephone," mouthed Maudie. "For you."

Instantly Mrs. Gorton laid down her hand. "Tom?"

All her secret thoughts were wrapped around Tom. Sara wasn't more completely involved with her son than the plump licensee of The Leather Bottle. To other people he was a young tearaway of seventeen, crazy as a bobcat and idle as a Biblical grasshopper. But you'd be wise to make your will and get it witnessed before hinting as much to his mother.

"They're waiting," said Maudie in the same awkward voice, and Elsie Gorton pushed back her chair and moved off without even apologizing to her partner.

"It's the hospital," Maudie confided, as they left the hall and started to walk down the passage that seemed a mile long, to the anteroom where the telephone extension was installed. "An accident, they said . . .

"What more did they say?"

"They didn't give me any details. Oh Elsie, don't look like that. It's the hospital, not the mortuary."

She hovered in the passage outside while Mrs. Gorton took the call. After a minute she heard her own name.

"Maudie!"

She sped in. "They're sending a car," said Mrs. Gorton.

At the other end of the line a voice crackled. "Get your things," Miss Deedes commanded, and she said into the mouthpiece, "Mrs. Gorton will be ready by the time you arrive."

"Tell her we'll come to the side door, don't want a lot of fuss, do we?"

She thought, How considerate!

"Tell her not to worry about bringing night things. If it's necessary for her to stay we can make arrangements."

At least that meant Tom wasn't dead, she thought. Probably speeding on his motorbike and run slap into a truck or something. She remembered hearing he was after some girl in Somerton; she wondered if the girl realized Tom was only seventeen. He looked a couple of years older, and bridegrooms of

137

nineteen were no rarity in the country. She went into the passage and there Elsie Gorton was, all her normal efficiency evaporated. Something to be said for being single, thought Miss Deedes, and added aloud, "You stay there, Elsie, I'll get your things. The blue coat, I suppose?"

They all knew each other's clothes, and Elsie's blue was almost a landmark. If you're a widow with a work-shy son you can't ring the changes in your wardrobe very often.

"You wait there," said Maudie Deedes, indicating the phone room. "I'll be along in two ticks."

A widow called Harrison was supposed to be in charge of coats, but she must have felt a call of nature or something, because there was no one there when Maudie went in. She found the coat and scarf with no trouble at all, and sped back by an empty passage. No one saw her come or go. The car, she repeated, was coming to the side door.

"Don't say anything," Mrs. Gorton besought her, pulling the coat across her comfortable bosom. "Just tell them at the table I won't be back. Don't want to spoil anyone else's evening."

"You can trust me," Maudie beamed. Sympathy oozed from every pore. Then the car arrived—must have traveled like the wind—a black Vauxhall, so sober you'd hardly have been surprised to see death at the wheel. Mrs. Gorton walked out—it was pretty dark and no one blamed Maudie afterward for not noticing the driver, who jumped down and opened the door—and climbed in without a backward look. The door closed quietly. The car moved away. With a bright smile on her plain horseface Maudie Deedes came back to the hall.

At first Mrs. Gorton lay back in the car like someone stunned, but when she felt she could trust her voice she leaned forward and asked, "How bad is he?"

"I couldn't say," said the driver, without turning his head. "I was just told to come and get you. Matron 'ull know," he added.

She balled her hands into fists and drummed them silently in her lap. She didn't look out of the window. Nothing would have appeared familiar if she had, since all she saw was the arid waste of her own mind. Presently, like someone coming out of an anesthetic, she put up her head and asked, "Aren't we taking a long time to get to the hospital?"

The driver sounded surprised. "He's not at St. John's," he said. "Greylands over at Backerton. That's where the accident took place."

"Backerton? He was going to take his young lady out to the movies. There's no theater at Backerton."

"He must have changed his mind then. The young lady didn't say anything about that."

"You mean, she was there?" As an afterthought she added, "Was she hurt?"

"Shocked, of course, but no bones broken. She was riding pillion."

"No," cried Mrs. Gorton coming suddenly awake. "You've got it wrong. Sheila never goes on Tom's bike, though he's a good driver. I've gone pillion with him myself. That's why they go to the pictures, see?"

"Sheila?" repeated the man. "I thought she said her name was Lesley. Or maybe Lily. Lesley's a man's name, isn't it?"

"Tom doesn't know any girls with those names." But there she stopped. Because how does any mother know for certain what girls her son meets? She only knows about the ones he names to her or brings home.

"Well, she knows about you," the driver told her. "It was her told us where to look for you, at the hall. She's gone home now . . ."

He heard a muffled groan behind him and pulled a cigarette case out of his pocket.

"Fag?" he offered. "Or don't you?"

"Easy to see you're a stranger," said Mrs. Gorton in a dead voice. "Smokes and sweets are my Sodom and Gomorrah. At least, that's what Tom always says."

"He'll be all right," the man coaxed. "He's young and . . ." He snapped on a cigarette lighter, a nice job, engine-turned, must have cost every penny of twelve pounds to the chap who bought it. "Concussed, and of course they have to notify the next-of-kin. Say there was an operation needed . . ."

"Operation?"

"You can never tell, can you, not these road accidents." Skillfully he turned the car around a hairpin bend. "They'll let you see him right away, I shouldn't wonder."

"That means he's on open order."

"Well, you're his mum, aren't you?"

She tried to accustom herself to the idea that this was Tom she was traveling through the darkness to see. And it wasn't only outside that the darkness reigned. The moment the news hit her it was all the lights in the world being extinguished in an instant of time. She hadn't had much luck in her marriage, Tom was all her compensation.

She began to feel calmer. The cigarette, perhaps, though it seemed a bit strong.

"What kind are these?" she murmured.

"Kind?" Again he didn't turn his head.

"The cigarettes."

"Oh, those. French. Nice, aren't they? A pal of mine brings them over. Like another?"

"They're a bit too strong for me," she said in the same confused voice. "Here, stop the car a minute, will you? I feel faint."

"Be at the hospital in another minute," he promised. "You can get a cuppa there, it's the shock, that's what it is."

She put out her hands, feeling for support, but the car seemed to have swelled, she couldn't find the sides; and the man in front seemed to be moving, swelling and receding—it must be dangerous when you were at the wheel on a dark night.

She tried to look through the black glass. "Are we going through a wood?" She couldn't recall any wood on the way to Greylands.

She didn't hear his answer, she was too far gone.

"That's right," he told her. "This is a wood and you're one of the babes all right, and you know what happened to them. Too bad there aren't any robins."

It occurred to him the whole incident had passed off as smoothly as a long drink of water.

11

Crook brought his party down to Maidment in the manner of a clockwork Derby runner. Denis said later that he hadn't murmured so many ejaculatory prayers in years. It was the next best thing, he assured Sara, to being in a circus. If this chap (meaning Crook) saw an obstacle in the road he jumped the car over it. It would hardly have surprised him if the Superb had taken wings and flown over the housetops. At Plowford, Crook drew up at the police station and bounced in.

"You!" groaned Sergeant Probyn. "If you've come about Mrs. Gorton everything's under control."

"And the other little matter I mentioned to the police—the identity of Stan's accomplice?"

"You've no proof there," snapped Probyn, who had been on the line to his colleague in Maidment and frankly thought Crook had a screw loose.

"Is he plannin' to leave the district?" Crook urged. And got the answer he anticipated.

"Is Mrs. Drew with you?" Probyn went on.

"What do you think?"

"There was a message," said the sergeant.

Crook offered to relay it, but the officer stood firm. He wanted a word with Sara himself. When Crook brought her in, white-faced, stiff with exhaustion, Probyn said, "There was a message, Mrs. Drew, some time earlier this evening. Some woman, wouldn't give her name, seemed to suggest Mike was missing."

"He is," Sara agreed.

Probyn looked shocked. "You didn't report it."

"She'll explain all that when she writes her autobiography," promised Crook, hastily. "Meantime, we're on the job."

"I told you, that was being taken care of."

"We're riding different horses," Crook pointed out. "Mrs. Gorton's your pigeon." (It never worried him to mix his zoölogical metaphors.) "No one's paying me to save her life. Mike Drew's another matter, and if my clients are always innocent it suits me better that they stay alive into the bargain."

Out he went again, dragging Sara after him, and on to Maidment to the Town Hall.

"What do we do here?" asked Sara, bewildered, as well she might be, by the speed at which things were happening.

"Collect Mrs. G. and find out how much help she can give us. If she got even a glimpse of the driver that's so much to the good. And, of course, we want her to come along with us."

"Will the police let her?"

"I'd like to see them try to stop us. This is still a free country, sugar, on paper anyway, and the police should be grateful to us really, specially if your hunch about the warehouse murder is so."

"You didn't mention that at the station."

"I do what I'm paid to do," Crook pointed out. "And I don't poke my nose in without I'm asked. Point is, is Red with his chum tonight? My guess 'ud be yes."

"He said something about them going for a holiday or something, so it would be inconvenient to keep Mike," Sara recalled.

"Fleeing the country I wouldn't wonder. Still, that's no skin off my nose. All I'm in this case for is to get Mike back for you. Not bring villains to the gallows or even the courtroom. Now, in we go."

The gathering at the Town Hall was thinning fast when a stout gentleman in a bright brown tweed suit—put him in a bracken bush and no one 'ud notice him, someone said—came bursting in, disregarding all protests, waving away any suggestion that he might have an invitation card or be anybody's husband.

"Do I look like a husband?" he roared.

He pulled Mrs. Drew in with him. At least that was the impression he gave, though actually he hadn't laid a finger on her.

"Like Attila in modern dress," said the Honorable Mrs. Abercrombie in outraged tones, and for once it was admitted she wasn't far off the mark.

"Give, sugar," Crook urged the girl. "Which of them is Mrs. Gorton?"

Sara looked around; she met innumerable inquisitive eyes, a few hostile, a few friendly. A few, of course, didn't look at her at all, but bent their attention on the young man following in her wake.

"I don't see her," said Sara in shaky tones. "How odd! I mean, she has the reputation of being a regular last-ditcher."

"Could be someone saw to it she could meet her last ditch tonight." Crook sounded grim. He saw someone standing like a grenadier beside him, her mouth opened to speak.

"Hold it, sugar. Crook's the name, Arthur Crook. No, I know you never heard it before, but one of these days you might be glad to remember. Been here all the evening?"

"Certainly," began Mabel. "I . . ."

"Looking for a Mrs. Gorton," Crook explained, and he could have sworn she jumped.

"So are we. The Committee's just going to sit down to supper." Her glance said they deserved a second Lord Mayor's

Banquet after the work they'd put in to make the evening a success.

"Nice work, if you can get it. Still, Mrs. G. may have to go hungry for once. Which one is she?"

A fluttering female, who had stolen up unnoticed like a smoky dawn, said in a voice that matched her appearance, "Mrs. Gorton's gone."

Crook swung around; he didn't even have a machete in his hand, he didn't even raise his arm, but poor Miss Deedes shrank back.

"It's the hospital. Her son was in an accident . . ."

Crook groaned. "That's the oldest tale in the book. Who says he had an accident?"

"The man from the hospital."

"Which hospital?"

"Well, St. John's, I suppose."

"You suppose. Did he say St. John's?"

"He said Tom had been in an accident and they were sending a car."

All around them the murmurs rose. They'd always said it 'ud come to this, silly young chap out to impress his elders, no patience, no thought for others, poor Mrs. G., a rotten husband and a tearaway son, why hadn't they been told before? But of course she'd always put others first, wouldn't want to spoil their pleasure. Was he badly injured, was he dead?

"When?" yelled Crook, sounding like an air-raid warning. "When did this chap ring? It was a chap?"

"Oh yes," said Miss Deedes. You didn't want to rejoice in other people's troubles, but it was nice to have a bit of the limelight for a change.

"Well?" demanded Crook, truculently.

"I think—they were playing whist. That would be an hour ago, no, rather more."

"Anyone but you see her go?"

"She didn't want anyone else told. Oh, Mabel"—she turned to Mrs. Probyn—"I was to tell you . . ."

"Happen to notice the car?" demanded Crook, in an unceremonious sort of way.

"It was black. I remember thinking it was first cousin to a hearse."

"You could be right at that," Crook assured her. "Driver?"

"It was a man—young, I think."

Crook bit back the comment that he hadn't supposed it was driven by a chimp and went on. "Wouldn't know him again?"

"I didn't really see his face. Does it matter?"

"Didn't notice the make of the car?"

"Well, of course not. I mean, I'm not a driver. They all look alike to me."

Crook sighed. "And you didn't notice the number, of course."

To his amazement Miss Deedes brightened. "Now there, I may be able to help. You see, I play the car game. You know, you take the letters on a license plate and try and make a word. Like CTH—that could be catch or cloth."

"Or cuttlefish. What were these?"

"ABC. Rather difficult really, till I thought of abietic. It came in a crossword last week—pertaining to a fir tree . . ."

"Abrazitic," capped Crook, "meaning not sparkling. Notice which way the car went?"

"Towards the high road."

"Anyone else in it? Or couldn't you see?"

"I don't think—well, the hospital probably wouldn't have anyone to spare . . ."

"Where's the phone?" asked Crook.

"Here are the police," announced Mabel Probyn.

"Have you seen Mrs. Gorton?" she demanded of the rather nervous-looking constable.

"Isn't she here?"

"God give me strength!" said Crook, piously. "Where's the phone? I'm going to ring the hospital and ask how young Tom Gorton is."

"Has there been an accident?" asked the policeman.

"That's what I'm going to find out. That is, I'm tooting sure there has been an accident, but I don't think it's happened to Tom."

Someone else, who was dying to know what was in the

wind, oiled up to say it had been a bumper gala, hadn't it, they'd taken twenty percent more than last year.

"That's nice to know," said Crook, heartily. "You'll be able to buy Mrs. Gorton a bumper wreath, won't you?"

That rocked them all back on their heels. The policeman began to question Crook, and Mabel started in on Sara.

"Get the deathhouse on the wire," Crook begged Miss Deedes. "If they've got the boy there I'll go about on hands and knees for the rest of my days—like Nebuchadnezzar, wasn't it?—eating the grass of the field?"

Off flew Miss Deedes (who said life in the country was dull?) and Crook and Sara stood up to a rain of questions.

"ABC," said Crook, cutting through the red tape with his usual lack of consideration. "That's not a county letter, is it?"

"CUU is the local one," the policeman said. "But, of course, a lot of people buy their cars second-hand."

"Some chaps like someone else to find out the weak spots," Crook agreed, "same as some chaps prefer to marry a widow, been broken in already, at least that's what they think."

This original view silenced everyone for a moment. Then Miss Deedes came back to say, "The hospital don't know anything about a Tom Gorton."

"It doesn't have to be St. John's," snapped Mrs. Probyn, feeling it was time she had the stage, sergeant's wife and all. "There are hospitals further afield."

Surprisingly Miss Deedes stood up to her. "I don't think it could be one of those. I mean, the car came so quickly, it must have been on its way . . ."

"I do like a lady who notices the trimmings," said Crook in grateful tones. "Daresay there ain't too many ABC cars here tonight for you to find out who this one belonged to. And you can forget about the hospital, sugar," he added kindly to Miss Deedes. "But I can tell you one thing. If the accident had been reported to the police, as it should, someone would have come up in person from the station to tell Mrs. G. Ain't that right, ma'am?"

"Of course." Mrs. Probyn and the police officer spoke simultaneously.

"Oh dear," murmured Miss Deedes in distressed tones. "I never thought . . ."

"No one was payin' you to think," consoled Crook in the same kind voice. "How about finding the car's owner?"

"If he's still here," said Mrs. Probyn sharply.

"Well, of course he's here, or he'd have missed his car. You don't imagine the boy friend's going to be considerate enough to bring it back. Could be putting his head in a noose trying that caper, and a noose is what I mean."

The police officer proclaimed silence in a manner that roused Crook's admiration, and then put his question.

"Is there anyone here with a car registered ABC, number unknown?"

A Dr. Penrose who had resignedly accompanied his wife, who claimed she never saw him except on such occasions as these, started forward.

"Don't tell me you're giving me a parking ticket?" he exclaimed. "The park was full, but that yard . . ."

"What's the number and make?" interrupted Crook, and the doctor answered him automatically.

"Black Vauxhall, ABC 9787. Why, what's happened?"

The police officer took over again. "Would you see if it's been moved, sir."

The doctor, looking troubled, hurried out of the hall. Mrs. Penrose said, "What is all this about?"

"It's possible it may have been—borrowed—for an illegal purpose," explained the policeman.

"They must be mad, taking a doctor's car."

"Maybe they didn't know it was a doctor's," said the policeman dryly.

"On the other hand, they may have thought a doctor's car just the job," put in Crook, obstinately. "I mean, if he had his bag in it . . ."

"Well, of course, it had his bag in it. Doctors have to be prepared for every emergency."

Then the doctor came back to say his car was gone, which was what Crook and the policeman had both anticipated.

Crook turned to his companions. "Seeing the cops have taken over, how about getting back on the trail, partner?" he suggested.

"Just a minute, Mr. Crook. As you say, the police are in charge . . ."

"They were in charge when Mrs. Gorton was lured away," Crook reminded him, unkindly. "It doesn't seem to have helped her none. Be with you in a minute, sugar," he added to Sara. Denis Carew took the hint and the two moved away to where the Superb was parked.

"If anyone's got the bright idea that Mrs. Drew could tell you more about this double disappearance than she's letting on, this latest development lets her out," Crook insisted. "She was in my company when Mrs. G. had her call, and though I know women can do a lot—leave chaps like us that play by the rules at the post—well, the Superb ain't fitted with a walkie-talkie, and Mrs. Drew was riding in her with me when this telephone call came through."

"Why should anyone want to abduct Mrs. Gorton?" Miss Deedes was in a perfect tizzy, but not an unpleasant one.

"Because she's the witness for the defense, if it comes to that. Now we're back where we started. We can't even prove such a chap as Stan exists."

"You need a very strong motive to abduct a child and then try and silence a witness," announced Mrs. Probyn, powerfully.

"Well, murder is a strong motive," Crook insisted. "No, I know there's no proof, but when we find Stan, there will be, because of the fingerprint. You explain," he added to the policeman, who looked as flabbergasted as anyone else. He moved away. They watched him approach two or three other people who were watching with their eyes on sticks. He nodded at the answers he got, then marched out.

Sara, sitting like a statue, had reached the same conclusion as Arthur Crook.

"They wouldn't have risked carrying off Mrs. Gorton if there was any chance of Mike coming back safe," she said. "I suppose in my heart I've known that all along."

"Lucky for us we didn't have to depend on you in the Battle of Britain," retorted Crook bluntly. "We'd have lost the war before your engine started revving. Now, let's see." He hauled out his big turnip watch. "As near eleven as makes no difference. They've got, say, an hour and a half's start on us. That's all, an hour and a half."

"And you don't think that's enough?" asked Sara, gently bitter.

"Point is, they think they've got twenty-four hours. Before any awkward questions are asked, I mean. They've laid the trail very neatly. Mrs. G. may be spending the night at the hospital so even if anyone rings the Bottle he won't expect an answer. And, believing young Tom's in a strange bed, he won't ring before morning. Even then it won't surprise anyone to get no reply. And by the time somebody starts putting on his thinking cap our young vultures will have flown."

"How about Tom? When he finds his mother isn't back . . ."

"It's a long time since I was seventeen," acknowledged Crook handsomely. "but Galahad here will bear me out that if you come home in the small hours and find the house dark, you thank your lucky stars and come upstairs in your stockinged feet. Last thing anyone wants at the end of a night out is a cozy chat with Mum. Mothers for some reason are always at the top of their form in the small hours, and Tom could be rather less—well, you get me. And he don't sound an early riser. No, our chaps must think they're batting on a champion wicket." He turned suddenly and put a large reassuring hand on Sara's cold ones. "It's all a matter of timing. If we can catch them before they've tied up the ends, well, Bob's your uncle." He started up the Superb.

"Where are we going now?" Sara inquired.

"Well," ejaculated Crook, "haven't you heard a word I've said? We're going to find Stan, of course. We know his hideout is past your cottage, though not outside the local phone area. What we have to hope for is that at the same time we find Mike and Mrs. G."

"How about Red?"

"Oh, I think he'll be there, too. Or, if not, Stan will lead us to him."

"But we don't know where to look. And while we're looking . . ."

"Get this into your head, sugar. Someone's seen him, if not Mike, and someone's been doing a bit of extraordinary shopping this past week. You can hide a little kid, but you have to get different things for him from what you get for the grown-ups. Extra milk, say, more bread, more meat, a bar of chocolate. Someone in one of the bungalows or cottages is going to remember and put us on the road."

"Have you any idea how many houses, bungalows and cottages, to say nothing of guest houses, there are within a radius of twenty miles?"

"You tell me. And you can wash out the guest houses, because you can't keep a little boy silent and he sounds a confiding little chap."

"If you're going to rap on every building we pass . . ."

"You're not with me. What we have to do is find the supplier of the extra stores. Well, that won't be a private dwelling, will it? Now, you do a bit of shopping at the Bottle?"

"Only drink and cigarettes. But I collect a lot of stuff there."

"But Stan ain't known there—well, obviously not, or Mrs. G. would have recognized the car. As she said herself, pale blue cars, especially racing models, don't grow on every hedge. So what we're looking for is a Leather Bottle or Woodland Stores on the further side of Fell Cottage. There won't be many of those. Of course, Stan could go further afield for his extras, but I don't suppose he'd think of that. They always slip up on some detail, like leaving that fingerprint."

They came swooping through Plowford and up the long dark road to The Leather Bottle. No lights burned here, but a stray beam of moonlight fell on the notice CLOSED FOR THE EVENING. Tom not back, then, but they hadn't expected he would be. Nearing Fell Cottage, Crook slowed down. Not likely Stan would have left a message, but no sense missing even a possibility. He nodded toward Denis.

"Take a looksee, in case there's a note in the porch."

"You mean, in case they've brought Mike back?" Sara cried. "But that would mean . . ."

Denis caught her hand. "Look," he urged, "Crook's got enough on his plate without you having hysterics. You stay here . . ."

But she wouldn't. She insisted on unlocking the cottage and she came back carrying shabby, loyal old Tigger.

"Mike will want to see him," she explained.

"What other sort of toys does he like?" Crook suggested. Keep her talking and you'd keep her from going over the edge.

"He's got a little globe, he'll spend hours with that, traveling round the world." Her voice laughed shakily, but it was a perceptible improvement. "Nothing bothers him. If he finds himself in the Arctic Ocean he takes a plane."

"Always assuming there's a plane handy, I suppose."

"If not, he finds a companionable albatross. You can't fault Mike."

"He's going to be a lot of help to us, a level-headed kid like that." Crook braked abruptly.

"Hedgehog," he explained. "Like any pedestrian, thinks everything should stop for him. And like pedestrians, he never learns any better." Delibrate, intent, apparently unaware of the death he had so narrowly escaped, the hedgehog snuffled its way through the ruts where the remains of snow were still visible.

"Let's hope his lady friend's worth it," murmured Crook.

Sara laughed again. Suddenly she was surprised to find her cold and nerveless hand warmly held in another. For a moment she thought she would pass out. It was more than two years since she'd taken confidence from a man's warm and energetic handclasp. Michael had had a grip like a vise. "Don't blame me if I drop the pan your steak's in," she used to warn him. You've probably broken half the bones of my hand. This was less gripping, but carried an equal assurance.

"Like a blood tranfusion," she said suddenly, and Denis

murmured something in surprise. Crook didn't bat an eyelid. If she'd started singing the cow jumped over the moon, it wouldn't have surprised him. Women are a law to themselves and, though he liked to say he hadn't much use for dames, it was a quality they both had in common. He boasted he had the hearing of a bat, which is higher than that of a man; he was listening for the sound of another car taking off, an invisible car. His great eyes, looking as large as those of the dog in the fairy tale who had eyes like saucers, roamed this way and that for the sight of a light moving through the woods. So long as he heard no car, saw no gleam, hope was not quenched.

Sara said suddenly, "He's such a little boy. And there are Stan and Red and probably some woman . . ."

"You thank your lucky stars for her," Crook told her simply. "Women 'ull poison their husbands, honestly, often without a qualm. 'Yes, I did give him rat poison,' a wife once told me, 'but I thought it was only dangerous to rats.' Oh yes, they'll knock out husbands and said husbands' girl friends or run a blackmailer off a cliff—I had one of those, too—but when it comes to a kid it's their heel of . . ."

"Achilles," supplied Denis.

"That's the one. Though, mark you, if his mam had had all her marbles, she'd have dipped him again holding him by the other foot."

"Aren't you forgetting the baby farmers?" asked Sara. "Or that woman who drowned her own two little girls . . ."

"Even the law lords had to admit she was mad. Granted we're all a bit wonky in the attics, it's my experience that a sane woman's the safest guard for a kid."

But, of course, every rule has its exceptions, and they both knew it.

Somewhere a church clock chimed. "We're nearing a village," said Crook. "Hold on, sugar. This could be it."

The big car, smooth and silent as a tiger, plowed on through the dark.

12

At approximately the time the Superb drew up at Plowford Police Station the young man, Stan Marvyn, said to a girl in the living room of a bungalow called Dunromin, "Red's late. He should have been here with the old girl by now." He went to the window and pulled back a curtain. "If he's messed things up a second time . . ."

"Second?" The word came in a whisper.

"Leaving that blasted fingerprint in the warehouse. But for that we'd be in the clear. That chap could never have identified us; stockings are like a winding sheet, make us all look alike." He laughed shortly, irritably. "Face the fact, Stell. Your brother may be Adonis 1963, but in our sort of job he's a damned liability, and it's a pity he didn't get himself knocked off instead of the old boy in the warehouse."

"Don't talk like that, Stan." If she'd been less haggard, if her spirit hadn't been dealt so many lethal blows, Stella would have been pretty; a year or two Stan's senior, with a nice figure and great deer's eyes that never left his face when they were together.

Now she burst out, "I don't like it, Stan. Why does it have to be this way? At the beginning you never said . . ."

"Oh, shut up!" cried Stan, roughly. His own nerves weren't quite as calm as he'd have wished. Where the hell was Red? If he couldn't manage an old woman he was no bloody use anyway. "You got your cut, didn't you?" he added, viciously.

"All for a measly three hundred pounds!" retorted Stella, in withering tones. "And you call yourself a businessman!"

"It was Lennie's top figure," answered Stan, as furious as she. "When you can't flog a thing on the open market . . ."

"Lennie doesn't hate himself much, does he? Anyone else would have given you five hundred. There was over a thousand pounds' worth of fags there."

"If your precious brother had kept his head and not knocked the old chap out we'd have got five hundred, possibly more. You can't blame Len for not wanting to be tied into a manslaughter charge."

"Manslaughter? What are you talking about? It was murder."

He looked at her in silence, and she began to shake. It was always the same. She could key herself up to contend with him, insist on her point of view, stand out for fair treatment, but let him once turn that particular gaze upon her, and she was undone. It wasn't terror, it was love, rising in her like a tidal wave, with no more sense than a tidal wave, poised for destruction. Sooner or later, most likely sooner, he'd destroy her, and she knew it. But he was the source of her living; she couldn't pull away from him without dying of the separation.

"Next time we must leave the planning to you," he was saying now, and there was no more trace of tenderness in him than there is in a stinging nettle. "You got to take the rough with the smooth, Stell. Nobody wins all the time."

"You must have been mad, rushing down Folly Hill just for kicks. You could have killed yourselves instead . . ."

"How were we to know that old fool would come marching

up? Or that silly woman be watching us from the woods? That's the trouble with life, too many nosy people everywhere. Once she came into the picture we didn't have any choice; she'd have talked, gone direct to the police and bleated like a little lamb."

"You never said you were going to bring a kid into it."

"Is it my fault she's got a kid? You stupid bitch! I didn't bring him in, he wandered in himself, and once there he'd got to be dealt with."

"Then you shouldn't have brought him here, not to me. He's such a nice little kid, the sort of son you'd want yourself . . ."

"He's a flaming danger, that's what he is. And I'm a flaming fool to have anything to do with you."

"And now there's this woman, this Mrs. Gorton," she persisted. She was like someone who sees the snake swaying closer and closer, but can't or won't run. "There won't be any end."

"This is the end," he insisted. By this time tomorrow we'll be in Spain, and we can put all this behind us." He saw her desperate tortured face, and softened a bit. "You know, Stell, you can't always fix things to the last detail. You have to take a chance. Like that night at the warehouse. We didn't know the old fool would put up a fight, and for a lot of rotten old cigarettes, that were insured anyway. It was him or us, can't you see?"

"He wouldn't have killed you."

"He'd have turned us in. And that woman on the hill would have turned us in, for the sake of an old fool she didn't even know. And if that one hadn't been round the bend anyway, she wouldn't have been trailing her miserable hound through the snow. Mercy anyway to put him out of his misery."

"But Mrs. Drew didn't go to the police."

"She would, if we hadn't stalled her."

"I suppose you're allowing we shall be out of the country before she gets the boy back. But what's to hinder her going to the police then? And Mike's no fool." She met his steady incredulous gaze. "You mean, you never meant to send him back?"

"Who do you think's the most important, him or me? When

155

you're in our business you have to accept the fact that obstacles are expendable. Think of a war . . ." But she wasn't listening, she moved away. His keen glance followed her. "I should have my head examined, getting tied up with that pair," Stan reflected.

"You always could talk the leg off a goat," she said, "but this time you've gone too far." Her glance fell on a clock. "Perhaps something's gone wrong, perhaps that woman wasn't foxed." She said it almost gleefully. Something going wrong might save Mike, though how—how—

"Did you ever hear of Arthur Crook?"

Stan's question caught her off guard. "No. Should I?"

"Don't read the papers, do you? He's the chap who found the old girl; and he's the one who came to the inquest and him and Mrs. Drew went off together. And Mrs. Drew was going to London tonight . . .

"You don't know . . . she was going to meet him, I mean."

"Well, she didn't expect to find her son there. Besides, I know her sort. Once Carew got blamed, sooner or later she'd come forward. Telling me about the witness, too. Dames 'ud be safer if they were born without tongues." Then he commanded her. "Go and take a look at the kid."

Mike was in bed, fast asleep. He looked all right, round and rosy, no marks of blows or ill usage. He was an adaptable child, easy to amuse, sharp as a needle. A ferret, corrected Stan. He was beginning to show too much curiosity about his mother, though. Why doesn't she send me a card? She must be *very ill*. If he'd been stupider it might have been better for him. Stella went and sat beside the bed. Mike's lashes lay tranquilly on his warm cheek. She had made him a little horse out of some toweling and fitted on a toy harness; he held it firmly, even in his sleep.

Her heart turned painfully in her breast. All she wanted was a home and a kid like this one and a chap coming back in the evening to the dinner she'd cooked for him, a drink at the pub at the weekend, a little car maybe and going out of a Sunday, a nice kitchen and one of those washing machines you saw advertised on TV—just the usual that everyone else had. And she had had her chances. More than one man had looked in her direction, and then she had met Stan, and that had been her undoing. All her peaceful dreams, her commonplace hopes, had gone like chaff before the wind.

When he was away she could be strong. I'll tell him I've had enough of it, my nerves won't stand it, he can get a job like everyone else, best in the long run, too, because sooner or later you always get caught, and what's the sense of living high if you have to do seven years in the Scrubbs or on the Moor? Then Stan would walk in, put his hand on her, twist her around to face him, smile, say something ever so ordinary—"Hello, sweetie." Or "How's the girl?" and she melted like butter in the sun. But this warring against a little kid was going too far. She'd tell him. I won't have anything to do with it. And I won't let you. I won't squeal on you, she'd say, but leave me and the kid out of it.

The door opened, Stan stuck his head in.

"Car coming," he said. "Action stations."

He sounded not merely relieved but joyful. She opened her mouth to speak; the words jammed, she found it difficult to breathe.

"Take it easy," Stan told her. "We've got plenty of time. We don't have to be at the airport before midnight at the earliest. The plane takes off at 12:30. Still, the sooner we're out of this place the better." He looked at his watch. "Not quite ten. Gives us nearly two hours." But he meant what he'd said a moment earlier. The sooner they escaped the better. Not likely anyone would stop them, but there are some risks it simply doesn't pay to take. Stella, he realized, was going to be their weak link. He cursed himself for ever getting mixed up with such an unreliable pair; yet it was Stella's personal devotion to himself, Red's absolute lack of nerve—he couldn't have spelled remorse if you'd offered him a thousand pounds—that had enabled Stan to preserve his own balance. Once in Spain, he thought, he could shake the pair.

Stella found her voice at last. "I'm not going through with it," she said, and was surprised to learn how calm she sounded.

"Come off it," he besought her. "You know you don't mean that."

"Oh you!" She made a gesture of despair. "You never listen to anything."

"If you were going to turn so bloody moral, why didn't you go to the police at the start?" demanded Stan, violently. "No, don't tell me. I'll tell you. Because you're like everyone else, you want money, but you want it the easy way. If you had to get it for yourself you'd be standing at a machine all day, or scrubbing some other dame's floor. This way you stay at home and, like I said, you get your cut. That's the worst of women, they always want to have their cake and eat it, and it can't be done. Well, if you don't mean to come with us you can stay here with the others, I suppose, but under the same conditions."

There was noise outside as though a slightly rusty cat had stopped purring. Stan went out to meet the driver of the black Vauxhall.

"I've got her," said Red in cool, untroubled tones. "She's out like a light. If we had her weight in gold," he added, with a grin, "we wouldn't need to do another stroke of work so long as we lived."

He stood there, tall and smiling, eyes bright as glass in the light streaming from the hall, as shallow, as brittle, too.

"What do you think?" inquired Stan, helping to lift the unconscious burden from the car and lug it into the house. "Your little sister wants to put us up the river."

Stella, who had come into the hall, cried half hysterically, "It's all your fault. Why did you have to lose your head and shoot that man? All the trouble stems from that."

"Do you shut your mouth or do we shut it for you?" inquired Red. "If you must know, I shot him because the old fool got in the way. Any reasonable jury 'ud bring in a verdict of suicide, only our laws are so haywire—heave, Stan."

Mrs. Gorton was a plump little woman, as cozy as a bolster when the two young men hauled her out of the car and finally dumped her on the vacant bed in the room where Mike slept tranquilly. Stan had rented the bungalow for three months, cash in advance, to obviate the need for references. At the time it had seemed a useful bolt-hole, fairly isolated, not too dear, in case of emergency, though neither had visualized an emergency quite like the one that had arisen. Still, it had proved useful enough when the necessity arose to intimidate that nosy bint on Folly Hill, who hadn't got the sense to see that in the civilized world of the nineteen-sixties, it's smart to mind your own business, and if the other chap goes under when the boat overturns, thank God you're still safe, and only a fool opens his mouth unless he wants it filled with seawater.

Stella, watching them, realized that to them Mrs. Gorton and Mike weren't an elderly woman and a child, both duped into captivity, but two bumps in their road who had to be ironed out. Whoever had lain awake worrying about old Larkin, it hadn't been Red. It's like a war, he had insisted once. They bring you up that murder's a crime, but in a war the criminal's the chap who doesn't pull the trigger or release the bomb. Life's a battlefield, kill or be killed. I don't mean to be killed.

"You won't get away with it," she assured them. "People may not worry much about the child, Mrs. Gorton's quite a person. Oh Stan, do think again. You're out of your mind, how can you hope to pull it off? Just get out, and Red, you'll make the plane, I shan't talk . . ."

Stan leaned forward and struck her sharply on the cheek. "Pull yourself together, it's too late to gab like that now. Do you want to wake the kid and land us all in the cart?" The gallows cart, he meant.

Red, as though she weren't even there, was explaining the situation.

"No one's likely to miss her till they start breaking up the party," he said. "Then they'll hear she went to the hospital, so it's not likely the ball will start to roll till sometime tomorrow, when Tom Gorton starts wondering where his mother is. By that time we shall be flown and lost in the mists."

"Lost," repeated Stella. That was how she felt. Lost in a hopeless, ill-fated love for Stan. As for him, he'd been lost from the beginning, something lacking when he was born, perhaps.

And yet loved by her, against reason, against any hope of happiness, as if some evil fairy had bewitched her in her cradle. She had grown to love the little boy, she pitied the older woman, but at the final moment she'd do what Stan said.

"You better get that car away, Red," Stan went on. "Any idea whose it is?"

"Does it matter, seeing we're going to return it—well, leave it for the cops to find?"

"And don't for God's sake go leaving fingerprints on it. Stell, you go with him and rub it up—handles specially, steering wheel—and don't leave a cigarette stub under the mat."

"Do what Gauleiter Marvyn says," Red mocked his sister. He pulled out his pack of cigarettes and lighted one, throwing the match carelessly away. Stella went out; thirty seconds later she had bounced back.

"Do you realize whose car you've taken? It's Dr. Penrose's."

"Who's he when he's at home?" Red inquired.

"I wouldn't mind having the pair of you under the wheels," Stan exploded. He was white with passion. "You bloody idiot! Of all the cars on the lot you have to pinch the doctor's."

"Well, for God's sake!" protested Red. "He's at the blasted party, isn't he? I told you, that won't break up . . ."

"A doctor's always on call. If they find the car's gone missing, and the old girl at the same time . . ."

"They won't suspect any tie-up there." Red remained unmoved. "Some chap's taken it for a joyride, it's being done all the time. Who's to know it was me?"

"I know one thing," Stan assured him, grimly. "You're not leaving that car anywhere near this place. For all we know, the word's gone out already that it's missing, the police will be told to look for a black Vauxhall—what's the number? Never mind, it doesn't matter. Stell, go and give him a hand. Don't forget about the ashtrays, it's all Lombard Street to a china orange he smokes a different brand."

"He doesn't smoke at all," said Stella, dully. "I went to see him once."

"That's a help. And get back as soon as you can. I shall want you here while Red ditches the car."

"I suppose you didn't touch the doctor's bag?" said Stella, sarcastically to her brother as they moved toward the door.

"What's that about a bag?" Stan exclaimed. "Might be useful. Bring it along, Stell."

"Why do you want it?"

"Yaketty, yaketty, yak," commented Stan. "Can't you do anything without asking why?"

"What are you going to do?" Resolute and miserable, Stella stood her ground.

"What does it matter? It won't make any difference in the long run. O.K., Red, you bring it in. Stell, give the car the once-over, and for goodness sake, do something to your face. If anyone sees you on the way out, they'll think it's the end of the world."

"They wouldn't be far out," muttered Stella, snatching up her bag and departing.

Red followed her, and lightly swung the doctor's bag out of the back seat.

"You want to watch your step," he advised her. "Stan's in no mood to play games. Come to that, nor am I."

He carried the bag inside the house. "A good thing she can't drive," he observed grimly. "I wouldn't put it past her to try and sell us up the river even now."

Stella appeared in the doorway, sheet-white. "You're not going to touch the boy," she insisted.

"I'm not going to touch the boy," Stan agreed. "Where 'ud be the sense hurting him?"

"I hope Lennie's done his stuff," said Red, as Stella went back to the car. "We don't want a breakdown at this stage."

"Oh, Len's O.K.," Stan assured him. "Old Len won't let us down. In his own interests," he added. "We know too much."

"Where's he meeting us?"

"At the airport. Stop fussing, Red, you're as bad as your sister. He'll have tickets, currency, passports, the lot. Even bringing a wedding ring for Stell." He chuckled. "The Spanish are very hot on female morality."

"I hope my sister isn't going to muck everything up. That's the worst of women, go sentimental on you without warning."

"I'll have a word," said Stan, confidently. "Here she comes. Did we tell you, sweetie, you're going to be a respectable married woman, traveling on your husband's passport? No, don't ask how. That's Len's job. And Spain 'ull soon turn you as brown as a cracker." He caught Red's eye and grinned. "I always rather fancied these colored gals."

"Might even settle," reflected Red. "The old country's had it. Nothing but a ratrace . . ."

"That doesn't affect anyone who isn't a rat," cried Stella. "Stan, do listen to me. You and Red go. I swear I wouldn't report you. Anyway, I don't know enough. Mrs. Gorton wouldn't be able to identify Red even if she was asked, and as for Mike, who takes a child's evidence?"

"Forgetting Mike's mother, aren't you? She'd know me again in an air raid."

"You'll be gone, you'll be safe. None of them ever saw me. Besides, once she has Mike back safely she won't care. I know women. And we know she hasn't been to the police."

"She's done a lot worse than that. She's gone to see Arthur Crook."

"You don't know . . ."

"Red and me know. Why else should she be going to London? Funny, I always thought you were kind of fond of me."

"Fond!" she breathed. "You couldn't begin to understand."

"But you'd put a kid and an old woman ahead of me when it comes to trouble."

"For your sake. Don't you understand? You'll have to live with this."

"Just so long as I live," said Stan, smiling, but a tide of hate, stemming from a secret fear, heated his blood. "After all we've done, Red, your sister's chicken. Now shut up, Stell, unless you want your own private bomb. That kid may be only four, though he looks more than that to me, but he's no fool. And if he can't go into a witness box he can gab to the police, can't he? Uncle Stan, Auntie Stell, even Uncle Red, I shouldn't wonder. Now, car O.K.? Right. Red, you better be going. Make sure she hasn't left any clues accidentally-on-purpose. I've got a small job to do, and then . . ." He nodded, picking up the bag and moving toward the bedroom.

Stella cast a despairing glance at the telephone, but she knew it was no use. She wouldn't get farther than the second letter before they'd be onto her; and anyway, how could she turn in Stan? No, she was tied to him forever and ever. She remembered a religious aunt in her childhood telling her that hell is the place where nothing ever stops and nothing ever changes, a far more alarming conception than the old-fashioned fire and brimstone. These thoughts ran pell-mell through her head as they went over the car once again, turning up cushions, brushing away mud—no need to look for matches, since Stan had his classy lighter.

"Now the back," commanded Red. "The old woman wasn't wearing gloves, she may have left a print."

Obediently Stella got to work. "Oh, Red," she murmured, "how did we get into this?"

"I'll tell you how we got into it," said Red brutally. "Our mum and dad fancied a bit of a roll in the hay, and so they went to the Town Hall and got a license—and lucky for you, my girl, they did, ran it pretty fine as it was—and that's about the size of it. We were in this, Stell, from the time we were born. That's what these goddamned elder statesmen never seem to understand."

When they got back to the house they found Stan at the bedside of the unconscious Mrs. Gorton. He had the doctor's bag open and was handling a syringe. It presented no mysteries to him, and no reason why it should; he'd been handling one for years. It was no wonder that a job at twelve or fourteen pounds a week was no good to him.

"Just for kicks," he'd say, but he hadn't managed to convert Red.

"I get my kicks other ways," Red would tell him.

"Here, Stell," Stan called. "Lend a hand."

She came like a machine, pushed up the coatsleeve, unfastened the cuff of the dress, held the arm steady. With a sure hand Stan pushed the needle home, slipping it in, giving it a slight twist, then releasing the morphine.

Lucky really he was carrying that. Never pays to take more chances than you need. He looked thoughtfully at the slumbering Mike. "Better not," he decided. "Don't want to risk waking him. He could start to yell. As it is, neither of them will know a thing. Here, put this back."

He held out the doctor's bag to Stella. "Just a minute, Red."

She wondered what he was saying as she ran back to the car, her handbag still hanging on her arm. Automatically she dusted it over with a rag as she settled it carefully in the back seat.

"We'll be at the crossroads in, say, half an hour," Stan told Red. "Get shut of the car as soon as you can. The Happy Goat stays open till eleven, so if you've got time to burn or we're a bit behind time, you can go in there. No need to attract attention." He caught Red's eye and laughed. "No need to tell you that, either. The bulls are scary about alibis. Innocent men never think they need 'em."

"Innocent men don't know they're born," retorted Red, "and mostly they aren't." Born, he meant.

"Give us a ring when you've ditched the car," continued Stan, "just to let us know everything's O.K. If we don't hear, we'll understand something's slipped up and you're on your own."

"Think of everything, don't you?" murmured Red. "First things first, I mean." And by first things he meant Stan Marvyn. "Pity really you couldn't have given my sister a shot; lucky for us she's nuts about you."

He met Stella on the doorstep; she looked absolutely whacked.

"Watch your step," he warned her. "Stan would slay me for saying so, but he's got the jitters. It's nothing to me what you do with your own life, but start trying to muck up mine . . ." He caught her arm and gave it a professional twist. With difficulty she suppressed a cry. Red started up the car and began to move off, with perfect aplomb. Nothing stealthy about his movements, nothing brash either; just another chap, like you or me, going home after an evening with the gang.

He went by the upper road, the long way around but safer,

since you could be pretty sure you wouldn't meet any of the roisterers from the Town Hall that way. Not that there was a dog's chance anyone would spot him, thought Red. Like most criminals, he was saturated with vanity, and didn't give dogs sufficient credit.

13

Back in the bungalow Stella had begun to polish the furniture with a bit of rag. Don't skimp it, Stan advised her. He was sorting papers, burning them carefully in the grate, reducing them to ash, so that even the cleverest cop couldn't make anything of them. There weren't many of them, mainly notes from Lennie about their escape. While Stella rubbed and washed, keeping her gaze from the two unconscious figures in the bedroom, Stan, wearing gloves now, went around closing and locking the doors, fastening the shutters at the front windows. At the back French casements opened into a little lawn; he bolted these, pulled the curtains, then methodically he stuffed up all the cracks with rags, blankets, even utilizing a small blue romper suit, a child's windbreaker. Presently he looked at the watch on his wrist.

"Red should be coming through any minute now," he said. "Provided he hasn't bungled it again."

Two minutes later the phone rang. It was Red. When Stan heard what he had to say he began to grin.

"Know what that brother of yours has done? Dumped the car behind the hospital with about half a dozen others. Last place they'll think of looking for it, and if it is seen there no one 'ull be surprised. Now, come on. We're all set."

He drove her out of the room; then crossing the bedroom with a light step he stooped to turn on the tap of an incongruous-looking modern gas fire. Out came the gas, puffing like an alderman. Stan switched off the light, came into the hall. The door had been fitted with a draft excluder, nothing to worry about there. He sent an anxious glare at Stella. She looked like someone carved in stone, or that woman in the Old Testament—Lot's wife, wasn't it? Not much to be done now, and what there was he did quickly. Then he caught Stella's arm and ran her out of the house. There was a detached garage alongside, and in it an innocuous-looking Ford car. He'd got rid of the Albion days ago: a respray, organized by Red, new license plates; now she was another fellow's property and nothing to show she'd ever belonged to a man called Stan Marvyn.

Stella, still wearing that inhuman look, got into the car, and they were off. They took the same road as Red had done.

"Don't want to chance running into any cars coming back from the gala," he explained. "Now take it easy. We've bags of time. Len doesn't want us hanging around the airport."

"I thought you said no one was going to notice us."

"Oh, wrap up," ordered Stan, disgustedly. "That woman could give a description, couldn't she?"

Stella let out an uncontrollable giggle. "You should have dyed your hair."

That angered him. He was vain of his appearance, worse than a girl.

"Stop that," he said. "For pity's sake, Stell, get a hold on yourself. This is serious."

That threw her into a paroxysm of mirth. "Don't mind me," she giggled. "After all, none of it's real, it can't be. It's just a nightmare. I shall wake up." Because it's only in nightmares that you gas old women and children. "It's what Hitler did," she burst out, "and look what we think of him."

He took one hand off the wheel and caught her wrist. She thought he'd break it.

"You make me sick," he said. "Honest you do. You came away from fairyland a long time ago. Can't you get it into your empty head that this is a competitive world, we've all got to fight for ourselves? It's kill or be killed. Of course, it can't work out for everyone; it didn't work out for that night watchman, it hasn't worked out for the boy and that interfering old cow who'd have reported the lot of us, but speaking personally, I prefer to be one of those that stay alive."

"And, of course, everything always works out for you, doesn't it?" agreed Stella, with a sort of gasp. "You want to be careful, Stan. You rush along at such a speed, one of these days you'll find you can't apply the brake, and you'll ride right over the cliff into the sea."

"Just so long as you're by my side," said Stan. And she shivered again. All impulse to laugh left her. She now sat very still; she looked as if she were praying. She hardly seemed to realize his presence, with her face pressed against the black glass, so still she might have passed out, too. For the first time he knew the pang of real apprehension. Until now she'd been like a glove puppet, always doing what he intended; now at last she seemed to have slipped beyond his reach.

'Stell!' he said sharply.

"I was thinking. Stan, when you were a kid, were you brought up religious?"

"Sunday school and all that bull?"

"Suppose it isn't bull? Suppose it's true?"

"I told you—you left fairyland a long time ago. It would serve you right if I was to chuck you out of the car, leave you to go home on your own feet. Only you'd run right to the cops, sniveling and whimpering. You're a liability, that's why we're taking you with us. Get that into your head. Don't suppose I'll forget how you've been carrying on. Remember Moll Lindsay?"

"Oh no!" He saw he'd scored a bull's eye there. Moll, sick of ill-usage and treachery, had betrayed her man, who'd been jailed in consequence. When he came out Moll was on the other side of the country, quiet and invisible as a bird on its nest. But not invisible enough. The thug in question tracked her down. After he was through with her she wouldn't have been any good to him or any man in her former capacity, even if she'd wanted to go back. They said she put cloths over all the mirrors. Ordinary decent people don't know, thought Stella. To them there's just right and wrong. To them she was just a rotten woman, must be to get mixed up with a chap like Stan. There wouldn't be a grain of sympathy for her when the story broke. But just as a stone, pushed off a cliff, must continue to fall, so, once you've got yourself linked up with a pair like Stan and Red, you just go on falling; all the moral welfare workers in the country can't change the law of gravity.

Stan turned the car at the top road and looked back. He glimpsed a light among the trees.

"The merrymakers return," he said. "We did it just in time. And if," he went on in a completely blank voice, "you had any idea of exchanging friendly greeting, just take a look at my left hand."

She glanced down involuntarily, and there it was, the wicked knife snapped into position and poised just beneath her breast. And she knew, because she knew Stan, that, just as Moll's fellow hadn't scrupled to use vitriol in settling his account, so Stan would have no compunction at all about thrusting the knife home, only curse her because he'd have to stop the car and conceal the body where it wouldn't instantly be found, and that might make him late for his rendezvous with Red.

The light they had seen had nothing to do with their pursuers. It belonged to a car bringing back a quartet from the movies at Martindale. They'd picked up Red and were running smoothly toward the airport before the Superb came nosing through the trees going more slowly now, looking for the inevitable clue.

The road turned to the right and ran past a few houses, a

riding school (we're coming up in the world, said Crook, look-ing hopeful, because a riding school means there must be peo-ple not far away), then the church whose chime they had heard.

Crook had slowed almost to a walk. "It'll be somewhere here," he said, and a moment later they saw it: a little squat building with two shop windows, a letterbox let into the wall, and a sign over the door. Woodland Stores. Ivy Lucas. Li-censed to sell tobacco. There were living quarters above, and if they were as dark as Sara's hopes that didn't mean a thing. People in the country go to bed early and rise ditto. It's only in towns as a rule that maniacs go to bed in the small hours and are up at seven. Crook halted the car and got out.

"Be ready to do your stuff," he warned Denis.

There was a side bell connecting with the living half of the building and he pressed this, keeping his finger on it till an upper window was flung up and an angry voice said, "What do you suppose you're doing? If you don't clear off at once I shall ring the police."

"No need," countered Crook, smoothly. "They're on your doorstep."

That sobered her a bit, as he had intended it should. She leaned out a bit farther, a big bonny woman, the statuesque battering-ram type.

"That's not a police car," she said, and Crook gave her a good mark for observation.

"Ever seen a police warrant?" he called back, and she said no.

"Praise the pigs," murmured Crook, inaudibly. "Now's your chance," he shouted.

The figure disappeared, the window was yanked down.

"You sell me up the river here," Crook warned Denis, who had left the car and was standing at his side, "and I'll put you in the river, and sugar here will hold you under to make sure you drown."

"What does a warrant look like?" asked Denis, unmoved. "I've never had the nerve to ask to see one."

Crook pulled a little leather-covered case from his pocket.

"This'll do in a pinch," he said. "Not that they ever let you get more than a glimpse of it. Now then, over the top."

Steps creaked down the stairs, the door was opened.

"What is all this?" Mrs. Ivy Lucas didn't look the kind that stands for any nonsense. "If it's one of those silly games they play . . ."

"Do I look the sort that plays games this hour of the night? No, we're hunting for a lost child—kidnaped," he added.

That did the trick, as he knew it would. Children and dogs—provided they're in trouble—are winners all along the line.

Denis put his hand in his pocket, brought it half out, and said, "Perhaps the lady would like to see our warrants, sir?"

"Inspector Crook, Constable Denis, plain-clothes branch," ad-libbed Crook sharply. In other circumstances he'd rather have enjoyed this, but he couldn't forget Sara's face, thin, sharp as a bird's, watching them through the glass.

Mrs. Lucas shook an impatient head. "Who'd want to call himself a policeman if he wasn't?" she demanded.

Mentally, Crook gave her a second good mark.

"When was this? I haven't seen . . ." Her sharp eyes pierced the gloom. "Are you the mother, dear?" she called.

Sara stepped out to join the other two. "They've had him nearly a week. I didn't dare go to the police before, they said . . ."

"Best come in," invited Mrs. Lucas. Her dark dressing gown covered her amplitudes like a monk's robe. In fact, she looked rather like a high priestess of some unknown sect.

"You the main shopping center here?" asked Crook, instantly approving the plaster Alsatian dog, the Victorian china basket, the large photograph on the wall, hand-colored—the dear departed no doubt.

"I do the local trade," Mrs. Lucas said. "Sit down, dear, you look all in."

"Oh please," breathed Sara. "Every minute counts."

Mrs. Lucas filled a kettle and put it on to boil. "Won't take a minute. Now, what did you want to know?"

"You'd recognize a strange kid suddenly turning up, wouldn't you?" asked Crook.

"I haven't seen one. Fact is, there aren't many kids round here. People with families want to live nearer a town—schools, see, and easier to get a baby-sitter. No, I haven't seen any strange . . . Wait a minute."

"Yes?" breathed Sara.

"That couple of Londoners, they said—rented the bungalow at the top—Dunromin, it's called. Not that they have."

"Have what?" asked Crook, enthralled.

"Done roaming. Gone off on a cruise and let the place. Mrs. —Mrs.—Marvyn, that's the name. Came in the other day and said she'd got her sister's little boy staying with them, while his mam had the new baby."

"You're on the ball." Crook nodded. "Didn't bring the kid?"

"Said he had a cold, but she wanted something to amuse him."

She got up and went through a door into the darkened shop. A light sprang up and the three followed her.

"I do a few toys, comics, cigarettes, on the side," she explained. "Not a great deal of demand, but . . ."

"What did she buy?"

"She bought one of these." The woman reached up and took down a small painted tin globe. "Said he had one at home . . ."

"Mike!" cried Sara.

Denis, forgetting his official capacity, put his arm around her.

"You're a policeman, even if you aren't in uniform," Crook reminded him, and at that moment the kettle behind them gave a great puff—of protest, of agreement, whichever way you liked to take it.

"Advertises it boils a pint in ninety-four seconds," said Mrs. Lucas, proudly, bustling past them. She was a big woman, but she seemed to move with the speed of light. She'd got the tea made before anyone could protest.

"Tell us more," Crook besought her. "How long ago was this?"

"Well, a week maybe. Mind you, I don't see much of them

here. The young woman comes in sometimes, and if ever she got that wedding ring in church my name's not Ivy Lucas."

She poured out a cup of tea, dredged the sugar into it and forced it into Sara's hand.

"Been buying extra food?" Crook forged on. "The sort of things a kid likes?"

"Cereals, chocolate, tinned milk. Funny thing, she never had the doctor to him."

"Would you, for a cold?" murmured Denis.

"Cold that keeps a kiddie in bed for a week is more than a cold," Ivy Lucas proclaimed. "Still, she was in yesterday, so . . ."

"They should give you a medal," said Crook. "Drink that up, Mrs. Drew, and we'll be off. How far's this bungalow, Mrs. Lucas?"

"Up at the top and turn right down Godstone Lane. Who thought of calling it that . . ." she shrugged. "Just ruts and potholes after the kind of weather we've been having, and nothing 'ull be done. Wonder it didn't pull the springs out of that car of theirs."

Crook pricked up his ears. "Lady came in a car?"

"No. But I saw her out early closing day. Had a chap with her. No sign of a boy." She frowned.

"Notice the car?"

"Little red job."

"Red," said Crook with satisfaction.

"That's what I said."

"I wish all witnesses were as reliable as you. Not got a license, I suppose?" He looked around hopefully.

She read him like a book. "If it's a drop of brandy—I can't sell it, of course, but you're welcome." She pulled out a chair, stood on it and reached to a high cupboard. "Our mother brought us up not to waste our time with doctors—of course they want you ill, how'd they make a living if you weren't—jamaica ginger for minor troubles, stomach aches and all that; if the ginger won't work, then brandy."

She stepped down with a bottle in her hand. "Have a sip in

173

that tea, love." She poured it in without waiting. "I didn't think to ask . . ."

"Officer and me 'ull get a cuppa when we're back at the station," Crook told her. He took the bottle. "Repay you four-fold," he promised, and she believed him, like a bird. Funny to think of him as a policeman, she wouldn't have believed . . . Crook saw the suspicion forming in her mind, and gave her a third point.

"Anything more you should want—I shan't be going back to bed for a while," she told them. "You send your young man . . ."

Sara put down the cup. "I won't forget," she said in a choking voice. They went out and piled back into the big yellow car, under Ivy's watchful eye. Crook signed to Denis to take the wheel. Inspectors don't drive themselves when they've got a dogsbody of a constable to do the job for them. And in his job you learned early that no sacrifice was too great, even when it involved the Superb.

Godstone Lane was everything Mrs. Lucas had pictured it. A broken surface, four bungalows dotted in an irregular row with plenty of room between them, sloping paths leading to sunken front doors.

"Not surprised they've gone on a cruise," ejaculated Crook. "Halfway to the graveyard already." Piously he thanked the God in whom he was still old-fashioned enough to believe, that he'd got the young man in tow.

Dunromin was pitch-dark and as quiet as—the word grave came into his mind again, but he chased it out smartly. He hadn't come all this way, and risked the Superb's axles, to be confronted with a corpse at the end of the road. Shutters covered the front windows, and Sara raced down the path and began to thunder on them. Crook dodged around the side of the house, closely followed by Denis. He made short work of the bolted French window, simply putting a huge fist in a heavy driving glove through the pane, and manipulating the bolt. Stan had thought of this and nailed up the catch. Denis came racing at it and caught it kersplosh with a heavy accurate foot. The bungalow hadn't been built for this kind of treatment, and within a few seconds they were inside. They could still hear Sara thundering on the shutters. In a couple of minutes she'd have waked the whole neighborhood.

The smell of gas had already penetrated to the hall. Crook slammed open a couple of doors but no soap. The third was locked on the outside, and the key was missing.

"Let her in," said Crook, distractedly, and Denis opened the door.

She smelled the gas at once. "Where is he?"

"Do a bit more of your footwork," Crook invited his companion.

But this door was made of sterner stuff. "If this was a novel we should fire a revolver into the lock . . ."

"That's a novel," Crook advised him. "In real life we should probably kill whoever was on the other side."

"Wait a minute," cried Sara. She twitched a key from one of the other doors. "If this is anything like the cottage you can make one key open more than one door."

Her hands were shaking so that Crook took the key from her; he went down on his knees, a little red-brown troglodyte, with no more thought for dignity than Red had for human life.

"What we want here is Bill," he muttered. "My partner, Bill Parsons. It 'ud be child's play to him."

"Tell him to open it," whispered Sara, almost frantic, and looking as if she'd twist the key out of Crook's hands.

"Don't shoot the pianist," Denis advised her. "He's doing his best."

For an agonizing minute that seemed like an hour, they watched Crook at work, intent as any bank robber, manipulating the cheap horrid key.

"Ever see the key of Barkstone Castle?" he inquired in a conversational tone, just as though there weren't two lives and one woman's sanity—to say nothing of his own reputation—at stake. "That's the sort of key to give you confidence. Why, you could knock a man out with it, and you need a page to walk behind you, carrying it on a cushion, if you aren't to end up with your arm in a sling. Ah!"

His breath came out like a rushing mighty wind, but nothing

to the way the gas came pouring from the dark room. He'd been working by flashlight, Sara realized; until this instant she hadn't noticed Denis was holding the light near the lock. Now he pressed the electric switch but nothing happened.

"Turned off at the main," interpreted Crook, flashing the beam over the room, and hurrying forward, half asphyxiated by the gas, to stop the supply. Denis went to the windows, and tore at the shutters. At the first beam of light Sara had raced across the room and picked up the blue motionless figure of her little son.

She carried him through the dark hall and into the patch of front garden. The life-giving air came pouring through the windows, dispersing the gas. And not before time, thought Crook, feeling remarkably hazy. He remembered the brandy bottle in his pocket and took a quick swig, passing it silently to Denis. Then they caught up Mrs. Gorton and between them dragged her out of the room of death.

"Get the police, get the ambulance, see if there's a local doctor on the telephone list," commanded Crook. "I'll try and find the main switch and we can get some light . . . Well," he added, irritably, "what are we waiting for?"

"You underrate Stan, really you do," said Denis, in such a close mimicry of Crook's own manner that Crook himself was startled. "He wasn't taking the remotest chance, and before he lit out he cut the telephone cord."

While Denis tore back to the Woodland Stores to borrow Mrs. Lucas's telephone, Crook, who had located the main switch and filled the cottage with light, came to squat beside Sara. She lifted a face of such despair that even he was shaken.

"I think he's dead."

Crook leaned over and took the child's limp body out of her hands.

"In that case, whatever we do we can't do him any harm. Now, don't panic, sugar. I've forgotten more chaps in extremis than you've so far had a chance to see."

It was strange that anyone who looked so like a bear and had hands like legs of mutton could be so gentle. He put his ear down to the child's chest. The heart was beating, but very faint, as if any second the effort would be too much.

"What we have to do is try to get the gas out of him," he said. He knew about artificial respiration, and he wouldn't have had a qualm about trying it on Mrs. Gorton, but this body was so small and limp it seemed it might break in his hands. He remembered the prophet who restored a child to life by stretching himself on the boy and breathing his own life into mouth and nose.

"We've got to get the gas out of him," he said to Sara. "Now don't stand there doing nothing. Pray as you've never prayed before. And if you don't believe in anything, you better get your faith back double quick.

She repeated "Pray?" in numbed tones, and he said, "Yes. That my luck don't run out on me. It never has, but there's got to be a first time for everything—only not tonight."

14

But even before Crook's spirited adjuration to Stella, Providence had started to do its stuff. Its instrument was a cocky and very ambitious prowl-car driver called Ede, who, having heard on his walkie-talkie about the stolen car, resolved to be the man to locate it.

"Now where would you put a doctor's car if you don't want it noticed?" he demanded. And answered his own question. "In front of his own house. So we look there first."

But it wasn't there.

"Guess again," suggested his co-driver, a cheerful extrovert who believed in doing things by the book.

"Hospital, of course."

"Or the house of any of his patients," suggested the extrovert.

"X wouldn't know who his patients were."

So to the hospital they went, and there it was.

"What did I say?" demanded Ede, looking as pleased as Lucifer after a soul hunt, and nearly as crafty. Stan and Red thought they were so blooming clever, but they made the usual mistake of not realizing that the chap on the other side can show just as much wit as you.

"Maybe he's in the hospital," said the extrovert, but Ede had no time for that sort of thing. A report to headquarters brought the Inspector around, with Penrose in tow. Penrose was furious that anyone should dare tamper with his car. When he was asked if anything was missing he pushed his head through the window like some old tortoise counting the fringes on the old rug he carried. He lifted his bag dubiously, then exclaimed, "Here, you—Inspector—you'd better see this."

The Inspector hurried forward. Under the bag, and hitherto concealed by it, was a bit of paper with a few words hurriedly printed in green ink.

Dunromin, it read. Godstone Lane. Gas. Hurry.

Stella, poor terrified creature, had found a way of defeating Stan, after all.

Instantly the wires began to hum. Penrose and his escort might be thundering through the woods looking for Godstone Lane, but a certain Inspector Poole, brought from his bed by the news, was snapping like the famous turtle.

"One thing you can be sure about," he said. "Stan and Company aren't staying cooped up in a gas-filled cottage. They'll have made their getaway by now, and my guess 'ud be they'll be leaving the country. Odds are they'll do the first lap by car. The country's littered with trains stuck in snowdrifts, and a man in a stationary train is always particularly vulnerable." All the same he put a man on to contact all main railway stations, with a warning to look for three people, two men and a woman—Stan's description followed—probably all under thirty. The names wouldn't be much help, since it was all Lombard Street to a china orange they wouldn't be using their own. Fake passports would be child's play to a gang like that.

But he didn't really expect the trio to use trains. That left two escape lines—ships and planes. There wouldn't be many boats leaving the country in present weather conditions at this hour of the evening, and the romantic notion that they might be sailing their own yacht across the Atlantic might look lovely in the films but somehow didn't appeal to his rugged common sense.

"Circularize all docks," he said, "but the airports are what we really have to watch. There are still some night flights operating, but I very much doubt if they can have reached any airport yet. Tell the officials to go through passengers with a toothcomb, examine passports, look out for disguises. They won't need me to tell them to watch for hands and ears, they're the features it's hardest to conceal. The odds are," he added more temperately, "it won't occur to our lot they haven't got a considerable start. The tickets will have been booked pretty recently, possibly by someone acting for them and booking on chance at a reduced fare. They'll travel together, you can bet your bottom dollar on that—they won't trust each other an inch. Probably the girl will travel as the wife of one of the others. Look out specially for charter flights, they may think they're less conspicuous. And whether they turn up anything useful or not, see the police are on the spot wherever it's possible for a plane to take off."

He didn't stop there; just in case they had by some miracle managed to outstrip the authorities, he had cables sent to all the European airports asking the officials to look out for the party and detain anyone remotely resembling them. "Tell them they're wanted for abduction and suspected murder," he said grimly. "If a few honest citizens are inconvenienced, they must put it down to experience. We spend a lot of time teaching citizens it's a privilege to assist the police."

He and Crook wouldn't have seen eye to eye in many things, but neither of them would have let himself believe that the criminals would get away. Not because the law of averages was against it or because they were stupider than most. "They've got me against them," Crook would have announced simply. And Poole would have thought the same, if he hadn't thought it advisible to put it into so many words.

So there was Nemesis chasing after Stan and his mates like a horde of wild beasts, but the three, reunited now, didn't even feel the hot breath on the backs of their necks.

And while Poole and his underlings were working like latter-day wizards to catch the criminals, there were others whose main thought was with the victims. The quiet of the woods and the normally empty country road from Plowford to Godstone was broken by the roar of cars and the sound of voices.

"All depends how long that car's been there," said Penrose, breaking a longish silence. "Whoever wrote the note—most likely a woman—must have thought there was some chance. Took a hell of a risk. If she'd been seen putting it there . . ."

"Well," said one of the policemen, "it's not likely the chap would want to risk leaving a fingerprint, handling it."

"Ho, that's how you see it, is it?" demanded the doctor. "Much more likely to be one of those conceited oafs who doesn't think a woman will dare blow her nose without his permission. I've always been against putting gas into houses," he went on—he was as intolerant in his way as anyone connected with the case. "The trouble I have—some old fool forgets to put a coin in the meter, fire goes out, she falls asleep, and quite often she doesn't wake again. Moonheads turn on the oven and then go and look for a match, phone rings or someone comes to the door. By the time they come back with the lighted match, they blow the roof up with themselves."

The police were worried under a reasonably calm exterior. Assuming there was anything in the theory that the kidnapers were identical with the two chaps who'd robbed the warehouse, it followed they were armed and not averse to using their weapons. And a copper who's seen one of his mates shot or coshed by the enemy is about as dangerous as a king cobra.

The light was still burning in Fell Cottage but there was no one there. "He was a cute little chap," said one of the policemen suddenly. He had a vision of Mike standing, legs astraddle, saying, "I might be a policeman when I grow up if they give me a car."

"Snap out of it!" rapped the Inspector. "He *is* a cute little chap."

"Yes, sir," agreed the constable. Who did the inspector think he was? The Lord Christ raising the dead?

A police car, following the Vauxhall, signaled that it was coming past. Reluctantly the doctor drew to the side of the road. Who the hell were the police? To them this was a chase after a murderer. He didn't give a tinker's curse for the crime, all that mattered to him were the victims. As he thought this, the devil seemed to enter into him. In sudden fury at this precedence of the lay authority in a matter of life and death, he put his foot on the accelerator, and "By God, he's gone out of his mind," cried the driver of the police car, seeing in his mirror the old black car apparently charging him like an infuriated rhino.

"*Dulce et decorum est*," said the Inspector, imperturbably. "You keep your eye on the road."

The driver swerved to avoid a yellow car—someone been robbing the British museum tonight—standing in front of the Woodland Stores. As the police car drew alongside, a woman jumped out like a genie from a bottle and shouted. "Your inspector went by some time ago. You want to watch it."

The genuine inspector groaned. "That's something we'll never live down," he said. For he had recognized the car. "Crook posing as an inspector. We shall be the laughingstock of the Force from now till the next war."

And it occurred to him that it was typical of Crook to steal the official thunder. One of these days he'd sneak an archangel's halo and come loping into heaven.

The bungalow, Dunromin, was ablaze with light. By it they saw an extraordinary tableau of a burly man with a child in his arms and an ashen young woman beside him. Not wishing to be blasphemous, the Inspector couldn't help being reminded of a Christmas group. Dr. Penrose, however, had no time for this kind of sentimental blah; he swung the gate open and came charging up the path like a human bull. Crook yielded up the boy; Sara, in response to a curt command, went to boil water. Crook went to where Mrs. Gorton lay, breathing like an engine. The police inspector came to stand beside him.

"She'd be a hard one to kill," said Crook, affectionately. He dropped down by her side. "No sense wasting good brandy yet, I take it?"

One of the policemen was talking to headquarters; he came back to say an ambulance was coming like the wind. Denis came shooting back in the Superb, with Mrs. Lucas beside him. Only right, she said, for that poor girl to have another woman on the spot; you couldn't count Mrs. Gorton, not the way things were.

"You'll be able to hold her head," said Denis obligingly, meaning Mrs. Gorton, of course. "You can leave Mrs. Drew to me."

"You great soft chap!" said Mrs. Lucas scornfully. "You don't suppose she'll look at you till she knows the boy's all right."

"Oh, he'll be all right," said Denis, confidently. "Crook's there, isn't he? What more do you want?"

She thought, as women have thought from time immemorial, he was as mad as a March hare, but seeing March hares are the females' only choice, you have to make the best of it.

Sara was standing as rigid as a pencil; she didn't even seem to notice when Denis went across and put a supporting arm around her shoulders. But when Penrose, after an age, said, "He'll do. Are they building that damned ambulance?" she turned her head and the tears came like a tide. She cried as if she'd never stop; even Crook felt some dismay. They had two patients on their hands as it was. But young Carew seemed neither alarmed nor distracted. You'd think he was the patron saint of Niobe. He just held her closer and let her cry. Oh, well, decided Crook, as good a way of breaking the ice as any. They made a nice pair, and if he had the good sense not to hustle his fences, you might hear the strains of the wedding march yet. Michael Drew might have been one hell of a good fellow, but being a widow is no profession for a young woman.

At Gosling Airport the big charter plane rested on the tarmac, looking like some huge Walt Disney insect. Most of those waiting to board her were gathered in close groups, discussing the project that was taking them to Spain. They were traveling on a shoestring and had let it be known that they had some spare seats at cut-throat prices that they would be prepared to sell to any interested parties. One of these, a broad dark man looking like a film villain, sat at a table, with a large envelope of documents in front of him, a nearly empty glass in his hand. His name was Len Harrison and he was watching the clock. There wasn't much life at the airport at this hour. Why people chose to fly after dark was beyond him. The truth was the charter plane had a return flight from Madrid during the morning and had been able to offer the party advantageous terms.

Len lighted a cigar and unobtrusively watched the door. A dull drizzle had started, which might slow up the car. Or something else might have gone wrong. Provided all three had been killed outright he wouldn't have minded if the car had gone over a precipice. Working agin the law was one thing, but drawing a rod and killing a man was quite another. He'd be a lot easier in his mind when these three were safely on the plane.

A door swung and someone came in, but it wasn't his crowd. This was another single man, who glanced around casually and then seated himself at another small table. He pulled out an evening paper, took a cigarette, but he didn't deceive Len.

Copper, he thought, feeling a squirm of unease down his spine. What's he doing here?

He toyed with the notion of getting up and walking out, but that might be just what this chap was expecting him to do. Or, of course, he mightn't be there on Len's account at all. There'd been a spectacular smash and grab in London a couple of hours earlier, and the thieves would want to rush the stuff out of the country at the earliest possible moment. All the same, there wasn't a flying machine in sight except the charter plane, and it seemed unlikely they could be going by that. He'd been congratulated on getting the last four this morning. He didn't intend to travel himself, but it seemed safer to buy the four and prevent a stranger muscling in.

An air hostess appeared from somewhere and an announcement was heard over the loudspeaker: "Passengers for the charter flight to Madrid may proceed to the aircraft." The others began to drift toward the doors. The solitary watcher looked across at Len. Len looked back, then picked up his own evening paper.

"Not going on this flight?" said a casual voice, and there was the chap standing beside his table.

Len shook his head. "Come down here to see some friends off and drive their car back for them, and it looks as if they'd missed it."

"Oh, they won't be taking off for another quarter of an hour anyway," said the man. "Being a charter flight they'll wait a bit."

Len found nothing to say. He hadn't the least doubt why the fellow was here. Red or Stan had muffed it again, somehow they'd got the coppers on the trail. He wished he'd kept the multifarious documents in his briefcase. It would look a bit conspicuous if he tried to dispose of the large envelope now.

The other chap was talking again. "Enjoy flying?" he was asking.

"No," said Len, who was terrified at the thought of being so far up, such a long way to fall, more frightened still of fire. "All right for the birds, I suppose."

His companion nodded. "Chap I know flew back from South Africa the other day. Funny thing, he was booked to come by sea, but he didn't feel too good. Got a slight throat infection, nothing serious really, so he and his missus decided to fly instead. When he landed his ears were humming like a hive of bees, went to a specialist, cracked his eardrum. All due to the throat infection. You never can tell, can you?"

Len knew he was just keeping him there, because his trio would make straight for his table when they arrived, there wouldn't be time for anything else. He wasn't going to be given a chance to warn them. He thought of saying he wanted to go to the gents but you could be sure they'd have a man watching.

You've got nothing on me, thought Len, but the three forged passports in the envelope seemed as if at any instant they might burst into flame, like a falling aircraft.

"I think I'll take a looksee, maybe I can spot the car," he murmured. "I've got the tickets, said I'd pick 'em up."

"Yes," agreed the man, "they'll need those."

Len pushed back his chair. "You waiting for someone?" he asked, disagreeably.

The man nodded. "The same parties as you're waiting for would be my guess."

"Why—something wrong?"

"I'll know that when I see them, won't I?" said the man. "By the way, did you say you had their tickets, Mr. Harrison?"

He jumped as if someone had pushed a pin into him.

"I never said . . ."

His companion indicated the briefcase, a rather showy affair with L.H. stamped on it.

"Of course, if I'm making a mistake I apologize," said the man. "I mean, you could reidentify yourself with your driving license."

Lennie's face hardened. "O.K.," he said. "Anything wrong with my name?"

"You should be able to tell me."

Lennie turned away and stared through the great glass shutter. The air hostess was standing on the tarmac, not impatient, not anxious, as gentle and eternal as Andersen's "Little Mermaid" by the waters of Copenhagen.

Suddenly there was a flurry of footsteps and they'd arrived. They looked a bit put out, but when they saw the plane hadn't taken off, after all, they straightened out a bit.

An airline official stepped from behind a desk. "You're traveling by charter flight, sir?"

"That's right. Car broke down enroute. Thought we shouldn't make it."

That was Stan, rapidly recovering his false bonhomie.

"We've been holding it, sir. If I could have your tickets . . ."

"We're picking them up here. We had to get some visas,

so . . ." He caught sight of Len and hurried forward. The man, who had disappeared behind a pillar, reappeared as Stan drew nearer. Abruptly Stan stopped, throwing a hurried glance over his shoulder. The official was waiting and you could be sure there were others behind him.

"You don't mind cutting things fine, do you, Syd," said Lennie in a hectoring voice, "or couldn't Sandra make up her mind which hat to wear? Well, I've got your documents." He flashed three dark blue booklets out of the envelope. "All present and correct. Mr. and Mrs. Syd Martin . . ."

The man's hand came over his shoulder. "I'll take those, sir, if you don't mind."

"Here, what the hell?" began Stan.

The girl didn't say anything. It went through the policeman's mind she looked as if she'd been put through the mangle.

The other flipped the booklets open. "Mr. and Mrs. Sydney Martin, Ponds End. Seems in order." He thoughtfully examined the photographs, looking from each to Stan and Stella in a grave, considering way. "Never pay you any compliments, these passport photos, do they?" he said. "By the way, sir, have you your driving license on you?"

"Driving license?" Stan stared.

"I understand you've just driven down."

"Yes." Stan put his hand in his pocket, pulled out a couple of papers, frowned, said lightly, "I don't seem to have got it on me. You understand, going abroad—I've always heard it's easy to lose things in Spain."

"That's a pity, sir."

"Look here," exploded Stan, "what is all this? You can't be going to hold us up . . ."

"Regulations, I'm afraid. If you don't have the license with you when requested to show it by authority"—he pulled his hand out of his own pocket to display his police warrant—"you have to call at a police station within a specified period . . . And seeing you're traveling to Spain on a single ticket . . ."

"I've got a license," interposed Red. "Matter of fact, I drove. Will that satisfy you?"

"Well!" The man hesitated, then put out his hand. Red displayed his license and would have put it back in his pocket, but it was taken from him.

"James Terence Stokes," said the man. He put out his hand almost casually, and picked up the passport still lying on the table. "There seems to be some mistake. This passport is made out for John Thomas Straker, so it can't be yours, can it? Unless, of course, you've got another in your pocket."

There was an instant's silence, during which the police official turned and lifted his arm. This appeared to be a signal understood by the air hostess, who had been waiting all this time on the tarmac. She nodded, turned and walked up the steps, which were then removed. The machine's engines revved, slowly it began to move; presently it left the ground altogether and zoomed away into the dark, still looking like some gigantic insect from a Disney film.

The silence in the airport hall was broken by Lennie Harrison.

"You bloody fool!" he exploded. For a moment it almost seemed he was going to spit in Red's face. "I hope they hang you as high as Haman!"

Red was carrying a light coat. Casually he shifted this from one arm to the other; then, like lightning, he flung it over the policeman's head and made a dart for the exit.

"Not to worry," said the copper, disentangling himself. "He won't get far."

Stella spoke suddenly. "But he's armed," she cried. "And they won't know."

A man standing near the exit put out his foot as Red drew near and kicked a small bag across his path. Red couldn't stop himself; down he came, tip over arse, and a minute later he found himself held and disarmed.

"This yours, sir?" asked an immovable official. "Do you have a license? Well, we'll hold onto it for the moment. Oh, we'll give you a receipt, of course."

A little farther off, Stan was saying hurriedly, "You can't keep us here. What's the charge?"

"Now, come, Mr.—what is the name? You know, I can't help

thinking that if you were to look again you'd find that driving license. And when you do I don't think it'll be in the name of Martin."

"Where's the crime in a pseudonym?" Stan demanded. "It's being done every day. Actors, writers, impresarios . . ."

"This is a passport," the man pointed out, patiently. "An official document requesting Her Majesty's representative to represent you abroad. Someone who doesn't legally exist. I mean you can't get a passport without producing a birth certificate, and how can you do that for someone who hasn't been born?"

"You've prevented us leaving the country," said Stan, stubbornly. "You can't hold us here. You haven't got a case."

"That's what you think. Never heard of a forged document?"

"A misunderstanding," insisted Stan.

"And Mrs.—er—Martin. How long have you been married, madam?"

Stella made no reply.

"Well, we can trace that through Somerset House, provided the marriage took place and we have your maiden name. But uttering a forged document or being a party to such a thing is compounding a felony. I'll have to ask you all to wait. You, too, sir." He turned to Lennie. "You were in possession of the passports."

"How long does this caper go on?" demanded Stan, sullenly. "I want to see my lawyer."

"A very good idea," said the officer in smooth tones. "I was just going to warn you you're under no obligation to answer any questions, but if you do . . ."

"Spare us," said Stan, contemptuously.

"It may be taken down and used in evidence."

He shepherded them into a waiting room and himself stayed with them. He was very polite. He offered them coffee, told them they could smoke.

"Do we spend the night here?" demanded Lennie.

"There could be other charges."

"Such as?"

"You'll see."

Stella lifted her head, cast an imploring glance in the man's direction. She was about to speak when Stan leaned across and caught her arm.

"Never heard silence is golden? You silly bitch, don't you see this is an act they're putting on? You talking is just what they want. Keep your trap shut. Let them do the work."

So they waited.

"Come on," said Crook to his companions. "The night is young and we've still got a job to finish."

"You can count me out," retorted Sara. "I'm staying at the hospital. They can find me somewhere to sleep, I daresay, and if not I'll sit up in the passage. I'm not leaving Mike now I've got him back."

"You're needed for evidence," Crook told her.

"You must be mad. What does evidence matter to me? This is *my son!*"

"Who's in first-chop hands. Face it, sugar, the staff here can do more for him than you can."

"And when he asks for me—hasn't he been through enough?" she demanded furiously.

"That kid isn't going to ask for anyone for hours," Crook assured her. "Leave his teddy bear with him, if you like, but tonight you come with us."

"I'll come tomorrow," she promised. "Why shouldn't they wait? I've waited nearly a week—you can't begin to understand."

Denis put in his oar, uninvited. "You're the one who doesn't understand. Mike won't be asking for you before morning, and that's the time you're proposing to be out of the way. You shouldn't be so foolish, Sara. You've had a small army out tonight in your interest, now it's your turn. Come on."

She looked at him in absolute disbelief. Crook grinned. That's the stuff to give the troops, he thought.

"But what—where—?"

"The sooner this is wrapped up the better," Denis continued. "I'll bring you back to the hospital, I swear it. And it'll be much better having something to do than just sitting on a hard chair in the passage—because surely you're not kidding yourself you'll sleep—oh, come on, Sara. You're holding up the entire brigade."

She took a final look at her son. The color was coming back into his cheeks, his breathing was normal; he still looked horribly frail to her, but the sister assured her she'd nothing to worry about.

The airport was so quiet it might have been sleeping. One incoming plane, delicate and shadowy and as yet silent, hovered and dived. The charter flight to Madrid had covered two-thirds of the journey.

"If you were going to keep us here all night," said Stan, "you should have offered us beds."

Red didn't speak, just smoked and smoked. Stella might have been dead already, slumped in a chair, all youth and beauty departed.

Then suddenly everything waked up as the pursuers, with Crook at their head, came surging in. Sara was at his shoulder.

"That's the one," she cried, pointing at Stan. "I could never forget him."

"You identify him as the man who approached you in the wood on the day of Miss Tite's death?" said the officer, formally.

"That's what I said. He threatened me—through Mike. And again in the market on the Saturday. Only I didn't know his name. Just Mike's Uncle Stan. You're not going to drag my son into all this publicity," she added furiously, addressing the patient police officer. "He's been through enough as it is."

Stella lifted her head; a faint light shone in her eyes. "You mean, he's all right."

"No thanks to you," remarked the policeman swiftly. Sara was going to speak but Denis caught her arm so fiercely she nearly cried instead. Then she realized that probably the two men didn't know about the act of treachery and until their bones were bleaching somewhere or other it was as well they shouldn't.

191

"See anyone else you recognize?" suggested Crook in a voice so smooth it made velvet look like emery paper.

Sara's gaze passed to Red. "But you're the one I met," she cried. "Do you remember—I told you I was going to London."

"So you did, sugar," agreed Crook, heartily, "but no one's going to charge you with accessory before the act. Still, it's always useful to know your enemy's move in advance. Ain't it, Red?"

"But, Mr. Crook, I didn't tell him I was coming to see you," Sara defended herself.

"Even chaps like Stan and Red can do a bit of elementary arithmetic," Crook reminded her.

"You haven't got enough proof to choke a flea," said Stan in the same contemptuous tone he had adopted throughout.

"They'll get it, though. Then the charges 'ull fly thick and fast. Murder of Larkin, manslaughter of Miss Tite"—he paid no heed to the officer's indignant outcry—"attempted murder of Mike Drew, ditto Mrs. Gorton—you left your fingerprint on the gas tap, didn't you know?"

"Mr. Crook!" shouted the officer, horrified.

"If he's going to plead not guilty he's got a right to the facts," Crook pointed out. "His lawyer's got his work cut out as it is, the poor boob."

This time it was the girl who uttered a warning. "Don't let him rattle you, Stan," she cried. "Can't you see he's trying to trap you? How could you have left your print on the gas tap? You were wearing gloves."

192

15

"'There be three things which are too wonderful for me,'" quoted Crook, "'yea, four which I know not: The way of an eagle in the air; the way of a serpent upon a rock; the way of a ship in the midst of the sea, and the way of a man with a maid.' And I suppose the reverse holds good," he added. "I'll never be sure if Stella said that bit about the gas tap on purpose. Mind you, she's thrown her bonnet over the windmill for Stan Marvyn . . ."

"How she could!" breathed Sara.

"So you don't understand, either. Well, you're in good company. One thing, they haven't been able to persuade her to turn queen's evidence."

"How would that help?" demanded Sara. "She was in it, up to the hilt."

"She saved young Mike's life—to say nothing of Mrs. G.—at the risk of her own. If that worthless brother of hers had noticed the bit of paper she dumped in the car, she'd never have got as far as the airport."

"It was you who saved Mike," Sara insisted. "You were there long before the doctor."

"If you locate a chap on a desert island and you're short of provisions he can still die of starvation," Crook pointed out. "Fair's fair, sugar. Another half an hour and it might have been too late, and you've got that girl to thank that it wasn't. From all acounts she treated Mike pretty handsome . . ."

"Leaving him to die in a gas-filled room?" retorted Sara, with a furious gasp.

"She did what she could and an angel could do no more—and it worked. That's what you want to remember, sugar—it worked."

"She could have done a great deal more," Sara insisted. "There were long stretches of time when she was in the bunga-low alone with Mike. She could have called the police, she could have found out where he lived and brought him home . . ."

"She could have taken a kitchen knife and cut her throat," Crook agreed. "Have you ever seen a girl whose face has been razored? I thought so. It makes the victim of a car crash look positively pretty."

Mike was out of the hospital and so was Mrs. Gorton. The police had identified the print found in the cigarette ware-house with one taken from "Red" Stokes after his capture. There hadn't, of course, been any print on the gas tap, Stan was far too smart, and the police were very cool about Crook's good intentions.

"Some chaps are never satisfied," he complained. "Here was I bringing you your case served up on a silver platter and you ain't even grateful. Of course," he added, "I didn't go to any public school myself and somehow I never caught on to the Queensbury Rules. And even if a chap wears his belt around his ankles I can still get in a pretty hefty kick."

"When did you start suspecting young Stokes?" Denis wanted to know.

"When you started bein' my client. It's my experience that the best way to clear your man is to shove the blame on another pair of shoulders, so I looked around to see what shoulders offered. And that brought me to Red Stokes. Now, I thought, you couldn't prove it wasn't your car that hit the old dog, but on the other hand the cops couldn't prove it was. It just could have been a cow. If only young Stokes had had the wit to keep a few of the hairs—and why hadn't he? I mean, he told Gladstone he thought your car might be involved while he was cleaning it. Well, he could have submitted the rags to the police. The lab would have showed something. But he didn't. He chucked 'em out. And why?"

"I'll tell you," said Sara. "Because there never were any hairs on the front of the car.

"That's the way it looked to me," said Crook. "Why should a fellow say there were hairs there if there weren't? Specially as when old Gladstone pointed out he hadn't really got a case, he climbed down at once. He'd done what he meant to, pointed a finger away from himself.

"It was pretty smart of him," acknowledged Denis, grudgingly.

"Chaps like Stan and Red are always smart, play about with razors like you and me could handle a paper knife. But in the end, mark you, in the end they always cut themselves, and quite often, like now, they end by bleeding to death. Mind you," he added reproachfully, "you didn't help us, coming forward with your cock-and-bull story about a cow flirting with Atalanta. Y'see, it's just the kind of yarn a guilty man would tell, can't be absolutely proved but can't be disproved either. And, of course, Stokes working in a garage he could deal with the transformation of the blue Albion without any record bein' kept, find a buyer, too, I daresay, with new plates and faked records.

"On the way down I dropped in at the station to suggest it might be worth the sergeant's while to find out if Stokes was thinking of making a move in the near future. Stan had told sugar here that him and his mate were plannin' a journey, so if Red turned out to be the mate—Stokes, that is—he'd be asking for his identity cards. Not," he added a bit gloomily, "that you can count on these young chaps doin' anything so normal. Just walk out and write in for their cards later. But that 'ud have meant giving some kind of an address, and that wouldn't suit his book. And Mr. Gladstone said, Yes, that was about the size of it. Came sauntering up to say he'd had the offer of a smashing job on the Continent, driving a millionaire—chaps like Stokes always lay it on with a trowel—so may he have his cards, please, and sorry for the inconvenience. Mind you, they'd been getting ready for some days, with good old Len to provide the passports. If he'd had the sense to use their own names they might have got away with it."

"You were sticking your neck out pretty far, weren't you?" suggested Denis, candidly. "I mean, you hadn't much to go on in the way of proof, that is."

"Gettin' proof ain't that hard," said Crook in his sweeping way. "Trouble is to get it in time. Ever wondered how criminals get caught? Because the cops are so clever?" He shook his big head. "It's the other side of the medal again, see? It's because, if you give 'em rope enough, criminals will always knot their own noose. You've only got to sit back, smoke a fag and do your pools, and sooner or later Mr. Big will come a cropper, and that's when the gentleman in blue will be waiting to do his stuff. No one, so far as Red and Stan knew, had tied them up with this warehouse job, and that's the way they wanted to keep it."

"Except Sara," Denis reminded him.

"Oh well, she's a dame. It's different for her. Sometimes, Carew, I envy dames, honest I do. They don't bother with reason or proof or any kind of logic—it's no wonder some savage tribes believe they're in league with the powers of darkness—they just put their little rose-tipped fingers on the spot and say—That's him—and the devil of it is nine times out of ten they're right," he wound up, generously.

"I still don't see how she got there. Even admitting that our precious pair were doing all they could to avoid the limelight, why should she have tied them up with this particular crime?"

"She wanted an answer and her answer had to be a crime, and this particular crime was there—and it could be tailored to fit. It was as simple as that. You might make a note of it," he added, thoughtfully.

"For future reference?"

"Just never ask a woman for her reasons, and one of these days you and the future Mrs. Carew could lay claim to the Dunmow Flitch—a side of bacon offered for the couple who've hit it off best in the course of the past twelve months," he added, gravely, "or so I'm told. I never competed myself."

"You make it all so clear," Denis congratulated him. "About as clear as a jungle."

"One thing about a jungle," said Crook, "you never have a dull moment. When a puma or something isn't jumping at you out of a bush, a little dark man is peppering you with poisoned darts. Your survival depends on the quickness of the eye. Well, there's matrimony for you, but it must have something to recommend it, because chaps have been making tracks for that particular jungle since the start of time. And anyway," he wound up cheerfully, "if you do miss the waterhole your bones 'ull whiten in A.1. company."

He spoke with the knowing air of a man who's worked hand in glove in his time with little Dan Cupid. He knew—he told himself—just how things were going to turn out for everyone, and the future proved him right.

Stan and Red stood their trial for the murder of old Willy Larkin, and though Stan tried to run out on his partner, saying he didn't know he'd got a gun, the jury chose to believe the word of the victim, when dying—"Let him have it, Red." So that disposed of them. Stella did nothing to help herself; she couldn't be tied up with the Larkin affair or the manslaughter of Miss Tite, but her share in the plot against Mike and Mrs. Gorton couldn't be ignored. She got a strong recommendation for mercy from the jury for her attempt to rescue the little boy at the eleventh hour and her sentence was comparatively light. She didn't seem to care either way. Once she knew Stan was going to die nothing mattered any more. More like a shadow than a creature of flesh and blood she moved away from the prisoner's dock. Crook knew that within a few weeks she wouldn't even be remembered.

Well, that wrapped it all up, except for Denis and Sara,

and they came to a matrimonial agreement about three months later while Crook was pursuing a very tricky fellow in East Anglia. The little box containing wedding cake followed him there and he ate it, sitting at the wheel of the Superb.

The things I do for my clients! he thought.

Not that he was surprised at this development. The nut experts tell you every man cherishes a death-wish in some form, whether he realizes it or not. Some, like Stan and his mate, go hunting for it with a gun, and end, as he did, in the little covered shed; others put their head into the matrimonial noose—and if they didn't Crook and his kind would be reading the Help Wanted columns years before they were due to draw the pension—while a third kind go out looking for trouble in ridiculous outdated cars, and even Old Man Death fights shy of them. You pays your money and you takes your choice, and he knew which his was. Forgetting the burden of his years, defying his digestion to play second fiddle to the lump of wedding cake he'd just devoured, and scorning the thought that there were chaps all over the place ready to take a potshot at him from behind any convenient lamppost, he patted the Superb as if she were his favorite charger and shot away toward the greatest of all cities, known to her lovers as Eldorado, and to penny-plain chaps like himself as The Smoke.

>>> If you've enjoyed this book and would like to discover more great vintage crime and thriller titles, as well as the most exciting crime and thriller authors writing today, visit: >>>

The Murder Room
Where Criminal Minds Meet

themurderroom.com

www.ingramcontent.com/pod-product-compliance
Ingram Content Group UK Ltd.
Pitfield, Milton Keynes, MK11 3LW, UK
UKHW022314280225
455674UK00004B/297

9 781471 910241